A Glimmer of Hope

BELINDA BENNA

Vinci Books

vinci-books.com

Published by Vinci Books Ltd in 2026

1

This work is a work of fiction. Names, characters, places and incidents are the product of the author's imagination or are used fictitiously. Any resemblance to actual persons, living or dead, places and incidents is entirely coincidental.

A CIP catalogue record for this book is available from the British Library.

Paperback ISBN: 9781036726614

The EU GPSR authorised representative is Logos Europe, 9 rue Nicolas Poussion, 17000 La Rochelle, France contact@logoseurope.eu

By Belinda Benna

Halifax Harbor Hospital

A Glimmer of Hope

A Twist of Fate

Miracle Glow

Love and Other Dreams

The Dreams We Share

The Sky We Seek

The Colors We Desire

The Dance We Remember

The Stars We Chase

Marie & Lukas

Promise Me

Show me the Stars

By Belinda Benna

All I Need

Every Step I Take

Foreword

I researched the medical aspects of this story with care and diligence; numerous specific details have been reviewed by medical professionals.

That said, we're all human, and despite best efforts it's conceivable that some inaccuracies remain or have been unintentionally left in. If you find any, I'd be happy to hear from you so I can correct them.

I wish you many gripping, moving and heart-felt hours of reading at the Halifax Harbor Hospital!

Yours,
Belinda

Trigger Warning

A Glimmer of Hope contains potentially triggering content. Readers are advised that some scenes may be considered disturbing.

Prologue

JUNE

Some truths we suppress for so long that by the time they surface, it's already too late. Others catch up with us precisely when we're least capable of handling them.

Mine is catching up with me now. In this moment, as Ashton teeters on the edge of life.

I press my thumb so hard against the emergency button that it hurts. Then I turn back to Ashton, who lies in the bed before me, his face contorted in pain. His skin is nearly indistinguishable from the white pillow beneath his head.

My gaze flicks again to the greenish-brown discoloration around his navel.

This can't be happening. Another new symptom. And one he hadn't had before, no less.

If that's Cullen's sign…

Oh God.

"Where does it hurt?" I ask him, but all I get in return is a gruff grunt, followed by a piercing scream. At least his hand points to his abdomen.

Okay, the abdomen. As always. He also has a fever—that's obvious. And he's shivering with chills.

"Can you breathe?" With trembling fingers, I reach for my stethoscope.

At that moment, the door bursts open—two nurses and, of all people, Dr. Young herself rush into the room.

My boss is going to think I've lost control of the situation.

And damn it, she's right.

This situation is slipping through my fingers.

Ashton is slipping away from me!

Sometimes a single moment can change everything.

Those were his words—the ones that, just a few days ago, turned the world I thought I knew upside down.

Deep down, I can feel that I'm living through one of those moments right now. Because everything I've ever cared about is shattering in this very instant.

Chapter One

JUNE

Two weeks earlier

The shared apartment is a complete battlefield. The pounding bass thunders in my ears, the smell of fresh paint creeps into my nose and mixes with the scent of pizza wafting from the boxes in my hands.

With my foot, I push aside the box with a whisk sticking out of it and close the door behind me.

"Hello?" I walk down the hallway toward the room where the music is blaring—our future living room. There I find Sonora—in a pair of torn overalls, wildly headbanging with her dark corkscrew curls and holding a power drill in her hand. "Hey, Sonora," I shout in vain over the music.

I turn down the volume, my friend lowers the paint roller and spins around. An excited expression flashes across her face. "Finally!"

"Wow, you got so much done." I nod appreciatively as I look around. The dusty pink on the walls is fantastic; it goes perfectly with the cream-colored couch currently hidden under a protective sheet. "The dining table goes here, right?" I point to the open corner where a ladder stands on a paint-splattered box.

"That's right," Sonora confirms. "Olive and Nyla are getting the decorations, Autumn's bringing her TV and a matching shelf."

"It's going to be amazing," I say dreamily. This room will be our cozy retreat. The place where, after long shifts at Halifax Harbor Hospital, we'll kick back and laugh together —hopefully. "When are the others coming?"

Sonora shrugs. "Olive's out shopping. Autumn texted that she got the job and is just signing the contract now. I haven't heard anything from Nyla."

"Then these are just for us for now." I wiggle the pizza boxes in my hands. "Hungry?"

"I hope you planned on two pizzas just for me." She grins.

While Sonora runs to the bathroom to wash her hands, I stack three moving boxes on top of each other and repurpose two more—filled to the brim with Autumn's books—into makeshift stools.

"Spill it. How was it?" my roommate asks a moment later, grabbing a slice of spinach pizza.

"In a word: grotesque." Frightening would probably be more accurate, but grotesque sounds less like I'm a coward. Chewing, she signals for me to go on. I pick an olive off my slice and pop it into my mouth.

"It wasn't a job interview, it was a military inspection. I had to make diagnoses at record speed." Instantly, I picture the tiny hourglass belonging to Dr. Victoria Young, the head of the diagnostics department. I have no idea what would've happened if I hadn't solved her hypothetical case studies before the last grain of sand squeezed through the neck each time. "On top of that, I found out from the other applicants that everyone got different cases." That was completely unfair.

"But you got the job, right?" Sonora wants to know.

With a sigh, I lower my slice of pizza. "Not yet."

"Why not?" She leans toward me, frowning.

"Apparently, the interview was only part one of the application process." I shrug casually. I don't want her thinking I'm rattled—even though I definitely am. "But at least I passed that part."

"I wouldn't have expected anything less from you." She takes a bite of her spinach pizza. "What's part two?" she asks, still chewing.

My stomach turns. I'd love to put my slice of pizza back in the box, but I don't let it show. "Dr. Young called it the practical stress test."

"That sounds unsettling."

You're telling me. "Today, the applicant pool was narrowed down to three doctors. We all signed a contract for a four-week trial period—one of us will stay in the end." That gives me a thirty-three point three, three, three repeating percent chance of getting the job. "Starting tomorrow, we'll see if we crack under pressure or turn into diamonds," as the boss put it with a mischievous grin.

"As if we didn't already have a doctor shortage…"

Maybe so, but it's different here. Dr. Young is the star among diagnosticians—everyone wants to work for her. "She can afford to do things like this."

"Brrr," Sonora said, reaching for the napkins. "Creepy woman."

Tell me about it. "Imagine—she kept calling me Barbie during the interview."

A mischievous grin spread across her face. "Well, lookswise, she's not exactly wrong."

"Just because I have light blonde hair and blue eyes doesn't make me Barbie." Not even close.

"Add the button nose, your symmetrical face, and those sexy curves," my roommate countered.

Barbie wears a size XS, I'm a medium—but that's not the point. The point is Dr. Young, who will no doubt haunt my dreams tonight with her dark sense of humor.

"Whatever happens tomorrow—even if she calls me Barbie in front of everyone—I can handle it," I say, steering the conversation back to more important matters.

"Well, I'm curious then." Sonora raises an eyebrow. "Have you met the competition yet?"

"Just briefly. At the end of the application marathon, they announced the list of those moving on to the next round. Alongside my name, there were two male names." Ben and Jaxon. "One of them had already left by the time they made the announcement."

"And the other one?" Sonora's tone carries a hint of tabloid intrigue.

"He was the only one besides me who was happy at the end of the day," I reply, sticking my tongue out briefly, fully aware that she was hoping for something entirely different.

Grinning, she crumples up her napkin and tosses it onto the floor, which is covered in painter's tape and newspaper. "Aha."

Not aha.

"Is he hot?" She scoots forward on her box of books and props her chin in her hands. "Come on, June. Under that lab coat, I bet he's hiding a six-pack that could burn your fingers if you even get close."

Now I lean in toward her, locking eyes. "Even if he were the hottest guy in the entire world, I wouldn't be interested."

She pouts in disappointment. "You've always got work on the brain."

"For good reason." Even though it's the last thing I want to think about right now, my thoughts drift to where my problem with men began.

To Ashton. The boy from back then.

And to that warm September day that changed my life forever.

"School is bullshit." My seatmate juts out her lower lip and flips open the math book.

"Well, I'm glad it's finally starting again," I reply, smiling as I glance around the classroom. Sure, vacations are great, but I want to become a doctor, and that means I have to study.

She shakes her head, sizing me up. "There's something wrong with you..."

The door swings open and our teacher, Mr. Simmens, bursts in. I quickly place my hands over my papers, so they don't fly away in the breeze stirred up by his hurried steps.

Suddenly, a heady, earthy scent hits my nose. A split second later, I know exactly where it's coming from.

Leather jacket. Dark hair. Stormy blue-gray eyes.

Wow.

Who's the guy walking behind Mr. Simmens who looks like a rockstar?

I'm pretty sure my mouth is hanging open.

Am I actually drooling?

No idea. But my heart is definitely beating faster.

"This is your new classmate," Mr. Simmens says as I stare at the new guy.

That roguish look. That smile. The way he runs his hand through his hair.

A tingling sensation spreads through my stomach.

"His name is Ashton West, and he just moved here from Toronto."

Ashton West.

What a name. Beautiful.

I rest my chin in my hands and let out a long breath. Maybe Mr. Simmens is still talking, or someone's asking a question. Maybe a bird just landed on the windowsill outside, or the fluorescent light above me is flickering.

Whatever's happening right now is completely irrelevant. All I want is for Ashton West to look at me with those stormy blue-gray eyes.

Stop. No. Get rid of that memory!

Ashton West has no place in my head. That's the only thing I should be thinking about. That, and the fact that there's no room for men in my life anyway.

I turn to Sonora to get back to what really matters. "I want this job. Desperately."

This is going to be a fresh start for me. Not just moving into this apartment. Also the specialist position in the diagnostics department at Halifax Harbor Hospital, which will hopefully be mine soon.

She raises her hands. "Got it. June's heart belongs to her job alone, which she'll one day marry so she can become the best diagnostician in all of Nova Scotia."

I raise my index finger with mock seriousness. "In all of Canada."

A smile plays at the corners of her mouth. "If you say so," she replies with a wink.

No. Not if you say so, but definitely.

But before I can say exactly that, Nyla appears in the doorway. Her doe eyes sparkle, competing with her oversized earrings.

I wave her over. "Where were you?"

"Had to take care of something," she replies vaguely, letting her gaze drift over the pizzas. Her short, tousled hair looks even wilder than usual. "By the way, there was some mail in the mailbox. It's on the stack of boxes in the hallway."

"Damn," Sonora mutters suddenly.

I turn to her and spot a wild mix of spinach, cheese, and tomato sauce clinging to the tips of her hair.

"It's always the same." With a sigh, she gets up, and Nyla and I nod in agreement. "Be right back," she says, disappearing through the doorway.

High heels clatter in the hallway. That can only mean one thing. Miss Perfect is back.

"Hey, Olive, we're in the living room!" Nyla calls out.

Olive's shoulder-length hair, parted precisely down the middle, is—as usual—perfectly in place when she enters the room. Just like her subtle makeup and her Marlene Dietrich-style trousers. How does she always manage to look like she just stepped out of a glossy fashion magazine?

"I'll get plates and cutlery," she says, her eyes on the pizza boxes.

Nyla and I burst out laughing at the same time.

"You're honestly the only person who doesn't eat takeout pizza with their fingers," Nyla says, shaking her head. Her earrings bounce in rhythm.

Olive casually shrugs, her silky, shiny hair brushing against her cheek. "Order is everything. You'll thank me soon enough when I make sure this apartment doesn't descend into chaos."

She might be right about that. Living together here is bound to be turbulent—after all, we're all starting our jobs at Halifax Harbor Hospital tomorrow. Well, everyone except me. I still have to prove myself before I can get a permanent position.

A cautious "Hello?" drifts toward us from the hallway.

Autumn's here. That makes our five-person apartment complete.

"Hey there!" I call out.

A few seconds later, Autumn joins us, her beloved book bag slung over her shoulder and her usual reserved smile on her lips. Her hair gleams as red as the fall foliage in Nova Scotia.

"Got it!" She holds up her employment contract, prompting the rest of us to cheer and applaud. Her cheeks instantly flush. Her green eyes, nearly hidden by her bangs, widen when she spots the pizza boxes. "Is there a Margherita?"

"What do you think?" As if I'd ever forget… I gesture to her and the others to help themselves.

With both hands on her stomach, Sonora returns as well. Wet strands cling to her mane of hair. "I think I've had enough pizza for today," she groans, joining us.

Autumn settles cross-legged on the not-so-clean floor, Nyla examines the food selection as if she's making a life-or-death decision. Olive pushes aside the transparent plastic cover on the couch and pats down the seat cushion before sitting.

I can't help but grin to myself as I undo my ponytail.

Moving in with the four of them—even though each of us could afford our own place—was the best decision I ever made.

We're all doctors, we all studied together, and for all of us, a new chapter is beginning.

We have so much in common, and yet we're all so different.

"You know what?" I glance around the group.

"Wha?" Autumn asks, her mouth full.

A warm smile spreads across my face. "I think this is going to be amazing."

Chapter Two

ASHTON

They say you can't run from your past. Instead, you have to process it.

What a load of bullshit.

If you really want to leave something behind, you need something entirely different: a boat.

I switch off the circular saw, take off my safety goggles, and brush the sawdust from my T-shirt. Silence surrounds me, broken only by the rhythmic sound of the surf in my ears.

Deliberately, I let my hand glide over the grain of the oak wood, its resinous scent having spread through my improvised workshop as I cut it. This piece is perfect.

To be sure, I pull the folding ruler from the side pocket of my work pants and glance at the wall—where I pinned the plans to the wood paneling years ago. On the third one from the left is the component I just cut.

The plank is supposed to be four meters and ten centimeters long. I hope it's long enough to stabilize the sailboat properly, but I don't have more space here in this half-collapsed barn anyway. It just has to be enough.

I measure again—the length checks out.

A plaintive meow reaches my ears, and moments later, I feel warmth against my shin.

I can't help but smile as I look down. "Back in town again, huh? Where have you been all this time?"

The red tabby stray looks up at me and meows again.

"So that's how it is." I stroke his head and take the dry food I always keep stocked for him out of the cupboard. Gently, I let some of it spill onto a clean wooden board.

He dives in immediately. "Not so fast, little guy, it's all for you," I say with a chuckle and watch him eat for a moment before getting back to work.

Time to shape the plank so I can attach it to the side of the bow tomorrow. Using the drawknife, I begin shaving the wood little by little to create the necessary curve. Beads of sweat form on my forehead, my arms ache and feel heavy as lead. Strange how exhausted I already am after barely three hours of work today.

A knock blends with the scraping sound of the drawknife. Seconds later, the door swings open.

My shaggy visitor takes flight with an alarmed hiss.

"Until next time," I murmur, watching him disappear through the widening gap in the door.

The low afternoon sun streaming into the barn from outside blinds me. Still, I can make out who stands in the doorway: Jeremy. Grinning artificially, surrounded by dust motes floating in the sunlight.

My smile vanishes instantly.

I straighten up and wipe the sweat from my forehead. "What do you want?"

"Happy birthday." He spreads his arms and grins stupidly.

This can't be happening.

I step aside and set my drawknife down on the workbench. "You're supposed to be in New York."

"I took some time off." He lowers his arms. "Thought we'd celebrate a little. After all, you don't turn thirty every day."

So that's why he's here? Because he wants to celebrate my damn birthday?

Is he still pretending this is just another day? Or has he really forgotten what we had to do on this exact day fourteen years ago?

With the worst stomach pain I've ever had, I stand in front of the mirror and stare at the black tie in my hand.

I take a deep breath and try again. "The wide end goes over the narrow one," I whisper, crossing the two ends with a clumsy motion, but a second later, the image blurs before my eyes, and once again I can't manage to tie the knot.

"We have to go. Are you ready?" I suddenly hear Father ask behind me, his tone cold.

No, I'm not.

Not for this.

I'll never be ready for this.

"In a minute," I reply anyway. My voice sounds hoarse.

Once again, I grab the two ends of the tie.

Despair grips me again.

Every part of me is trembling.

Father steps up beside me. Our eyes meet in the mirror. "You're sixteen years old. Don't be such a wimp," he mutters and yanks the tie from my hands.

With harsh movements, he ties a knot while I watch in the mirror as fat tears push their way out of the cursed corners of my eyes and drip onto my black blazer.

"Don't you dare start crying now," Father snaps, pulling the tie so tight I lose my breath for a moment. "You have no reason to, understand?"

No reason?

"Mom is dead," I whisper soundlessly.

Just like that.

Dead.

I still can't comprehend it.

My nose is swelling shut, my head feels heavy. And dull. And full.

She'll never hold me in her arms again. She'll never look at me with that understanding gaze again, even when I've acted like a complete idiot. She'll never secretly comfort me again, because she always knew when I needed it—even if I never would've admitted it myself.

I look at Dad pleadingly. "Mom is dead," I repeat.

"And why…?" he begins, but Jeremy cuts him off, appearing behind him in the doorway.

His gaze lands on me, and my brother rolls his eyes toward the ceiling. "Come on, Ashton…" he grumbles, annoyed. Be a man, he adds silently.

I want to. More than anything.

But I can't.

Mom. Is. Dead.

I glance back and forth between the two of them. Like me, they're wearing black suits, but they're not sad.

"Don't you realize where we're about to go?"

"And what we'll have to do there?"

I bite my tongue until it bleeds, but it doesn't stop the tears from falling.

Now Father digs his fingers into my shoulders. His icy stare pierces through me. "Stop crying right now," he hisses at me. His grip tightens. Painfully. "Or you'll have a real reason to cry soon. Got it?"

"Got it," I force out. Then I rush past them and out the door, just to get away from them.

The dreadful feeling that everything good in my life left with Mom stays with me. Just like the grief.

"Ashton?" Jeremy's voice pulls me out of my memory, but not out of the emotions it stirs in me.

Back then, I thought the day of the funeral was the darkest day of my life.

Today I know that, in that moment, I had no idea how dark a day could really be.

After my mom died and everything that followed, I learned to be tough.

And I still am.

"Come on, let's toast to your birthday," I hear my brother say.

"Not in the mood," I reply, because there's no point in explaining why I don't feel like celebrating, and I turn back to the plank. It'll take hours to shape and sand it. Tomorrow I've got a temp job and won't have time for my boat.

Out of the corner of my eye, I see my brother shove his hands into the pockets of his tailored suit. "I've been on the road for five hours and skipped an important hearing to be here today."

"No one asked you to." I reach for the drawknife again and get back to work. Can't he just leave already?

For minutes, he does nothing. He says nothing, doesn't move, doesn't leave my workshop. I ignore him—eventually he'll get the message that this conversation, and his visit, is over.

"What's the point of this boat, anyway?" he suddenly wants to know.

I shoot him a poisonous look. "None of your business."

As if he doesn't get that he's not wanted here, he walks toward me, shaking his head. "Don't be like that—tell me."

I straighten up. My breathing is heavy, hot air trapped beneath my long-sleeved shirt. "It might surprise you, but I want to sail it."

"Sail it where?"

Away. Just away. From him, from this goddamn backwater, from this life.

From the memory.

Deliberately, I turn away. "You'll see soon enough." The tool grows heavier in my hand; my fingers can barely hold it anymore. A split second later, the drawknife slips from my grip and crashes onto the wooden floor.

"What's wrong?" Jeremy is already beside me, studying me intently. He even reaches out, as if to place his hand on my forehead. "Are you sick?"

I pull back before he can touch me. "Don't."

He narrows his eyes, scrutinizing me. "Do you have a fever?"

Bullshit.

"This," I say, pointing to my workshop and the half-finished sailboat I've been building for years, "is hard work. Not something you'd know about, I get it. But here's a little secret: when you do physical labor, you sweat sometimes."

He presses his lips together as if he has to stop himself from telling me what he really thinks of me. But he doesn't have to—I already know.

"Spit it out, Jeremy. Come on, don't be so shy. Tell me what an asshole I am." Then I'll tell him no one asked him to show up here with his damn perfect-world face, and that he should finally get lost.

I notice his nostrils flare. "What did I ever do to you?" he asks, trying to stay in control.

"Get lost," I reply instead of answering.

Screw him—and not just today.

The moment I say the word, my stomach cramps so violently that I lose control of my body for a moment. I double over, unable to stifle a cry. My brother is at my side instantly, offering his arm to support me.

"Hands off," I snap at him and lean against the workbench.

He shakes his head with a mock-concerned expression. "You're sick."

"Just an upset stomach," I mutter, even though the next wave of pain hits me—far too intense for just an upset stomach. It knocks me down onto the sawdust-covered floor of the shed. The fine wood shavings scrape at my lungs.

"I'm calling an ambulance." Jeremy's voice sounds strangely distorted.

I force my eyelids open. "No!" It is supposed to sound forceful, but even I can't hear myself.

Too weak.

I am far too weak.

"Right, Ashton doesn't need any help." He pulls a phone from the breast pocket of his blazer. "Ashton wants to be alone, grumbling at himself and the trees."

That's exactly what he wants.

"But let me tell you something." With a hard expression, he unlocks the screen. "What Ashton wants right now—just to put it in your language—I don't give a damn."

My eyelids grow heavy, and I feel like I am on fire. The center of the flames is my stomach.

Jeremy dials a number and raises the phone to his ear. "We need an ambulance at 27 Church Road, Peggy's

Cove," he say a moment later into the phone. "Follow the narrow path that branches off from the last house for about two miles, then you'll see a trailer and a barn. We're in the barn."

"I don't need a..."

Oh God.

The fire inside me blazes high, and the only thing I can still hear is my own piercing scream.

Chapter Three

JUNE

The five cups of coffee I drank this morning to make my body forget the sleepless night have made me way too jittery.

Sitting on the narrow bench in the center of the communal changing room, I stretch out my fingers. They're trembling.

Take a deep breath, June. You've got this.

The door swings open, and a cool breeze brushes against me. Instinctively, I jump to my feet.

It's Ben, the doctor who celebrated with me yesterday when the results were announced.

"You must be June," he says with a crooked smile, tucking his shoulder-length hair behind his ear, though it immediately falls forward again. "Hi, I'm Ben." He seems more nervous than I am, thanks to my caffeine overdose.

"Nice to meet you." I nod at him and give him a warm smile. Just because he's something like my competitor doesn't mean we can't be friendly.

"Likewise." His attempt to sound relaxed falls flat.

Is he already thinking about how to get me out of the way?

He turns into the area for the male staff. I hear him walk over to one of the lockers and take off his shoes.

A strange silence spreads, broken only by the buzzing of the fluorescent light overhead.

I get up and wander over to the window. I'd love to have something to do, but I've been ready for half an hour. The pager is clipped to my waistband, and my laptop, which I brought for research, is waiting in my locker. I reach for the thin silver chain at the back of my neck and pull out the pendant that's always hidden beneath my T-shirt.

I gently stroke the metal daisy.

Many years ago, it was one of my lucky earrings. Ever since I lost the second one, I've worn it as a pendant. It helps me when things get tough. During every exam, whenever I feel like I'm about to drown. It reminds me to hold on, even when everything seems hopeless.

I press the pendant to my chest and take a deep breath.

"A prayer won't help you, Number Two." Dr. Young's cheerful tone makes me flinch.

I quickly tuck the pendant back into the neckline of my top and turn around. Ben stumbles out of the men's section toward Dr. Young, who's leaning in the doorway. Even though she's a head shorter than me, she fills the entire room with her presence.

With a sharp puff, she blows the bangs of her chin-length bob out of her face and looks around. "Number Three has already given up? Interesting."

Number Three? She must mean that Jaxon guy. "Maybe..."

Dr. Young raises a finger. "There's no such thing as

'maybe' here. 'Maybe' means people die. And we don't want that, do we?" she asks with a wink.

I shake my head with a noncommittal smile. My shoulders stay where they are—she should see that I can handle the pressure here.

At that moment, a guy strolls into the locker room. Wearing tinted glasses perched on a freckled nose, chewing gum, a leather jacket casually slung over one shoulder.

"Good morning to you too," Dr. Young remarks sharply. "How lovely of you to grace us with your presence."

So this is Jaxon.

He rubs his unshaven chin. "Morning? It's the middle of the night," he replies with a smug grin.

What's he thinking? Doesn't he realize who he's standing in front of?

The boss tilts her head and smiles kindly at Jaxon. "Congratulations, Garfield, your shift just got extended from eight to twenty-four hours."

I'm slowly starting to understand her sense of humor, and I'm even on the verge of giggling. Garfield suits his round face, tired expression, and reddish-blond hair perfectly.

"Want a twenty-four-hour shift too, Barbie?" the boss asks, turning to me.

I meet her gaze. "If the job requires it, I'm ready."

A flicker of surprise crosses her face. "Follow me and make it snappy." She gestures broadly for us to come along.

At the door, Ben squeezes past me like he absolutely has to be first. It's childish, so I let him go ahead. Out in the hallway, I trot after Dr. Young, who sets a brisk pace despite her short legs. Thanks to my running training, I can keep up easily as she alternates pointing to the right and left.

"On-call room. Trauma bay. Admissions," she says,

before stopping abruptly and turning around. "This is the nursing station." She nods to the left. "The staff knows you're here. I expect you to introduce yourself and only ask for help if absolutely necessary."

I peek into the room, where two clearly exhausted male nurses and a female nurse are drinking coffee and discussing patient records. It's obvious the shift handover is happening, yet all three glance over at us.

I give a friendly wave, which they all return with a smile. "Nice to meet you." No sooner have I spoken the words than I realize the others have already moved on. With an apologetic look, I say goodbye and hurry after the boss.

I catch up to her at the end of the hallway.

"This," Dr. Young's index finger points to the glass door on her left, "is my office—I strongly advise you to enter it only if you have a very good reason."

While I try not to let my uncertainty show, I hear Ben panting beside me. Jaxon, on the other hand, doesn't seem to be here. Out of the corner of my eye, I see him casually ambling down the hallway about twenty meters away.

If he treats his patients with the same lack of respect as the boss does, things won't end well for him. She may present herself as a joker, but that doesn't necessarily mean she finds what we do funny.

"Across from here is the library, which also serves as our meeting room." The boss opens the door and motions for us to follow her.

In the middle of the room, lined with bookshelves, stands a long wooden table with five chairs on each side. The seat at the head of the table—an imposing leather chair—clearly belongs to the boss. It's far too big for her, yet she climbs onto the seat and gestures for us to sit. Her legs dangle in the air.

Better not to stare too obviously—that wouldn't be appropriate. With my gaze lowered to the tabletop, I take a seat and pull out my pen.

"I don't care where you come from or what you've done so far. Your grades don't interest me, and your recommendations even less," I hear the boss say. "This is my arena, and here, I make the rules."

Even though my stomach knots up, I lift my eyelids to look at her. I suppress the urge to fidget with the clicker on my pen and rest my hands on the table, trying to appear relaxed. Just a few seconds later, I notice the wood beneath my palms starting to fog up.

Don't move now, June.

"Don't worry, the rules are simple." Dr. Young fixes her gaze on Jaxon. "Even half-asleep, you should be able to understand them."

"I'm wide awake," he replies with a smug grin.

She continues to hold his gaze. "Rule number one: What kind of person you are doesn't matter. All that counts here is what kind of doctor you are."

She can't be serious. You can't just let anyone loose on patients! Humanity and respect are just as important as medical expertise. That's what Dad taught me, and if anyone knows that, it's someone like him.

As if Dr. Young can read my mind, she turns to me. "Your personal opinion has no place here." She raises her eyebrows so high they disappear beneath her bangs. "Rule number two: In this game, there are no second chances. Everyone only gets one life. If you don't win, you lose."

I hold my breath as Ben nods beside me, his expression hard as stone.

"Whoever solves their case first gets the job." The rustling of medical files, which Dr. Young now pulls toward herself, breaks the tense silence in the room. "Whoever loses their patient is automatically disqualified."

Is this one of her jokes? Or is she actually serious?

"Cheating, trickery, and lying also lead to disqualification." Dr. Young raises a warning finger. "And anyone who shows up at the hospital outside of their shift is immediately out."

I nod as her gaze lingers on me. At least that sounds fair. Except for the small detail that Jaxon, with his little stunt in the locker room earlier, has unintentionally gained an advantage—as I now realize. He has a full twenty-four hours today, while Ben and I only have our regular eight-hour shift. "But..."

She raises her hand, which immediately silences me, and picks up the top medical file. Almost ceremoniously, she opens it and lets her gaze glide over the cover sheet. "Number one."

"Yes?" Ben's voice sounds hoarse.

"Patient P010424-062. Female with hemoptysis and accompanying syncope. Room 302." She closes the file and slides it across the table toward Ben. He does his best to catch it, but it still sails to the floor. "I hope you're more skilled with a stethoscope, Clumsy," Dr. Young murmurs as Ben, his face flushed deep red, retrieves the folder.

I watch as he skims through the patient information. Coughing up blood and fainting—there could be many causes. Pneumonia, tuberculosis—where will he start with his diagnosis?

"Number two."

Immediately, my attention snaps back to the boss. Seconds pass as she silently examines the cover sheet of the next file. Damp heat builds between my back and the chair, and I can barely keep my legs still.

Please let it be a case I can win. Please, please, please.

Now she looks at me expectantly. "Patient P010424-060. Male with abdominal pain and pyrexia. Room 320."

Abdominal pain and fever? That sounds manageable. The file flies toward me faster than I can react. Luckily, it collides with my notepad. I pounce on it with both hands like a bird of prey on its catch.

"And then we have number three," I hear the boss say next. "Patient P010424-065. Male with leg pain after hockey practice. Room 309."

Seriously? Of all people, Jaxon gets something so simple she doesn't even bother using a medical term for it?

One last time, the scraping sound of paper sliding across the tabletop breaks the silence. Jaxon stops the file with the casual confidence of a poker player who knows—without even looking—that he's been dealt the best hand at the table.

"We'll meet tomorrow at eight o'clock for the first case discussion." Dr. Young climbs down from her chair and strides toward the exit. She stops beside Jaxon. "Eight in the morning, understood?"

He flashes her a charming smile. "I won't need any longer than that to solve the case."

Without replying, she heads for the door. Once there, she turns to face us and lifts the corners of her mouth. "Welcome to Halifax Harbor Hospital."

Chapter Four

JUNE

On my way to room 320, I study the patient file while trying to dodge the colleagues crowding the hallway. Snippets of conversation, laughter, and a chaotic blend of disinfectant and deodorant fill the air around me.

Just a few minutes ago, I was pleased about what seemed like a straightforward case. I should have known it wasn't. No one ends up on the diagnostic ward if their illness is easy to identify.

I delve into the file, reviewing the initial examination notes from yesterday afternoon and the lab results. Elevated inflammatory markers, fever, severe pain in the lower right abdomen. The colleague in the emergency room suspected a perforated appendicitis, which made perfect sense.

Nevertheless, the emergency physician appears to have transferred my patient to surgery a bit hastily, so his inflamed and allegedly near-burst appendix could be removed in an emergency operation. Her medical history seems incomplete, as if she didn't have enough time to examine the patient thoroughly after the ultrasound proved inconclusive.

The ER was probably swamped. You have to make quick decisions there, and an acute appendicitis was indeed a likely assumption.

I turn the page and focus on the surgeon's notes.

The appendix vermiformis presented during the surgical procedure without any pathological findings, with normal morphology and unremarkable appearance.

So the surgery was unnecessary, the diagnosis incorrect. Pensive, I turn the page again, but there's nothing more. All I have is fever, abdominal pain, elevated inflammatory markers, and the certainty that it's not appendicitis.

First, I'll fill in the gaps in the patient's history. That should provide some clues I can follow up on.

"Alright, let's see what's going on here," I say, motivated, closing the medical file and tucking it under my arm.

Room 320 should be the next door. I head straight for it and knock.

A dull, two-voiced "Yes" comes through the white-painted door.

It's time to begin.

With a professional smile, I push the door open. At that very moment, I realize I've already made my first mistake. I don't know my patient's name. Apparently, I was so focused on the medical details because of the competitive situation that I overlooked it.

The door is already open, and there's no time to check the medical file. I have no choice but to improvise.

I step in briskly. "Good afternoon, I'm Dr. Taylor, your attending…"

I fall silent mid-sentence. My patient lifts his eyelids, and suddenly, I'm aware of nothing else.

That blue-gray—stormy like the sea on a winter's day.

That is… that is…

Oh God.

The medical file sails to the floor, the pages rustling loudly.

"Ashton West," I whisper soundlessly, and the memory hits me—stronger than every single time over the past thirteen years.

I'm no longer Dr. Taylor, the ambitious doctor who has her life under control, but simply June. June, the seventeen-year-old girl whose heart was shattered in an instant.

An A in math. Yes!

Grinning, I shove the math book and the test we just got back into my locker and grab a chocolate bar.

I've totally earned this.

Top of the class! Mom is going to be so proud—and Dad even more! If my grades stay this good, I'll definitely get into med school.

I lean against the row of lockers and take a satisfied bite of the bar, when a commotion at the end of the hallway catches my attention.

Is that…?

Leather jacket. Black hair. That casual stride.

My Ashton radar is going off.

I instantly feel hot. To calm myself down, I shove the rest of my chocolate bar into my mouth whole, then shake out my hair so it falls casually across my face.

Stomach in, chest out.

He walks up to his locker, his expression unreadable. Distant. And impossibly hot.

Will he look at me today?

Does he even know I exist by now?

"Hey, June," someone chirps behind me.

Was that... my mom?

I turn around. Yep. It's Mom, charging down the hallway toward me with the wild gestures of an air traffic controller. Her T-shirt is stained. "You forgot your gym bag, princess," she calls out loud enough for everyone to hear.

My gaze automatically flicks to Ashton, who's staring at my mom. His jaw tightens for a moment, then he lets out a scornful snort.

He thinks she's embarrassing.

A wild mix of embarrassment and discomfort spreads through me. I can feel myself blushing. By the time Mom reaches me, my whole face feels like an overripe tomato.

"Not so loud, Mom," I whisper, shooting her an accusatory look. "You're embarrassing me."

"But you need your gym clothes." She presses the bag into my hand, then tilts her head. "Are you okay, princess?" Before I can react, she places her hand on my forehead. "You feel hot."

A giggle drifts over from Ashton's direction. I glance that way. It's not Ashton who's laughing, but one of his friends. That doesn't make it any better, though, because Ashton is still staring at us like he's in a trance. His chest is rising and falling rapidly.

The last thing I need right now is for him to think I'm Mommy's little darling. That is so uncool. Casually, I brush Mom's hand away and sweep my hair into my face. "I'm fine."

She steps back, disappointed. "What's wrong with you?"

I try to signal with my eyes that this is a really bad time, but she only raises her eyebrows questioningly. In desperation, I nod toward the exit. "Thanks for the bag. I've got to go."

"Yes, of course," she replies, but instead of finally leaving, she takes a step toward me and tries to kiss me on the cheek goodbye.

God, why can't she see she's making me look completely ridiculous?

"Mom!" I jerk away from her. "Don't you have something urgent to do?" Once again, I try to signal with my eyes that she should really leave now. "We'll talk at home."

"All right." Shoulders slumped, she turns to go. "Have a nice day, princess."

My stomach twists—her words sound so hurt. I didn't mean to hurt her, but... Ashton...

Damn.

Ashamed, I turn to my locker. Out of the corner of my eye, I see Ashton slam his shut.

What must he think of me after that scene with Mom?

He probably thinks I'm a little kid who can't manage anything without her mommy. But I want him to see me as a woman.

Great.

Just great.

Now he's walking over with his friends in tow. I can't help but watch him.

My heart flutters with excitement.

I give him a hesitant smile. My fingers instinctively reach for my lucky earrings, hidden beneath my long hair.

Just three meters left. His expression is intense. Daring and untouchable.

Oh God, he's just so cool.

My heart pounds excitedly against my chest, and my palms grow clammy.

Just two meters.

He's talking to his buddy, looking the wrong way.

Just one meter.

Suddenly, he looks straight at me.

Oh man, is this what a heart attack feels like?

"Hey," I hear myself squeak.

He doesn't respond. Instead, he just looks at me in silence.

Only a few centimeters left.

"Hello, Ashton." That was better, right?

He stops.

Oh God.

He fixes me with his inscrutable eyes.

Can someone get the defibrillator? We're going to need it any second now.

A charming little crease forms between his brows. I want to reach out with my index finger and trace it.

My lips lift automatically, higher and higher, until I'm beaming at him.

Now he scrunches up his face, just like last week in biology class when we had to dissect the frog. "You're supposed to be a princess?" he spits at me in disgust. His eyelids narrow. "Bullshit. You're a fat pig."

What? How?

Confused, I gasp for air, but before I can say anything, he pushes past me.

"Did you see the fat pig?" he asks one of his friends.

"Totally gross," the other replies. "Good thing Mommy brought her gym clothes—she really needs them."

Both of them laugh.

I can't breathe. Frozen, I stare after them.

Ashton thinks I'm fat?

Suddenly, the three of them turn toward me. "Take a look in the mirror, fat pig," one of Ashton's friends yells down the hallway so everyone can hear.

My eyes meet Ashton's. They're cold, his expression unbearably hard.

My heart shatters into a thousand pieces.

Every— and I mean literally EVERY— student at Halifax High turns to look at me.

They stare at me.

Whispers.

Snickers.

My chest tightens—I can't breathe.

"Fat cow," I hear someone shout.

I stumble, the hallway tilts, and my classmates' faces twist into grotesque masks.

Mocking laughter fills the corridor.

"Fat cow."

"And now, all together!" Was that Ashton's voice? Or his friend's?

"Fat cow! Fat cow! Fat cow!" they all shout in unison.

I have to get out of here. I have no idea where I'll find the strength, but I have to. Without knowing where I'm going, I start running, faster and faster down the hallway, through the chorus of voices that won't stop insulting me, all the way to the bathrooms.

I burst in and press my back against the door.

Tears burn in my eyes. They blur my vision, but even so, I can still see myself in the mirror opposite.

I see my disappointment. The shame.

The shouting in the hallway turns into a whooping that only slowly dies down, and I don't know what feels worst in this moment.

The humiliation in front of my classmates? The knowledge that no one will ever forget my new nickname?

Or the fact that Ashton—my amazing, legendary, sleep-stealing Ashton with the mysterious, stormy blue-gray eyes—is an asshole.

Today, thirteen years later, he looks hotter than ever—but that doesn't affect me in the slightest.

Because inside me, along with all the panic that the memory of that time stirs up, there's only hatred for that idiot. And from the look on his face, I can tell he feels exactly the same.

We stare at each other. For seconds. Maybe minutes.

This man nearly destroyed my life. And now I'm supposed to save his?

Abruptly, I turn around and stumble out of the room. I leave his medical file on the floor, the door hanging open behind me.

Someone calls after me. A voice that doesn't belong to Ashton. Was someone else in the room?

Doesn't matter. I break into a run. Any direction will do.

As long as it's away.

And never back to Room 320.

Shaken, I reach the library a short while later, throw open the door, and storm inside. Just like back at Halifax High, I press my back against the door, as if I could keep the past trapped out in the hallway before it swallows me whole.

Why does he have to be my patient of all people?

This isn't going to work.

I have to get rid of Ashton—as quickly as possible. Yes, that's the only way.

"Case closed?"

Was that Dr. Young?

It was. On the opposite wall, she's drawing a chart on the whiteboard with a blue marker.

Above the columns, she writes the numbers one, two, and three.

What is that?

"Guess not," she remarks, the corners of her mouth lifting slightly.

"I…" How do I even say this? No matter how, I have to convince her to assign me a different patient without making her think I can't handle it. "Um… so… my case… it's just that… maybe I could…"

"I thought I made that clear. *Maybe* doesn't exist here. *Maybe* means people die." Without turning to face me, she places her pen on the first line of column two. "You get five points for correct observations and findings, and I deduct five for every question," she explains in a deliberately neutral tone. "So, number two—do you have a finding or a question?"

"Neither," I reply, my voice rough.

"Three points off for the unnecessary interruption."

She can't be serious. "You're joking. Right?"

She shrugs one shoulder, turns around, and just like that, a bold minus three appears in my column.

I stare at the whiteboard. Swallow hard against the awful feeling my failure stirs in me, and recall what she said earlier:

There are no second chances in this game. Everyone gets only one life.

Everyone gets only one life. Earlier, I thought she was talking about us doctors. Now it dawns on me that she might have meant our patients.

Everyone gets only one patient. Just one chance.

If I ask her to assign me a different case, would she disqualify me?

"Another two points deducted for standing around doing nothing," Dr. Young commented, crossed out the minus three, and replaced it with a minus five.

Great. Five points behind right from the start.

Thanks for that, Ashton West.

She turned to me with a serious look. "Do you owe the Grim Reaper something, or why are you making things so easy for him?"

"I…"

She raised her eyebrows. "Your patient? Might die without the right treatment and all that?"

Let him, then.

No, June, that's not right, I scolded myself immediately. I can't think like that—not even about him.

"I could disqualify you right now for failure to render assistance. That would save us both a lot of work."

No!

"I just forgot my pen, that's all," I reply quickly, step up to the table, and drop to my knees.

"Well, if Barbie doesn't have her lucky pen, of course she can't work—that's obvious," she comments, amused.

I reach under the table, pretending to pick up a pen, even though I pull it from the pocket of my lab coat, and then stand up as energetically as possible. "Got it." No idea why I'm grinning now, holding the pen up like it's a trophy.

"Bravo, I'm very impressed." She smirks, and I make my escape once again as fast as I can.

My God, how did I end up in this nightmare?

Chapter Five

ASHTON

Shaking his head, Jeremy looks toward the still wide-open door through which June just fled. "Who was that?"

The woman I never wanted to see again in my life. Because she's so inextricably tied to all the shadows I've been trying to escape for so long. That would be the right answer.

"No one," I reply anyway, begrudgingly, because it's none of Jeremy's business. My brother turns to me. Against the white hospital wall, he looks like a far too polished outsider.

"What did she do to you?"

"Weren't you just about to leave? I need rest." To prove my point, I gesture to my freshly operated stomach beneath the sheet.

He walks to the door, but only to close it. When he comes back to me, there's sadness in his eyes. "Actually, I'm waiting for you to thank me."

For what? For clinging to me like a damn leech and, for

once, pretending he cares about someone other than himself?

I sink deeper into the pillow. The exhaustion and the lingering fever make it hard to keep fighting. "If I thank you, will you finally leave?"

He grips the metal rail at the foot of my bed. "Probably not."

"You're probably missing an important court hearing." His work is how I get to him. He's always only wanted to satisfy his own ambition. Feed his ego. Be the best.

With determination, he steps forward and sits down on the edge of the bed.

I pull my legs to the side to make sure he doesn't get too close. "Don't get all up in my space, man."

He studies me with that piercing lawyer stare. "Should I be worried your doctor's going to smother you in your sleep out of revenge?"

Admittedly, that could happen. I'd been a real asshole to her.

"Come on, spit it out." He raises his eyebrows, his forehead creasing. "Who was it?"

"June Taylor."

God, I hated her. From the moment I saw how horribly she treated her mom, I hated her with a passion.

She had what I had lost. What I would've given anything to have back. And what did she do? She trampled all over it with her damn feet like it meant nothing.

At first, I barely recognized her, the way her body had changed. And her long hair doesn't constantly fall halfway across her face anymore like it used to. But that same ungrateful damn face is still there—and her cold-hearted nature probably is too.

That same old rage rises in me again. That uncontrollable fury I swore I'd never feel again. She pushed away her loving mom without a second thought, while I had no idea how to go on living without mine.

The tips of Dad's hair tremble. "One more word about your mother and you'll regret it, you useless failure," he yells at me. Tiny droplets of his spit land on my cheeks.

But I miss her every damn day. That's what I should say, but inside me there's this helplessness. The feeling that I'm no match for him and his ignorance.

"Now hand over the photo." He reaches for the picture of Mom. Maybe he does want to hang it up, like I just suggested?

I hand it to him. "We could..."

Before I can finish my sentence, he hurls the photo into the trash can next to his desk. Mom's picture lands among crumpled paper, plastic wrappers, and banana peels.

That's where Mom is now. Like in a second grave.

He can't do that!

"But..." I'm seventeen, yet I feel like I'm only three. Small. Helpless. Weak.

I don't want that. I want to be strong, to be in control, to stand up to him. But what do I do? Just stand there like an idiot, fighting back these stupid tears.

Dad drops into his imposing desk chair. "Why can't you be more like your brother, huh?"

I'm trying, I really am, but no matter what I do, I can't measure up to Jeremy. "I'm sorry," I mumble and hate myself for being such a pathetic loser.

"That's not good enough." His icy stare pierces me.

And yet I'm trying so hard, doing everything he wants from me. But it's like he only has to look at me to hate me. Like there's something in my face that drives him up the wall.

"And stop crying right now. Or you'll have a real reason to, got it?" he snaps at me.

I do everything wrong.

Anger boils inside me. At him. At myself. And at Mom and Jeremy too, for leaving me alone with him.

Screw it.

I turn away and leave his shitty office—the only place he's stayed in since the funeral.

I've got better things to do anyway, so I escape to the shed at the very back of our yard. The only place where there's still something like hope.

Shit. I didn't want to think about that anymore. But just one encounter with June is enough to bring the memory back to life.

With a sigh, my brother leans against the foot of the bed and pulls one leg up. "And what about this June Taylor?"

"Nothing." My God, why is he still here? Doesn't he have a life of his own anymore?

Pointedly, I look toward the window, beyond which the masts of the boats in the harbor stand out. A lone seagull glides through the pale blue sky. Even if he pretends otherwise, he doesn't want to know. He's never cared about anything that happened back then.

"She's hot," I hear Jeremy say. "So I'm guessing you broke her heart—in some really nasty way, judging by the way she looked at you."

Hot? June Taylor?

I shoot him an exasperated look. "Pfft," is all I say, it's that ridiculous. Just because she lost—what, I don't know, maybe twenty kilos—doesn't make her hot. And just because now her high cheekbones and waist are more defined, that doesn't either.

June Taylor is only one thing: the living shadow of my past.

"Whatever." Jeremy grins, clearly entertained. "Looks like she's your doctor now."

"She's definitely not coming back," I reply. Not after what happened between us. Besides, there's nothing left to treat. The appendix is out, the scar will heal soon. And that's a good thing. Because being near her feels like I'm seventeen again, and reliving that hell is the last thing I want.

"And what if I do?" My brother wiggles his eyebrows.

Why is he grinning like an idiot? "Then feel free to ask her out," I mutter.

He pushes out his lower lip and rubs his clean-shaven chin. "Maybe I will."

Great. I roll my eyes. "Go ahead. But don't even think about…"

Inviting me to your wedding, I want to say, but at that moment the door opens and—unbelievable as it is—June is back.

"Well then," my brother murmurs to me, though I barely hear him.

My eyes are locked on June Taylor.

On her long, blonde hair. That same cold, selfish face. The doctor's coat, with her hands shoved into the pockets. They're clenched into fists—I can see that clearly.

And that's when I realize it's time to form fists of my own under the blanket. Because that's the only chance I have to keep the past—and all the pain sleeping inside it—at bay.

Chapter Six

JUNE

"Good afternoon, I'm Dr. Taylor, your attending physician," I say, offering Ashton a professional smile while trying with all my might to suppress the panic rising inside me. I don't dare let my lips go slack—they'd surely start to tremble.

He continues to stare at me, unmoving. His expression is unreadable. The guy in the tailored suit standing next to him, despite his slick appearance, actually comes across as more approachable. At least he offers a lukewarm counterbalance to the chill radiating from Ashton.

But that cold won't affect me anymore, not in the slightest. The days when I let him tear me down are long gone.

He's my patient, and I'm going to treat him. Because I'm a professional. And, well, partly because I don't really have a choice.

I can do this.

Period.

With a deliberate clearing of my throat, I bend down to retrieve the medical file from the floor. "I'm sorry to inform you that your abdominal pain isn't associated with appendicitis." I don't dare look at him. He says nothing, so I assume he understands I'm referring to his nonexistent appendicitis, and I continue. "You've been transferred to the diagnostic ward so we can determine the cause of your symptoms."

He falls silent again.

I lift my eyelids and look into his eyes for a moment—eyes that are, even today, as blue-gray as the sea on a stormy day.

Oh God.

I quickly avert my gaze. "Did you understand that, Mr. West?"

No response.

"Is there a problem?" My palms start to sweat.

The man in the suit pushes himself off the wall. "Hi, I'm Jeremy, Ashton's brother."

Ashton grumbles irritably, "Shut up, Jeremy."

Unfazed by his sharp remark, Jeremy smiles at me. He comes off a bit slick, but at least he's talking to me.

I nod in Ashton's direction. "Does he have a problem?"

"He's a bit shy around people," Jeremy explains to me.

Shy around people? Yeah, right.

"Well, this is about his health, so personal sensitivities are out of place," I say, because I don't know what else to do. Professionalism is the best shield against the fear Ashton's presence stirs in me.

A strained breath comes from the hospital bed.

I immediately turn to him. "Yes, Mr. West, that's right. Your symptoms could have serious underlying causes." I should really stop there, but my fear pushes me to keep talking. "Autoimmune diseases, Pel-Ebstein fever due to Hodgkin's lymphoma, various forms of cancer…" I deliberately use only medical terminology. Hopefully, it'll intimidate him enough to keep him from attacking me.

"Come on, June," Ashton snaps at me. "It's just some infection—I've had it a thousand times."

His words cut right through me. Still, I tilt my head to the side with feigned nonchalance. "Well, look at that—he can talk."

If looks could kill, my heart would've stopped on the spot.

And his probably would've too.

Though I'd kill in self-defense. He, on the other hand, would do it just for fun.

"Great, if that's the case, then you can finally answer a few questions for me." I flash him an overly friendly smile and pull out my pen. I'm no longer the chubby little June he could provoke endlessly until I had no choice but to fight back with whatever means I had. Not anymore. Today, I'm the June who doesn't take anything lying down—not from the start. I won't make the mistake of waiting to push back again. I strike back, and I do it immediately. "Are there any hereditary diseases in your family?"

Silence.

"No," Jeremy answers for his brother, shoving his hands into the pockets of his suit pants.

"Do you have any allergies?" I ask, turning my gaze back to Ashton.

He stares back, hoping I'll look away.

He'll be waiting a long time for that. "Well?" I raise my eyebrows, my breathing shallow.

"No," comes the answer again from Ashton's brother.

I force myself to keep holding Ashton's gaze. "Are you currently taking any medications, including over-the-counter drugs or dietary supplements?"

He looks at me with the expression of a stubborn toddler. Out of the corner of my eye, I see his brother shrug apologetically.

Long, dragging seconds of silence pass as Ashton and I continue our stare-down.

What will he do next?

Is he going to make my life hell again?

The hatred in his eyes gives me the answer.

Yes, he will.

I have to beat him to it.

"If that's the case, your body will give me the missing answers. I'm ordering a lumbar puncture." I keep a straight face. "This involves inserting a slightly longer needle into your spinal cord to collect a sample. We'll also run a drug test—just to be sure."

His eyelids narrow, his nostrils flare. And I could swear the color of his face is starting to match the white of his pillow.

Now would be the right moment for him to give in and answer my questions. No one undergoes a spinal tap voluntarily. I'll give him a little more time to admit he's lost.

"I…" he says at last, and I see the tension drain from his facial muscles. He's giving in. Thank God!

I exhale in relief. "Yes?"

"I…" He fidgets with the port on the back of his hand, clears his throat.

Come on, Ashton, let's not go back to where we left off, I silently plead with him. If he says the right thing now, this could work.

His eyes glint as he looks at me so piercingly it makes my stomach turn. "I'd like to speak to your superior," he says, bone-dry.

My smile freezes instantly.

He can't be serious!

"Ashton, come on," I hear Jeremy say urgently from somewhere off to the side. "She's just trying to help you."

Almost imperceptibly, my charming patient shakes his head. "No," he says wistfully, "she's not."

Of course I am. Because it's the right thing to do. He should stop acting like a child.

Before I can point out that we're both adults now and should be past our history, he raises his eyebrows. "Well?"

Inside, I shrink, feeling like a helpless baby who can't get anything right.

"Don't do this to me, Ashton."

"Not again."

Struggling to keep my composure, I snap the medical file shut. "As you wish, Mr. West." I act unfazed, even though the thought of Ashton complaining to the boss about me ties my stomach in knots.

"Fine." His hard expression hits me like a punch.

"Fine," I reply firmly, turn on my heel, and stride out of the room on unsteady legs.

I'm a mess inside, but one thing is crystal clear: I can't let Ashton destroy my life again.

Not at any cost.

Chapter Seven

ASHTON

Jeremy shoots me an accusatory look. "What the hell is your problem?"

I unclench my fists under the blanket. "Stomach pain and a fever."

He inhales sharply through his nose. "That's enough, Ashton," he snaps at me, as if he had any authority over me.

"Don't act like you didn't hear her trying to order pointless tests just to get back at me." Even Forrest Gump would've figured that out. She wants revenge—for everything I did to her back then. Yeah, I was an asshole, and yeah, that was anything but okay. She has every right to hate me, but this is about my health. I didn't think she'd go so far as to mess with that out of spite. Then again, recklessness has always been her thing, and clearly, she hasn't changed.

"Because you wouldn't give her any information." Jeremy unbuttons his jacket and steps up to my bed. "You started this, Ashton."

Because she's so… she is so… damn it, I can't have her around me, can't bear the memories. "Stay out of it. This is between her and me."

"What is it with you two?" my brother asks, clearly annoyed.

If he's that fed up with me, he should just leave. It'd be better for both of us.

I glare at him, furious. "Nothing that concerns you," I say defensively, because explaining it without ripping open the deepest wounds of my life is simply impossible.

Sighing, my brother raised his arms. "Okay, I give up. Do whatever you want."

There we go. Finally.

A petite woman with chin-length black hair swept through the door like a miniature hurricane. She held a medical file in her hand—probably mine.

"Good afternoon, I'm Dr. Victoria Young. How can I help you?" she asked with a charming smile.

Jeremy started to say something, but I beat him to it. "I'd like a different doctor."

"This is a hospital, not an ice cream parlor, Mr. West. All our doctors are highly qualif—"

"She wanted to order unnecessary tests," I said, sitting up in bed. My surgical scar hurt, but I didn't let it show.

Her brow furrowed as she opened the medical file. "Are you a doctor, Mr. West?" she asked pleasantly, scanning the notes.

"No, but—"

"Then how can you assess which tests are appropriate and which aren't?" she asked calmly, flipping the page, nodding with her lower lip slightly protruded, and tilting her head to the side.

"With my common sense, of course." I just have a fever and stomach pain.

"Which measure do you believe is unjustified?" She lifts her gaze and looks at me directly.

What was it called again? "That spinal-whatever puncture," I mutter gruffly.

With a maternal expression, she closes the medical file. "That spinal-whatever puncture is necessary to rule out a meningitis infection," she explains to me.

Bullshit. She's clearly in cahoots with June.

My eyes flick to Jeremy, who's leaning casually against the windowsill and actually seems to find this amusing. Now he raises his hands in a defensive gesture. She's right, there's nothing I can do, it means.

Bullshit. Of course he can. He's a lawyer—twisting the truth until it fits is literally his job.

"I'm sorry, Mr. West, but I don't see that my colleague has made any mistake here," June's boss chimes in, just to make matters worse.

She hasn't? Can that be true? "But…"

"What I do see," she says, frowning, "is that you apparently failed to provide some information."

Fuck.

"Look, here." She walks over to me and shows me the file. With her finger, she taps the third line. "Dr. Taylor noted that you remained silent when asked about your current medications."

That's true—unfortunately. What am I supposed to say to that? "I still want a different doctor," I reply, desperate. How could I possibly let June be the one to treat me?

That's simply not an option.

Dr. Young tilts her head and taps her foot on the floor. "On what grounds?"

There's more than one. Aside from the memories, there's also the fact that she'll kill me out of revenge if she gets the chance. But her boss won't believe that, and I definitely can't tell her the other reason. "She…"

Her attentive gaze fixes on me. "Go ahead, spit it out."

I stay silent because I just can't think of anything I can tell her.

"I'm sorry, but doctors don't grow on trees around here." With that, she steps back and tucks the medical file under her arm. "Give the colleague a chance. I'm sure once you two get to know each other, you'll get along just fine."

Hell will freeze over first.

Her gaze shifts to Jeremy, who is still leaning idly against the window. "Make sure he gets some rest. The surgery took a toll on him, and the anesthesia might still be affecting him. That kind of thing can muddle your thoughts."

"I will, thank you," he replies, while I bite my tongue so hard I can taste blood.

Chapter Eight

JUNE

Sonora's eyes had been on the verge of closing, but now they widen as if I've suddenly turned into a ghost. "Excuse me?"

I take a sip of my extra-strong black coffee to go and stare out at the sea. Where water meets sky, the first rays of sunlight break through the clouds. Below me, waves lap against the wooden posts of the Halifax Waterfront Boardwalk.

My friend, who was immediately assigned to a twelve-hour night shift in surgery, yawns. "And what did you do?"

"I informed Dr. Young," I reply, shrugging as casually as I can. She doesn't need to know that my heart rate was over two hundred while I did it.

We keep strolling. The air tastes of salt, mixed with the sweet scent of freshly brewed coffee from the nearby cafés.

Sonora pulls her jacket over her hospital scrubs. "Hardcore. Respect!"

"What else was I supposed to do?" He wouldn't have backed down.

"Weren't you scared?" she asks.

A shiver runs down my spine when I think back to the moment I informed my supervisor yesterday about my patient's request. I was in the right, after all. At least mostly. "I didn't do anything wrong."

Sonora nods thoughtfully. "Did she see it that way too?"

"She docked me another ten points." Because my patient filed a complaint against me, and because she needed some kind of justification for a spinal tap that wasn't strictly necessary. That puts me at minus fifteen points, while my colleagues are still holding steady at zero. "But the tests were approved," I add quickly, because I'd rather focus on the positive. At least that worked out. I don't even want to imagine what would've happened if she had reversed my orders too.

"That point system is bullshit," Sonora says, linking her arm through mine. Together, we stroll along the pier. This early in the morning, hardly anyone is around—just a few fishermen loading their boats. A jogger passes us.

"I'll catch up," I reply with determination, because I won't allow myself to think otherwise. "I should get the first lab results today. And the boss herself said that only one thing matters: Whoever diagnoses their patient correctly first gets the job."

She fights against the heaviness in her eyelids. "I'm keeping my fingers crossed."

Something in her expression makes me pause. Does she actually think I won't be able to handle it? Ashton won't break me!

"I've got this." I lift my chin defiantly. "And the faster I solve his case, the sooner I'm rid of the guy. Win-win, basically."

"Why is he acting so weird anyway?" Sonora frowns so deeply that her overly long lashes brush her eyebrows.

I squint against the increasingly bright sunlight. "No idea. He hates me, always has, and clearly he hasn't matured since back then."

"Maybe you'll uncover that mystery too?" She pats my upper arm.

No need. "There's no mystery."

He's an asshole. Period.

It happens.

"You're probably right." She rests her head on my shoulder and lets her gaze wander over the pier, which is slowly coming to life. "I'd love to keep chatting with you, but I really need to get to bed now."

"But you haven't even told me about your first shift." So far, we've only talked about my start at Halifax Harbor Hospital. I'm sure she had plenty going on too.

"Okay, the short version." She sighs, picking at her fingernails. "Exhausting, dramatic, mysterious—but also incredibly beautiful."

"Mysterious? You'll have to tell me more about that once you've had some sleep." I lean my head against hers, feel her nod.

"Mhm," she murmurs. "Whenever that might be."

"Anyway, it was nice that we got to chat for a bit." With our work schedules, it's not easy to find time. Even the shift patterns vary from one department to another.

"I think so too." She pulls away from me. "Have a nice day."

"Sleep well." I raise my hand as she turns and shuffled down the pier. Children swirl around her, laughing, while couples stroll hand in hand along the boardwalk.

I drink the last sip of my coffee and continue walking in

the opposite direction. Behind the quaint wooden huts housing bars and restaurants, the Halifax Harbor Hospital rises with its continuous glass façade and the wraparound terrace halfway up.

I can't help but wonder what awaits me there today. What will Ashton do? Will he keep trying to make my life difficult?

Even though I don't want to, I feel the fear creeping in at the thought of facing him again. It is a sensation that gnaws at my stomach, makes my heart beat heavier, and tightens my chest.

It is exactly the feeling I have sworn I'd never experience again.

"I can't go to school, Dad." I press my forearms against my stomach for emphasis.

With a concerned look, he places his hand on my forehead. "You don't have a fever."

"But I feel really sick. And dizzy." I look at him pleadingly, hoping I can get away with it.

Dad furrows his brow. "I'm a doctor, remember?" He looks at me gently. "What's really going on, princess?"

Damn, he doesn't believe me, but I can't back down. "I have cramps. Like something's twisting up in my stomach."

Absentmindedly, he smooths out my blanket. "Did you have too much chocolate?"

"Maybe it's an infection or something."

He just looks at me for what feels like forever. As if he could find something in my face if he stared long enough. Then he exhales wearily. "Strange kind of infection that always shows up Wednesday morning and clears up by Friday afternoon, don't you think?"

Crap. He noticed?

"What's going on at school on Wednesdays, Thursdays, and Fridays?" he asks again.

The same as on Mondays and Tuesdays. The stuff I can't stand for more than two days in a row. "Nothing at all," I reply glumly, even though the correct answer would be everything.

I have biology every day.

With Ashton.

And math every day.

With Ashton.

Another wave of nausea washes over me just thinking about being in the same room as him. My eyes fall on my lucky daisy earrings on the nightstand. They've gotten me through so much, but not even they can help me at school right now.

"Last chance." His expression turns stern.

I press my lips together and do the one thing that convinces him every single time.

In my mind, I picture Ashton. His effortlessly cool hair, those stormy blue-gray eyes, that dark, mysterious expression.

I see him in front of me, walking toward me. I feel my heart pounding, triggered by his nearness, and something I can't fight, no matter how hard I try—the hope that there's a completely different person inside him than the one he lets me see.

My God, how ridiculous is that?

"Well?" I hear Dad ask amid my crazy thoughts.

It has to happen now, so I do it.

Because it's still better than going to school. I picture Ashton's face twisting into a hideous grimace. The way he looks at me, full of hate and rage.

He still calls me a fat pig and snaps at me not to cry when I tear up because of him.

Stop bawling right now. Or you'll have a real reason to cry soon, got it? his voice hisses in my head even now.

Just the thought of having to face that again today is enough to make my stomach rumble so loudly that Dad could probably hear it.

"Oh God," I groan. Not just because the nausea is overwhelming

me, but also because these thoughts are making it hard to breathe. Then I throw back the blanket and rush toward the bathroom.

There's one good thing about it—I definitely won't get any fatter if I keep throwing up. And who knows, if I even lose weight, maybe Ashton will stop tormenting me. After all, he wouldn't have a reason to call me a fat pig anymore.

Suddenly, I feel Dad's hand on my back. "It can't go on like this, Princess," he says gently.

He's right about that. But what's the alternative? If I tell him there's a boy I still have a crush on—even though he's making my life a living hell—he'll think I've lost my mind. And he'd be right. I should hate Ashton for everything he's done to me. But part of me still hopes that deep down, he's someone else entirely.

And if I only tell him about how mean Ashton is, he'll want to take action against him. Ashton could get into trouble—serious trouble.

I don't want that. I just want him to stop. And for us to maybe become friends. Maybe.

That's so messed up. Completely insane.

Exhausted, I pull myself up and wash my face. "I'm going to bed," I say, ignoring Dad's words, and drag myself out of the bathroom.

The memory of that vicious cycle that started spinning faster and faster around me—just two months after I first saw Ashton—still makes me feel sick to this day.

With my eyes locked on the hospital, I march steadily toward the clinic, while tourists armed with cameras and maps stop to capture the picturesque maritime backdrop of the Halifax Waterfront Broadway.

In an hour, the first team meeting takes place, where I'll have to present my case. And until then, I want to draw as many conclusions as possible from the lab results.

"Symptoms. Diagnosis. Treatment," I remind myself. That's what matters.

Because I know: today, I'm so much stronger than I was back then. And there's one crucial difference between then and now: seventeen-year-old June was completely infatuated with Ashton. So much so that she held on far too long to the hope that beneath his tough exterior, there was a sensitive person hiding.

Thirty-year-old June has her heart firmly in check—and that's how it's going to stay.

Chapter Nine

ASHTON

"If you do that, you're dead to me," I hiss into the phone, my eyes fixed on the IV line in the back of my hand.

"But Dad needs to know you're sick," Jeremy replies on the other end of the line. "I should tell him."

Dad doesn't need to know a damn thing. I don't owe that asshole anything—least of all any information about how I'm doing.

"I can manage just fine without him." No, that's not right. I can manage even better without him—just like everything else.

For a while, I hear only the engine of the car Jeremy is sitting in. "Okay, whatever you want," he says eventually, yielding. "I can be there in thirty minutes if you need anything."

"No, I don't need anything." I switch the phone to my other ear.

He hesitates for a moment. "You sure?"

"I'm already feeling much better. I'll probably be discharged today," I reply.

I looked it up. My appendectomy was the day before yesterday; some patients are released as early as the following day. I only had to stay because of the fever and persistent abdominal pain, and both have pretty much disappeared today. I'll be out of here by this afternoon at the latest.

"Okay, then I'll head straight to the airport. But if you need anything—anything at all—just call me." He sounds uncertain. "And in three weeks, I'll come visit you."

Somewhere inside me, it feels strangely warm that he wants to be there for me like this. Which is insane, considering I know I'm better off without him. And it doesn't change anything either. Would've been nice if you'd visited me back then, I'd like to say. Instead, I say, "All right," because he'd ignore anything else anyway. Besides, I don't want to talk about it. Or even think about it.

Still, after Jeremy says goodbye with a ton of unnecessary advice, my thoughts drift back to that very past.

The smell of paint creeps into my nose. Intense and intoxicating. I take an extra deep breath, inhaling the fumes like a drug.

I feel dizzy, but not enough to make me forget. It never is.

I set the can down on the wobbly shelf and, like so many times over the past few days, pull my phone out of my pocket.

Once again, the screen shows no new messages or calls.

Why isn't he getting in touch?

Fuming, I open my chat with Jeremy.

Hey, call me, we need to talk, *I wrote him yesterday.*

I scroll further up. Three days ago, I already made an attempt. Can we talk? When do you have time?

No reply.

Last week, when I had to hide from Dad every damn day to escape his hatred for me, it was especially bad.

I need to get out for a bit—can I come visit you?, *I texted Jeremy.*

Things are busy here, tough classes, exams, you know. I'll be in touch, *was his reply.*

He never got in touch, so I shouldn't be surprised he isn't doing it today either. He'd rather hang out at dorm parties thousands of miles away from the place where he left me alone with Dad.

"Screw it." I hurl the phone into the corner of the boathouse. "I don't need you, asshole."

What would I even say to him?

That I'm going through hell? That I've never felt so lonely and broken in my life? That I'm angry—at Dad, at myself, at the whole damn world? And that I don't know what to do with all that rage?

Screw it. Screw everyone.

I'll get myself out of this.

Determined, I grab the brush, dip it into the can of paint, and wipe off the excess on the rim. Then I turn to the boat I've been building for nearly two months and start applying the paint.

I've got ten months and thirteen days left to finish it. Then I'll be eighteen. And then I'm getting the hell out of here.

Forever.

This boat is going to save me. It'll take me wherever I want to go. And I don't care where I sail to—whether the sun blazes down from the sky, a winter storm rages, or a typhoon swallows everything in its path. The only thing that matters is that I'm far, far away from Halifax.

"Screw it," I say out loud again today, trying to push the memory away, even though I don't need any convincing that my brother is the last thing I need. I set the phone down on the nightstand.

Then I throw back the covers.

Time to go.

My boat has to be finished—today more than ever—so

that this one wish, the only one that's ever mattered to me, can finally become reality.

When I sit up, a wave of nausea hits me. I ignore it and swing my legs out of bed. Instantly, my head feels hot.

"What the hell?" a woman's voice snaps at me out of nowhere.

June. Perfect.

"I'm leaving," I reply curtly and pull the cannula from the back of my hand. It burns. I clench my teeth to keep from showing any reaction.

Just as I try to get up, she steps in front of me. "No way."

Snorting, I look up at her. Stray strands of hair frame her face, and if I didn't know it was impossible after everything I've done to her, I'd think she actually cared about me. "And what are you going to do about it?"

She crosses her arms over her chest. "I can have you tied to the bed. For your own safety."

Why the hell does she want me here? She should be just as glad not to see me anymore as I am about her. There's no way she wants to go through all this crap again.

Exhaustion hits me, and even though I should fight it, I don't have the energy. So I prop myself up and exhale wearily.

"What do you want, June?" I ask, just to get this over with.

Instead of answering, she swallows noticeably several times.

"You don't want to deal with this crap either. So let me go." I'd shrug if my shoulders didn't feel so heavy. The queasy feeling in my stomach turns into a cramp.

It's because of her presence and the past she brings back. Once I'm out of here, I'll feel better.

She remains silent, but I can see in her eyes that she feels the same way. I have no idea why she still won't step aside.

"Your symptoms could be signs of a serious illness. You need to get that checked out." Her voice trembles.

"Move," I reply, pushing myself up from the bed in a way that ensures we won't risk touching each other.

No sooner have I shifted my weight onto my legs than a burning pain shoots through my thighs. My knees feel like they're being tortured by a thousand needles at once. A scream escapes my lips. I stumble backward and bump into the edge of the bed. Eyes wide with alarm, June steps toward me, her arm reaching for mine. Even though I don't have the strength, I swat it away.

No one touches me.

No one.

"Leave me," I hiss through gritted teeth as the pain continues to spread down my legs, forcing me back onto the hospital bed.

What the hell is going on?

"Okay." To my surprise, June raises her hands and puts some space between us. "Where does it hurt?"

"It's nothing," I answer through clenched teeth, even though the whole thing scares the shit out of me. Then I exhale in short, ragged bursts.

The burning subsides.

Thank God.

My eyelids droop shut; I feel beads of sweat tracing their way down from my temples.

Something touches my ear, there's a beeping sound. "One hundred and four degrees."

This can't be happening. I have a fever again? And that high? Why? I keep my eyes closed, refusing to look at June, and even more determined not to think about what this means.

"Looks like you'll have to stay," she comments unnecessarily, then reaches for my medical chart and pulls out a pen. "For now, I'm prescribing Novalgin intravenously. It should work both as an antipyretic and an analgesic," she murmurs to herself.

Anal... what?

Frowning, I open my eyes. Does she really have to put on this show with the medical jargon again? "I don't want that," I say, just to be safe.

"Yesterday you said you didn't have any known allergies." Is she just pretending to be confused, or is she actually confused?

Standing there in my hospital room, against the white-painted walls, wearing that ridiculous coat and the stethoscope draped around her neck, she plays her role perfectly. So perfectly that I might even believe her—if I didn't know exactly what I'd done to her, and how serious it was. Serious enough that there's no way she could forgive me as generously as she's pretending to now.

"I'm not allergic to anything either." The burning in my legs flares up again, and there's a throbbing in my temples that's hard to ignore.

She tilts her head to the side, looking at me with something close to pity. "The Novalgin is for the fever and the pain. But if you'd rather go without..."

Oh. I see.

She could've just said that from the start.

With a distracted wave of my hand, I signal that I agree. I just want to feel better as soon as possible.

"Okay. Can you tell me exactly where you feel the pain

and what it's like?" she asks, jotting something down in my medical chart.

Yesterday, I would've either lied to her or refused to answer at all—just to shield myself from her and everything she represents. "A burning all over my legs, a stabbing pain in the knees," I say today, worn out.

"Mmm," she murmurs thoughtfully, tapping the chart with her pen. "Anything else?"

I shake my head silently. If she were another doctor, I'd ask what's wrong with my legs and what it means. When I'll be able to walk again—and if I ever will.

Oh God, what a thought!

"The nurse will be with you shortly to insert a new IV and hook up the Novalgin," June explains in a pleasantly soft tone. "I'll check on you later."

"Okay," I mumble, knowing full well I ought to thank her instead.

She should be leaving now, but she's still standing by my bed, shifting from one foot to the other.

"It's going to be fine, don't worry," she blurts out suddenly, turning so abruptly that the curtains beside her lift in the draft.

Gazing at the brilliant blue sky beyond the window, I listen to the fading sound of her footsteps, the scrape of the door, the click as the lock engages.

She's gone. And nothing would make me happier than if she had taken my worries with her. But they're still here—with me—and scaring the shit out of me.

Chapter Ten

JUNE

Dr. Young passes her whiteboard marker from one hand to the other. "Okay, number one, three points for your diagnosis. What tests do you order?"

Ben exhales visibly. "Chest X-ray, blood cultures, and a bronchoscopy."

"Is that all?" the boss asks in a tone that clearly implies there must be more, glancing around the room. Her gaze stops on me, as if she can tell I have ideas. "Number two. Any additions?"

I slide forward in my chair. "Pneumonia is certainly the most likely reason for Ben's patient coughing up blood. Another possible cause would be tuberculosis. I'd order an interferon-gamma release assay and a Mantoux test."

"Pfff," I hear Jaxon mutter, slouched in his chair like this is a sports bar and not a hospital conference room.

He immediately draws Dr. Young's attention. "Yes?"

He lets out a long yawn. "The Mantoux test is from the last century. Plus, it takes forever and the results don't even tell you whether the disease is active."

I turn to him. "That's true, but it's another clue that helps narrow things down," I counter.

Out of the corner of my eye, I see Dr. Young smirk. Our back-and-forth seems to amuse her. "Number one, it's your case. You decide."

Ben fiddles with his patient file until the cover tears noisily. "Well, um, I…"

I glance over at him, trying to signal what I would do. Even though he's technically my competitor, I want to help him.

"Yes, I would order both tests," he finally says.

Immediately, my attention shifts back to the boss. She scrutinizes Ben intently, then turns to her whiteboard. "Do that." She removes the cap from her marker. "However, the points for that go to number two, and of course, I have to deduct them from you," she says, and marks a full three points for me, raising my score from minus fifteen to minus twelve.

It's a start. And that's exactly how it needs to continue from now on.

"Good, now to you, number two. Medical history, differential diagnosis, treatment plan."

Up until thirty minutes ago, I was fully prepared for this. Then Ashton developed these new symptoms, for which I haven't yet found an explanation in the short time since.

For a moment, his pain-contorted face flashes through my mind. A solid eight on the ten-point Visual Analogue Scale. Just like before, it makes my heart skip a beat. No one deserves that kind of pain—not even someone like him.

"Barbieland, come in." The boss's laughter makes me flinch.

"Sorry," I say quickly, shaking the thought of Ashton from my head—unsuccessfully. A bit disoriented, I briefly outline my case's history and add the results of yesterday's lumbar puncture, which ruled out the already unlikely diagnosis of meningitis.

Ben twirls his pen between his fingers, Jaxon yawns without covering his mouth, and Dr. Young taps her foot on the floor.

"The drug screening was also negative. However, there are now additional symptoms: joint and muscle pain," I say finally, and with that, I've reached the end of what I know.

"Those aren't additional symptoms." Jaxon rolls his eyes. "Just side effects of the fever, nothing more."

Dr. Young pushes out her lower lip, and Ben's pen clatters uncontrollably onto the tabletop.

"No, that was more than ordinary joint pain," I counter, because I'm sure of it. "The patient couldn't put weight on his legs, described the pain as burning."

And his eyes looked so tormented that even the furious stormy blue-gray disappeared for a split second. There was something else—something deeply emotional. Something that made my heart feel heavy.

"Possible causes?" the boss asks.

Well, if only I knew. I open the medical file and pretend to study it while I frantically search for an answer.

"Is this going to happen today or what?"

Oh man, she probably thinks I'm an idiot.

Great job, June.

"Of course." I clear my throat. "The symptoms could be caused by a viral or bacterial infection, which would also explain the patient's fever and elevated inflammation markers," I say, just to contribute something.

"Both were ruled out during the initial admission. Otherwise, the ER wouldn't have diagnosed appendicitis." The chief sounds exasperated. So it's official: she thinks I'm a complete idiot. "Tell me something I don't already know."

I force my chin up. "That leaves tropical diseases, inflammatory bowel diseases, or other infections like mononucleos…"

A fake snoring sound cuts me off.

It comes from Jaxon. "Way too far-fetched," he says, leaning back in his chair and lacing his hands behind his head.

Is it? A wave of nervousness hits me, but I push it aside quickly. If I want to prove I belong here, I can't let him rattle me. I give him a tense smile. "I wasn't finished."

"Sorry, didn't realize you had more straws to grasp at." He gives a dumb grin. "Please, go on."

Damn it. Did he interrupt me on purpose to throw me off? If so, it worked. I have no idea where I left off.

"Or an autoimmune disease," I say quickly, turning back to the chief—after all, those are known for triggering all kinds of symptoms.

Dr. Young shrugs. "Well, that's going to cost the hospital a pretty penny if you want to test for all that."

Jaxon lets out a mocking laugh; Ben gives me a consoling look.

"Well... the patient's well-being..."

"...in no way justifies the incompetent behavior of his attending physician," my boss cuts me off. "So, Barbie, what's your next step?"

She fixes her gaze on me.

Stay strong, June.

"I'll assess the likelihood of tropical diseases through a diagnostic interview," I suggest, even though the thought of having to squeeze more information out of Ashton doesn't thrill me in the slightest.

The boss continues to stare at me. "And?"

My thoughts race as I search for the right answer. "Acute arthritis." Yes, that could be it. "The sudden onset of joint pain supports this. There also appears to be an inflammatory infection that could trigger such a flare-up."

It makes sense. So much so that even Jaxon doesn't feel compelled to deliver a scathing remark.

When no one responds, I add to my proposed treatment plan. The silence that follows is almost unbearable.

Dr. Young pushes out her lower lip and looks up at the ceiling. "Hm," she says eventually. "Well, why not. Give it a try."

Yes!

Inside, I'm cheering; on the outside, I don't let it show.

"Three points for number two." The boss adjusts my minus twelve to a minus nine. I'm still behind, but the comeback has definitely begun.

"Number three, you're next," she continues before turning forward again. "What's going on with your hockey player and his leg pain?"

"It's either tendonitis or a strain. I'll prescribe diclofenac, that should do it." Jaxon pulls the corners of his mouth down, as if the case annoys him.

"How did you arrive at that diagnosis?" the boss wants to know, prompting him to yawn as he outlines his differential diagnosis and the examinations he performed.

Is this guy high or what?

I try to catch a glimpse of his pupils while he explains his suspicion—which, admittedly, is quite plausible. "What does the X-ray show?" I ask anyway.

He rolls his eyes. "I don't need an X-ray."

"Excuse me?"

"Looks like you're in the lead, Garfield," Dr. Young

remarks before I can respond. Then she glances expectantly at Ben and me in turn. I immediately feel awful. And the feeling only gets worse when she awards Jaxon a full five points.

What kind of scoring system is this? He had the easiest patient and gets more points for a simple diagnosis than I do for my complex case?

"Ben minus three points, June minus nine, Jaxon plus five." The chief sets her pen aside. "That's a solid start—at least for one of you."

Don't worry, I'll make up for the deficit, I let Dr. Young know with my expression. I'm not giving up that easily. Not with her, not with my competitors, and definitely not with Ashton.

"Then out you go, your patients are waiting. Next case review tomorrow at eight." She signals for us to leave the room.

We get up and head for the door.

"Anyone else want a coffee?" Jaxon asks as we step into the hallway.

I stare at him in disbelief. How can he be thinking about coffee right now?

He shakes his head like he's disappointed in me. "Don't look at me like that, I just finished a twenty-four-hour shift."

Right, he's been on his feet for an insanely long time. Suddenly, I feel ashamed of my thoughts. He must be completely exhausted.

"Go home, I'll put the support bandage on your patient, it's no problem," I say apologetically. He's my colleague, and even if he's way too lucky for my taste, I should help him.

"You do realize I'm taken, right?" he asks with a grin.

As if I'd ever be interested in an arrogant guy like him. I

answer that useless remark with an eye-roll. "My heart is breaking."

"Sorry." He shrugs with a mock-sad expression. "Can you still make sure my patient gets his diclofenac?"

I hesitate for a moment. It's not really a big deal. Besides, maybe I'll get bonus points for it, and I could seriously use those. "Did you note the prescription in the file?"

He scratches the back of his head and looks around as if searching. "No idea where it is." He yawns widely. "But I'm sure you'll find it."

"Sure," I reply, begrudgingly.

He nods at me gratefully. "You're not as bad as I thought."

Whatever that means. "Good night, Jaxon."

"Bye, Barbie."

"I prefer June," I reply, turning away from him before he can take further advantage of my civility.

Chapter Eleven

JUNE

With the cold packs in hand and a firm resolve to handle this as professionally as possible, I enter Ashton's hospital room.

Someone has cracked open the window, letting in cool sea air that fills the room. In the distance, the waves can be heard crashing. It could be peaceful, comforting even—if not for Ashton and the fear his presence still stirs in me.

"Let's get started." Smiling professionally, I walk over to him and check the setting on his Novalgin drip, which is already running.

"She's back." He grimaces, maybe from pain, maybe to show his disapproval.

"How are you feeling?" I ask, ignoring his nasty remark.

Once again, he doesn't answer me. Which is still better than if he were lying. To get the information I need, I study him more closely. The IV bag is already half empty, so the medication should be taking effect, yet his eyes still gleam with the same feverish intensity. A thin sheen of sweat coats his flushed cheeks.

I lift the bag of cold packs. "These will help with the joint pain."

He watches skeptically as I unpack the pads. I pretend not to notice and reach for his bedsheet, just as I would with any other patient. "They need to be placed directly on the aching joints."

"Not necessary." He instantly presses his arms down onto the sheet. "It doesn't hurt anymore."

Yeah, right. And I couldn't imagine anything better than having him as a patient. "What's going on?" There's a hint of unease in my professional tone.

This is about nothing less than the job of my dreams. If he keeps sabotaging me, the goal I've worked so hard for over the years will vanish into thin air.

"That's just how it is," he replies hoarsely.

That makes me take notice. That—and the way he smooths out the yellow-and-white striped fabric—is strange.

Is he afraid?

In front of me?

No, Ashton West isn't afraid of anyone. And certainly not of June Taylor.

"Don't look at me like that, it's not my fault," he says accusingly.

No, Ashton, you can't fool me. Something's not right here. You don't want to show it, but I can sense it behind your mask. "So you're feeling better?" I shove my hands into the pockets of my lab coat. "I'd like to see that."

He furrows his brow, pretending not to understand what I mean.

"Out of bed, walk to the window and back." I sound a bit like a military commander. Ridiculous. But what else am I supposed to do?

If I show weakness now, I'll have to fight for every treatment and every exam with him. I don't have time for that. And if there's a serious illness behind his symptoms, neither does he.

We both want the same thing. Doesn't he see that?

He deliberately looks away from me, probably not even thinking about getting out of bed.

So that doesn't work either.

Great.

I stroll over to the window and lean against the sill. The sunlight streaming in warms my back as I search for another way to persuade him to join in.

This can't go on like this. We have to put our past behind us. Doesn't he see the risk his behavior carries?

Thoughtfully, I let my gaze wander over his face, seeing his angular chin, the stubble on his cheeks, the throbbing temples.

And finally, his eyes.

They're as inscrutable as ever.

Still, I meet his gaze. What I'm about to say is something I would never say to a patient. But Ashton won't understand unless I make it crystal clear. "Are you aware that this could end fatally for you?" My question echoes in the silence between us.

With his lips pressed together, he turns his head toward me.

There's something in his eyes that cuts right through me. Something I feel in my chest, like the warmth of a small flame struggling against a gust of wind.

Is it sadness? Or pain?

I have to clear my throat to keep speaking. "We can only get through this together, and I think you know that."

He blinks, the tension in his jaw easing.

"Believe it or not, but I want to help you." It's unbelievable that I'm saying these words with such gentleness.

The corners of his mouth lift into a wistful smile.

The little flame inside me flares up. I nod at him. "Let me apply the cold packs."

A crease forms between his brows, and I sense I'm about to lose. He's going to shake his head any second now.

What's his problem, anyway? This isn't about painful exams or medication with nasty side effects. Why is he refusing something as simple as cold packs?

Because I'm the one who would do it? Because he still hates me so much that he'd sacrifice his own comfort just to avoid me? Even though he doesn't even know half of what happened between us?

Swallowing hard, I turn toward the window and fix my gaze on the shimmering waters of Halifax Harbor. I watch a flock of silver gulls gracefully gliding through the air.

This can't go on like this. He has to tell me what's going on.

"What are you afraid of?" I dare to ask softly, feeling for my daisy pendant through the fabric of my T-shirt.

I hear his breathing—uneven, shallow. He remains silent for minutes as I press my palm against the slight bulge the pendant makes beneath my shirt and feel its strength.

"Okay, but I'll put them on myself," he says eventually, exhausted.

This moment should feel like a victory, but it doesn't. Instead, I push myself away from the windowsill with a conflicted feeling. So he doesn't trust me to place cold packs properly. If it weren't for that strange expression on his face again, I'd tell him straight out that I'm perfectly capable of doing it.

But something holds me back.

He bites his lower lip as I step closer and reach for his sheet once more. Even though he's already given me permission, I look at him questioningly.

He gives a faint nod, as if all his energy is draining from his body.

How sad he looks. Almost as if something inside him is breaking.

My gaze lingers on him—just for a second, yet it feels like a small eternity. And everything that happened back then seems, for the blink of an eye, so far away. So far that I can't grasp it anymore. So distant that, for a moment, I forget who's lying in the bed before me.

I can't help but wonder if I ever truly knew the man with the stormy blue-gray eyes. If what I thought I felt thirteen years ago might still be buried somewhere inside him—the tender heart that might just be hurting.

Ashton West, June. That's asshole Ashton West!

Right.

I shake the confusion from my head and pick up a cold pack. Absentmindedly, I fold the sheet back just enough to expose his knees and a few inches of his thighs.

Then I hand him the first cold pack, which he places on his knee. "Now wrap it," I say.

With a pained expression, he lifts his knee slightly to follow my instruction.

That's when I see it.

Right where the sheet ends. On his skin.

What is that?

A scar?

I push the fabric higher and discover more scarred areas. All of them are the same perfectly round shape.

"Hands off." Ashton yanks the sheet down abruptly.

I step back, confused by what I've just discovered. Did he try to get rid of me earlier so I wouldn't see those scars?

No. That's not Ashton West. He couldn't care less what others think of him. There must be another reason.

Or is there?

"Cold packs," he comments, motioning for me to hand him another one.

Right, that's what I should be doing.

Mindlessly, I grab the next pack and place it in his hand. "Other knee."

He places the pack. Instinctively, I look for scars there too, but find none.

"Is that it, then?" He sounds exasperated.

"Two more for the ankles," I reply distractedly, bending down to pull them from the bag.

As soon as Ashton has positioned them, he pulls the blanket back over himself and gives me a look that probably means something like "and now get lost."

"What... are those scars?" I want to ask, but the words won't come out.

Instead, I study him thoughtfully, not entirely sure why myself.

He shakes his head, his expression more guarded than ever since he was admitted here.

Okay, I should end this. Right now.

My job is done. I should leave and stop wondering what's behind his behavior.

Yes. That's what you should do, June. Now.

I tear my eyes away from him and head for the door. "Get some rest," I say, reminding myself that he's not my only patient. Jaxon's hockey player is waiting for me, and I'm also covering for my colleagues when they're off duty.

Still, Ashton lingers in my thoughts as I step out into the hallway.

Chapter Twelve

JUNE

Although I should be focusing on Jaxon's patient, I can't stop thinking about Ashton.

About the way he looked at me. About his scars. About the small fire he sparked in me.

It's been like this ever since I left his hospital room. Even when I'm treating patients who deserve my full attention. Neither the woman who sees everything blurry for no apparent reason, nor the little boy with the unexplained weight loss could distract me.

"Is everything okay?"

The question from Jaxon's patient pulls me out of my thoughts. "Yes." I quickly give him a smile.

"You look kind of sad." The man is unusually pale, his eyelids heavy.

"I'm fine." I wave it off and begin applying the compression bandage. As I go about my work, he yawns conspicuously often. "Do you often suffer from fatigue or trouble concentrating?" I ask thoughtfully.

He sighs. "Constantly."

I fasten the end of the bandage. "Shortness of breath, heart palpitations, dizziness?"

As if he has to think about it, he taps his chin with his index finger. "Yeah, that could be. Sometimes my circulation doesn't cooperate in the mornings."

A patient who talks to me so openly—what a blessing. Why did Jaxon have to be assigned this case?

"My little daughter loves it when I whirl her through the air," he tells me now, a tired smile on his lips. "But these past few weeks, she's gotten so heavy."

Kids don't gain weight that quickly. Something's not right here. "So heavy you can't lift her anymore?" I check the tightness of the bandage.

"Sometimes it completely exhausts me," he says flatly. "But I do it anyway—she loves it so much."

My heart tightens.

"Higher, Daddy, higher," she squeals then, her whole face lit up." He blinks rapidly. "How could I deny her that?"

"I understand," I say, even though I'd like to ask him more questions. Because what he's telling me about his condition is more than concerning. Why hasn't Jaxon mentioned any of this in the team meetings?

I immerse myself in his medical file, which I found earlier in the locker room beneath the shoe racks.

If the boss knew that Jaxon was so careless with patient records, she'd dock him at least ten points. And rightfully so.

"Has your attending physician also talked to you about the other symptoms?" I ask thoughtfully.

"He said they're from overexertion during hockey, just like my leg pain," he replies, yawning again.

Jaxon really took the easy way out there. There's a lot to suggest that the patient is suffering from anemia. I would have at least ordered a blood test to determine the red blood cell count and hemoglobin levels, but I can't find any such directive in the records.

"Mhm," I murmur absentmindedly, making a mental note to bring it up with Jaxon. After all, anemia can point to all sorts of conditions—some of them serious and in need of immediate treatment.

The man has a family. A young daughter who needs him.

I close the medical file, suppress the anger rising in me over Jaxon's negligence, and focus on my patient. "Does it tingle or hurt under the bandage?"

He shakes his head.

"No numbness?"

"No, it's perfect," he replies with a smile. "And believe me, I've had my fair share of support bandages, so I can judge these things."

"I'm glad to hear that." I smile at him, a warm feeling spreading in my chest. "Well, that's it for today. Do you have any questions?"

"Who do I have to bribe to make you my doctor from now on?" His hopeful look gives me a brief moment of warmth. "The other one seems a bit… disinterested."

If only he knew how much more I'd rather treat him than Ashton.

"My colleague is an excellent doctor," I say anyway, because it's the right thing to do, and I suppress the melancholy in my voice as best I can. "Don't be fooled by his detached demeanor. You're in good hands."

Hopefully.

And if not, I'll make sure of it. Our patients are what matter most—something Jaxon seems to have forgotten.

"Pity." He pushes out his lower lip.

Yes. A real pity, I think. "All the best to you," I say, give him a quick nod, and turn to leave.

There are still what feels like a thousand differential diagnoses for Ashton's symptoms that I want to rule out. I'm going to do my work thoroughly so that I don't come across as clueless again during tomorrow's case discussion. I have catching up to do, after all.

A few minutes later, I'm wandering through the tenth-floor cafeteria, my laptop in one hand and a jumbo mug of coffee in the other. I spot Autumn's red mane peeking out from behind a potted plant and head toward her.

"Is this seat taken?" I ask.

She closes her book and adjusts her shirt. "Afraid there are actually two free."

Thanks to Jaxon's patient, I'm late—and even though our meeting was casual and Autumn knows how unpredictable a doctor's schedule can be, I still feel guilty. "Sorry."

She waves it off and sets her cutlery down on the empty plate. "No big deal."

I sink into the chair across from her. Sunlight streams through the glass façade, warming my side. Lost in thought, I take a sip of my coffee while Autumn, eyes lowered, reaches for her napkin.

"Is everything okay?" I finally ask, unable to shake the feeling that something's weighing on her.

"Just work." Autumn brushes her bangs from her face and stands up. "Being a pediatrician is both a blessing and a curse."

That's the nature of our job—a real rollercoaster. And

when kids are involved, it's bound to be tough. But it's always the beautiful moments that help us get through the hard ones. "It'll get better," I remind her.

She nods, and now her smile even seems a little more carefree. "Guaranteed."

"Have you heard about Sonora's mysterious boss?" I ask her conspiratorially, trying to cheer her up even more.

"Not only that, I've actually seen him—unlike her," she replies with a wink. "But don't you dare tell her."

I press my index finger and thumb together and pretend to zip my lips shut. "And?"

She leans toward me. "He could pass for a pretty attractive fairytale prince, if you ask me."

"And Sonora is Cinderella?" I can't help but grin. Just because it doesn't suit her at all.

"That, I wouldn't know," she replies with a smirk, grabs her tray, and blows me a kiss goodbye. "Alright, I'm off. See you soon."

"Hang in there," I say, watching her disappear between the half-empty tables of the cafeteria.

I lean back in my chair and gaze outside through the glass front. Unfortunately, there isn't much time to let my eyes wander over the water or watch the bustle in the harbor. I enjoy the view for just a brief moment and take a few deep breaths, then my thoughts return to Ashton and his strange scars.

Where could he have gotten them? They were pale, no swelling, no redness. He probably got those injuries months ago—maybe even years.

Does he have more somewhere else?

Maybe even fresh ones?

Uncertain whether this discovery should factor into the

diagnosis or not, I open my laptop. But before I can read up on this type of scarring, my phone rings.

I can't help but smile when I see who's calling. Of course, I answer right away. "Dad, how lovely."

"So, how's it going?" he asks after a brief greeting. "I bet you're ahead of the pack."

There's so much joyful anticipation in his voice that I have to bite my lower lip. "It's coming along, looking good."

"I knew it!" I hear him slap his thigh with excitement. "See, Emma, I told you. Our daughter's going to win."

I sink back into the wooden chair. "Well…"

"That's fantastic, Princess. Really great. My colleagues are going to be thrilled. I've already told them about my successful daughter," Dad cuts in.

"Nice," I reply meekly. My heart leaps with joy while my stomach twists into knots.

In the background, I hear footsteps. "We should plan a party to celebrate your new job." That's Mom, shouting into the phone from a distance. "Sunday in four weeks, that's when your probation period ends, right? Would that work?"

"I don't even know…"

"We should get started with the preparations, or it'll be too short notice. How about we invite Aunt Lou and your cousins? They'll be so impressed!"

…if I'll even get the job, I should say, but the truth is I don't even know if I would've been able to say it out loud if Mom hadn't interrupted me.

If I showed them how uncertain I am, they'd be disappointed—and that's the last thing I want. She believes in me so much that it doesn't even occur to her I might not get the job.

Someone claps their hands. "I'll bake a butter tart. Or maybe a maple pie?"

"That's really not necessary, Mom." I shake my head, even though neither of them can see it.

"No, no, a success like this must be properly celebrated," she insists.

I hear the pride in her voice, warm and settling on my chest. "Okay," I say, even though I should probably temper her excitement a little.

This feeling is too good. Far too good…

"June Taylor, get down here this instant!"

Whenever Dad calls me by my full name, I always get a little queasy. Today is no different—the nausea rises as I walk down the stairs of our single-family home.

What did I do this time?

"Yes?" I ask as innocently as possible when I step into the living room.

He looks up from a sheet of paper, takes off his glasses, and points at the couch with them. "Sit."

Not good. Not good at all.

I slip past him and try to sneak a glance at the paper in his hand.

It's my last math test.

Fuck.

With clenched teeth, I sink onto the sofa, just as Mom appears in the doorway. Blinking rapidly, she studies me.

Dad turns the test over in his hands. "What is this, June?" he asks, looking at me with such a disappointed expression that I feel completely sick.

I shift around on the sofa, but I can't find a comfortable position. "What?" I ask in desperation. Of course I know what he's found.

"Please don't pretend you don't know," Mom says in a worried tone. "What's going on with you?"

"Nothing." And everything.

Dad sets his glasses down on the coffee table. Next to a stack of folders—all of them mine. From school!

Oh no…

He taps the top folder. "Nothing?" he asks, his voice flat. "So you think it's completely normal to fail every test for months?"

I slide my hands under my thighs and lower my gaze. "Don't know."

"Are you having trouble keeping up with the others? Do you need a tutor?" I hear Mom ask gently.

"No! That's not it."

"It's because you're always sick. You miss too much and trying to catch up on everything by yourself is impossible." That was Mom again.

"Is that true, June?" Dad asks, his tone intense.

Still keeping my eyes lowered, I shrug. What am I supposed to tell them? That I can't concentrate on studying anymore because of a boy I both hate and love?

They'd think I was crazy—and they'd be right.

"Look at me when I'm talking to you, June," Dad says, his voice strangely flat. Yesterday, I was still his princess. Today, I'm just June. That hurts.

I blink before obediently lifting my eyelids. His eyes have a watery sheen—he is that disappointed in me. Behind him, all his awards gleam in the glass display case.

The newspaper article about his practice. The continuing education certificates. The award for Best General Practitioner in Halifax. The Canadian Medical Association trophy for outstanding achievement.

My chest tightens.

"I don't understand. You were always an excellent student." He tries to smile, but it fails miserably.

If only I knew what to say to that. Ever since things started with Ashton three months ago, all I've been doing at school is trying to avoid his clique and his hatred toward me. The insults, the attempts to stick gum in my hair, the deliberate ball attacks during gym class.

Mom sinks onto the couch beside me. "What's going on? What's changed?"

"Nothing," I reply, because I just can't tell them.

With a swift motion, she pulls me into her arms. "It's okay, June," she whispers, her voice choked. "You'll just be a waitress or a store clerk—it's not a big deal." Her tone tells me exactly how disappointed she is in me.

Dad forces the corners of his mouth upward. And I know it hurts him the most to give up on me and our shared dream.

"I can do this," I insist, because I can't handle the feeling of letting them—and myself—down. "I'll work harder, study more, catch up on everything."

"Oh, June." Dad pushes himself up from his chair. "We love you, no matter what happens. You know that," he says gently, but I can tell it's not the truth. He's sad—so deeply sad—that I won't carry on his legacy.

And I am too.

"See you at dinner." Dad turns away and leaves the living room.

I watch him go. Watch the way his back trembles and his shoulders slump forward.

"Come on, let's get ourselves a nice piece of chocolate cake. That'll cheer you up," Mom says, trying to sound cheerful as she hugs me.

No. I don't want a damn piece of chocolate cake. I look at her with determination. "I can handle this, Mom, I swear."

A wistful smile crosses her face. "Of course, sweetheart," she replies lovingly, and that's when I realize something has to change.

From now on, things have to be different. I'm going to stand up to Ashton West. He's going to learn what it feels like to be taken down. If I have to, I'll do it the hard way.

"Oh, June..." Mom breathes into the phone today. "You can't imagine how much your success means to us."

Oh yes, I can. It doesn't just mean the world to them—it means everything to me too. Back then, I managed to pull myself out of the quicksand Ashton had pushed me into. He almost broke me, but I fought back—with everything I had, and admittedly, not always fairly. But he left me no choice.

"Thanks, Mom," I murmur, touched, and in the very next second, I realize I need to step it up if I want to land this job. "I have to go, work's calling," I say, wedge the phone between my shoulder and ear, and type my password for the medical database into the laptop.

"Don't let us hold you back. Talk soon, Princess." Dad's tone is warmer than the rays of the morning sun.

I'm a grown woman now. But whenever Dad calls me Princess, I still feel like I'm something special. Like I'm his treasure, guarded as if I were his most precious possession.

It took years of relentlessly proving that I deserved her trust before Dad called me that again after what Ashton did to me. I won't risk losing it again for anything in the world.

Chapter Thirteen

ASHTON

Yesterday afternoon, June came into my room again. Without looking at me, she handed me the cold packs so I could change them, checked my temperature, and muttered something like "There you go, that's better." Then she was gone again.

Maybe I should've asked her what's wrong with my legs or how much longer I have to stay here. But she might've looked at me with that pitying expression again and asked questions that cut too deep.

Questions like "What are you afraid of?"

Questions like "What are those scars?"

I can do without that.

And today more than ever. I can feel that I'm getting better. The pain in my legs is gone, and my head no longer feels like a nuclear bomb went off inside it.

Even though dawn is only just breaking, I throw back the blanket, sit up, and swing my legs out of bed. Carefully, I place my bare feet on the gray linoleum floor. Its chill makes me shiver, but I stand up slowly nonetheless.

It feels surprisingly good.

Bravely, I take a step. My muscles ache a little, but nowhere near as much as they did yesterday. The stabbing pain in my knees is completely gone.

Whatever June did, she was right. She helped me, took away the pain, and brought me closer to my goal.

Soon I'll be back home, working on my boat again. The schedule is still on track—within a few weeks, I'll set sail.

And then… then I'll finally leave all of this behind.

A sense of anticipation and relief spreads through me. I actually feel good enough to stretch my legs a bit. Since being admitted four days ago, I haven't left the bed. Being able to move now feels like breathing pure freedom.

Smiling, I take a pair of sweatpants from the waist-high cabinet next to my bed. Turns out it really was a good idea of Jeremy's to bring me clothes and those ridiculous slippers.

I pull the pants on over my boxers, slip into the shoes, and stroll out of the room. It's wonderful how my legs are slowly getting back into motion, becoming more flexible with each step.

Sighing with pleasure, I stroll around. There's not much going on in the hallway—no surprise, it's barely six in the morning, as the large clock on the wall tells me. From the staff lounge, the delicate scent of coffee and carefree laughter drift over to me. In the distance, dishes clatter.

Leisurely, I continue on. It's incredible how fit I feel. And even more incredible is that I have June to thank for it.

Inevitably, her face appears in my thoughts. The blue eyes. The intense way she looks at me, making me feel as if June can see right through what I did to her and into my dark soul. The symmetrical features, the high cheekbones. The little lines that form around her mouth when she purses her lips. When we saw each other again, I thought she was still the same ungrateful bitch as back then. But what if I was wrong? What if she doesn't want revenge at all, but actually wants to help me?

"Why exactly did I want to become a doctor again?" A female voice pulls me out of my thoughts. It seems to be coming from the changing room, whose door is only slightly ajar.

"To save lives, of course." That's June.

I stop in my tracks.

"You're way too idealistic. People are dumb," says the other woman.

June's bright laughter reaches me. "Not all of them."

"True. You, for example, are not dumb," the other replies affectionately, followed by a metallic clatter, as if someone is closing a locker. "Or… wait a second… no. You're dumb too," she adds, mockingly defiant.

"And you're completely sleep-deprived, so I forgive your mean, mean words." Instantly, I picture June in her doctor's coat, hands on her hips, grinning.

"These twelve-hour night shifts… a nightmare…" Someone lets out a loud yawn. "But whatever, I'll be in bed soon, then everything will be fine. But tell me, why are you already here? I thought we were meeting at home."

Oh, the two of them are roommates!

"Couldn't sleep." Fabric rustles.

"Because of your asshole patient?"

Oh. That must be me. Now things are getting interesting. I lean against the wall and tilt my head toward the crack in the door.

"I can handle it, Sonora, really, it's not a problem," says June, accompanied by a soft clinking sound.

This Sonora grunts in agreement. “Have you figured out what’s wrong with him?”

“Empathy,” June replies dryly.

Okay. I deserved that.

For a moment, no one says anything. I try to imagine what’s happening in there right now. Maybe June’s conversation partner is giving her a long, hard look. Maybe she’s raising an eyebrow.

“I don’t know. Not yet,” June finally says, a good dose of determination in her voice. “He’s still completely uncooperative, apparently doesn’t want me to help him. But…” She falls silent. Wood creaks.

“But what?” the other woman asks gently.

With my back pressed to the wall, I inch closer to the door to peer through the crack.

The two of them are sitting on the narrow wooden bench in front of a row of lockers. June’s jaw is tight, and her colleague watches her with raised eyebrows.

Now June shrugs. “I think he needs help.”

The warmth in her words takes me by surprise, and once again, there’s not the slightest trace of insincerity in her tone. She means it—she’s genuinely concerned about me.

“But he’s getting that from you anyway,” says the doctor with the brown corkscrew curls.

“No, not medical help.” June exhales heavily. “Psychological.”

Excuse me? What the hell is that supposed to mean?

“Because he refuses treatment?” Sonora asks, frowning thoughtfully.

June shakes her head, then gestures for the other to come closer. She lowers her voice, and I stop breathing so I won’t miss a word.

"He might be hurting himself," June whispers so quietly I can barely make it out. "There were scars on his thigh. Old ones, yes, but that doesn't necessarily mean there aren't fresh ones somewhere else… but…"

Damn, she saw them. The memory creeps up inside me —dark and painful. It has to go. Now.

"I don't know," Sonora says evasively, lowering her gaze to her fingernails and starting to pick at them.

"Yes, you do. They looked like someone had pressed a hot lighter head into them." There's something in June's expression that erases even the last trace of doubt in me: compassion.

Genuine, empathetic compassion. For me. The boy who tormented her day after day thirteen years ago. Guilt settles heavily on my chest.

"What if he's not an asshole at all, but actually has serious problems?" she asks, her voice trembling.

I bite my tongue to drown out the pangs of conscience burning through my soul.

The other girl picks at her fingernails more and more intensely. "Then you refer him to psychiatry as soon as your treatment is over. Problem solved."

"I…" Chewing on her lower lip, June looks up at the ceiling.

Sonora grabs June's upper arms. "You're taking this way too seriously, June."

June presses her lips together. "I knew him from before," she admits quietly, and once again I'm surprised.

I've been her patient for two days, and her roommate knows nothing about our shared past?

What does that mean?

"Okay." The brunette gets up from the bench and takes off her lab coat.

"We really went at each other." She sounds ashamed.

What does she mean by that? Why each other?

"And I did some awful things too. But he started it," June adds quickly.

Absentmindedly, she gazes out the window, where the day is finally beginning to break. She looks sad.

So sad that it couldn't possibly be an act.

If I had any feelings for June, the sight of her now would make me melancholy. My heart might skip a beat at the sight of her despair. And I'd probably feel the urge to pull her into my arms to protect her from whatever is making her whole body tremble.

Sonora scratches her left thumb with the nails of her right hand. She looks like the conversation is making her uncomfortable.

June shrugs. "One time I told the principal he'd kicked the school mascot—the cutest hamster of all time."

What?

Confused, I furrow my brow, struggling to form a coherent thought.

Could that be true?

Impossible.

Or is it?

Was it actually her who got me into trouble back then?

"You stomped on a hamster?" Dad towers over me, furious. "Have you lost your mind?"

I lower my gaze. Not because I feel guilty, but because I don't want to see the hatred on his face. "I didn't."

He waves the paper in his hand through the air. "Then why is your principal informing me that you've been suspended from school for a week because of it?"

How should I know? "I didn't do anything to the hamster. I swear."

"Stop lying to me!" Dad yells. The crease between his eyebrows deepens into a canyon. "Do you know what you are? A useless failure who'll never amount to anything in life."

I stubbornly hold his gaze.

Screw him.

He can't hurt me. I've long since gotten used to the way he talks to me.

He'd probably be happiest if I were dead too, but I'm not giving him that satisfaction.

With a dismissive wave, he turns away from me. "Useless, that boy," he mutters to himself. "Damn brat, ruins everything."

Bullshit. He's the one who ruins everything.

But I'll fix it.

If I catch the one who snitched on me to the principal, they're going to regret it.

Fuming, I turn to leave.

"Make sure I don't see your face next week," Dad yells after me.

"Got it," I snap at him.

"Did I give you permission to speak?"

With my back to him, I silently shake my head. And now, the very tears I'd managed to hold back start to well up in the corners of my eyes.

Like I'm some little girl.

Fuck.

Fuck. Fuck. Fuck.

"For heaven's sake, don't start crying now," he growls, clearly exhausted by the burden of having to endure me as his son.

"Screw you," I snap at him.

"What did you say?" His tone turns threatening now. Threatening and ice-cold. "Get out of my sight before I lose control." His fists clench so tightly the knuckles turn white.

With trembling fingers, I reach for the doorknob, push it down, and get out of there. The moment the door closes behind me, the chaos inside me takes over. The rage needs out.

With all my strength, I kick the glass panel of the hallway cabinet. It shatters into a thousand pieces with a crash, glasses tumble from the shelves. But it's not enough. I kick it again.

Once more.

And again.

Harder and harder, until the damn cabinet collapses.

Panting, I stare at the wrecked piece of furniture.

My anger still burns inside me, unchanged, and I know it will consume me if I don't do something about it. So I focus on what matters most right now.

Finding the one who pinned that hamster nonsense on me.

And making them pay for it.

I never found the culprit. Not until today. There were just too many people I didn't get along with. How did I not realize back then that June was the one who ratted me out to the principal? Maybe because she always acted so innocent.

What else did she try to use to fight back against me?

"That's a pretty harsh thing to say." Sonora rolls up her coat with stiff, jerky movements. "I mean, animal cruelty…"

"I know. But he left me no choice," June replies intensely. "Whatever happened—Ashton West was a bastard." Suddenly, she seems weak, so incredibly weak. "I was just defending myself—I had to."

Hearing that hits me like a punch to the gut.

Distracted, I push myself away from the wall. I've heard enough to suspect that neither the cold, heartless June nor the innocent, helpless June from back then is the real one. But if she's not who I thought she was—then who is she?

An empathetic, helpful woman who even cares about someone like me? If that's the case, then… then I owe her more than I could ever make up for. Or is she a fighter, striking back in secret? In that case, she's probably playing a game with me today that's even crueler than the one I once played with her.

"I understand," comes a voice from the changing room to my ear.

"Good, then we can get back to the things that really matter," is the last thing I hear from June before I'm too far away from the two of them.

Dark shadows follow me on my way back to the room. Deep, dark shadows and the certainty that I have to uncover the truth—no matter how I'm supposed to do that.

Chapter Fourteen

JUNE

His silence is different today.

I had actually worked up the courage to ask him about the scars, but now I slip the thermometer back into the pocket of my lab coat without even trying.

"Normal temperature," I say, noting it in the medical chart. "How's the pain?"

"Gone." He studies me so intently, it's as if he's searching for something very specific in my face.

Do I have a yogurt stain from breakfast somewhere? Or what is it that's got him so preoccupied?

Better to pretend his strange behavior doesn't faze me. "Even in your knees?"

He nods. "Everything's great."

"And the muscles?" I gesture with my pen toward his legs, hidden beneath the sheet.

"Listen… I…" he says, and I notice that the usual hostility in his expression is gone. In its place is something else. Maybe embarrassment? Yes, that could be it. But why?

His behavior unsettles me deeply. We've made progress

lately, even if only tiny steps. Has that all been lost again today, or is he avoiding me for some other reason?

Hesitantly, I reach for the visitor's chair and sit down. "Do you have any other symptoms? Maybe new ones or ones…" I wanted to ask, ones that embarrass you?, but I can't bring myself to finish the sentence. "Tell me about them. We've got all the time in the world."

"You don't have any other patients?" he asks, his voice rough.

I look him straight in the eye, with all the inner conflict that has been churning in me since I discovered his scars yesterday. "No one as important as you," I reply with urgency, because it's the truth. In the case review starting in just a few minutes, I have to present findings to Dr. Young. For that, I need to know whether my treatment has worked.

He exhales slowly and reaches for the water bottle on his nightstand. "The muscle pain has subsided," he says, at least answering the question I asked earlier.

Involuntarily, I smile at him. But a split second later, I realize it's entirely inappropriate.

"But it's still there," I say quickly, letting the corners of my mouth fall. It shouldn't be—not with his body temperature. "Then it's not related to the fever." Disappointed, I jot a note in his file. Maybe he does have a tropical disease, even though my research yesterday made that seem unlikely. "Have you been abroad in the past three months?"

He looks at me with a pained expression. "That's not what I…" he begins, but then cuts himself off.

What's going on, Ashton? I ask him silently.

He looks like he's fighting with himself. Maybe he was away, and something happened on that trip that he doesn't want to reveal.

As calmly as I can manage, I set the pen aside. "I just want to help you, Ashton."

He doesn't answer, just stares at me again in that strange way that sends a queasy feeling into my gut and screws the cap back on the water bottle.

Stop it and tell me what I need to know, I want to beg him. Instead, I bite my tongue and hold his gaze, while his bizarre behavior gnaws at something deep in my chest.

"What's going on, Ashton?" I finally ask in a soft voice, because I can't bear his heavy silence any longer.

He gives a barely noticeable shake of his head, opens his mouth, then closes it again.

"Just answer the question. Please." My God, I'm begging him now—what else am I supposed to do? Drop to my knees in front of him?

"Or you answer mine," he replies, gripping the water bottle tightly.

What is he talking about? "Stop trying to change the subject. Were you abroad or not?" I shoot back, folding my arms across my chest.

I don't like where this is going.

"June…"

What, June? What is that supposed to mean? Is he trying to confuse me? "Cut the mind games," I snap at him, a little too sharply thanks to my nerves.

"Okay, I get it." With his lips pressed together, he sets the water bottle down on the nightstand. "You fooled me for a moment, but not anymore. You're the one playing mind games." His gaze is hard, his jaw clenched. The vein in his neck is throbbing.

"Stay cool, Ashton. Or do you want me to have the nurse draw up a dose of Valium for you?" I ask, because I honestly don't know what else to do.

"On what grounds?" He sits up in bed. "What are you trying to stir up this time to get your revenge?"

Why this time?

"Go on, run off and tell everyone your lies." His breathing is labored. "That's what you're best at, isn't it?"

"What the hell are you talking about?" I shoot back, even though I already have a feeling what this was about.

How does he know about that? And since when?

"Don't make a fool of yourself. I know it was you," he counters. His cheeks turn so red I fear his fever might be coming back. "You were the one who spread that crap about the school mascot to get me in trouble." His expression is a twisted mix of hatred and pain. "And more than that, right?"

My mouth falls open, and shame takes hold of me. And beyond that, I feel a wound inside me tear open—one I thought had healed years ago. The pain sweeps away everything I'd built. Dr. Taylor no longer exists. Only June remains—the hurt girl from Halifax High.

"You made my life a living hell!" I scream\at him, hurling my rage, my anguish, and my suffering at him with trembling lips. Everything that now pours from my wound, dragging me down into a darkness I thought I'd already escaped.

My eyes burn, and the hospital room threatens to blur. But one thing I see all too clearly: the deep pain in Ashton's eyes as he looks at me.

Chapter Fifteen

ASHTON

I can't argue with that. It's true. I was a damn asshole to her. "But I wasn't the only one who screwed up, was I?" I ask, exhausted.

She gasps, her cheeks flushing red. "I… I… I…" she stammers, agitated, and slowly, memories start to resurface—ones that had seemed unimportant until now. Suddenly, they carry weight.

"Everywhere I went, you showed up. I saw you hiding behind ledges, under the bleachers at the sports arena, behind the fire escape where my boys and I used to sneak smokes." I look at her challengingly. She can't deny it, because that's exactly how it happened.

Shaking her head, she wraps her arms around herself.

"You were there to spy on me." Yeah, that must've been it. That old anger starts to boil up inside me again, and I can't control it. I know it's wrong, but it's there anyway. "Every damn chance you had, you ran to the teachers with your half-truths and made up the rest."

"I had to defend myself!" she snaps back. Her fists

clench, her nostrils flare, and suddenly, her fierce anger melts into painful sadness. "You bullied me," she says, her voice cracking.

Shit, yeah. And I'm anything but proud of it. "I did," I admit. The anger has left my voice, too. Maybe because she looks so vulnerable right now. Maybe because seeing her like this breaks something in me. Maybe because years of fighting this rage have finally worn me down.

She sniffles. "You called me a fat cow and made my life a living hell every day with some new cruelty."

I shouldn't have done that, but in that moment... the way she was with her mom... "And you made sure everyone called me 'Hamster Horror,'" I reply, trying to keep the memory from coming back up.

Aside from Dad's lecture—which only made an already bad situation even worse—everyone thought I abused animals. After that, I had no choice but to double down on playing the tough guy who didn't give a damn about anything.

June shakes her head so violently that strands of hair come loose from her ponytail. "I had good reasons for that," she says, fists clenched.

Same here—sort of. Maybe. I don't know. "What else did you do?"

With a hardened expression, she bites down on her lower lip.

So there's more.

It was a mistake to bring it up. This isn't leading to any kind of clarity—just more confusion. On top of that, it's dragging back all those awful memories. I don't want them. I want them gone.

"You'd better go now," I say firmly, already deciding to do the same. Halifax Harbor Hospital isn't the only clinic in

Nova Scotia. Even if my health issues come back, I don't have to be here of all places.

I can hear her breathing—uneven and strained. She doesn't move, or at least I don't hear any footsteps. What the hell is she still doing here?

"Do you remember March fifth, back in eleventh grade?" she asks into the silence between us.

That was thirteen years ago. How am I supposed to remember that? I turn to her, searching her face. "No."

"But I remember it like it was yesterday." She blinks rapidly. "I could tell you every detail from every single day of that school year."

Impossible. No one can do that.

A tired snort escapes her lips. "March fifth was the day you put melted chocolate in my biology book."

My stomach twists into a knot.

"You knew I'd open it at the beginning of class. And you were prepared." A pained expression spreads across her beautiful face.

I don't want the memory to surface. I fight against it.

"After Mr. Simmens entered the classroom, you announced you needed to use the restroom," she says haltingly.

And suddenly the memory floods back. I passed by her desk on my way out. I walked extra slowly, keeping an eye on the biology teacher.

"When Mr. Simmens asked us to open our books…" Her voice falters, but she doesn't need to say anything more.

I remember standing next to her. Burning with anger and hatred toward her damn perfect family, after I'd had to spend a whole week in hell at home because of that stupid school mascot incident. I slammed the biology book right into her face with all my strength.

My buddies took a photo of her chocolate-smeared face. And then... "The flyer..."

"This software can do the sickest hacks." My buddy boots up his old man's computer and uploads the picture he took today of that fat cow in biology class.

I burst out laughing immediately. I hit her face dead center—she looks like a perfectly round chipmunk with bright cheeks. Even the hair that always falls over both sides of her face got splattered with brown spots.

God, it feels so good to finally laugh at something again.

"Come on, let's really blow her up. Give her a pig's nose and that Miss Piggy hairstyle," my buddy suggests.

I rub my fists together. "This is gonna be epic."

Grinning, he moves the cursor to her button nose, grabs the chocolate-smeared tip, and pulls it upward. The nostrils stretch longer and longer. "Like this?"

"Make them wider too. They should be nice and round," I suggest.

As soon as he's done, I double over with laughter. "And now give her a double chin."

"Coming right up." It only takes a few clicks and now the fat pig looks another sixty pounds heavier. "And here comes the Miss Piggy hairstyle."

"Awesome," I comment. "We still need some text. Like a piece of art, you know? They always have names too. Write Fat Pig Eating Chocolate."

He types the words in all caps at the top of the image. "We'll print it out and hang it up at school."

I love the idea. She's going to suffer—even more than I do—and she should, that ungrateful cow.

When I hold the printout in my hands a few minutes later, I'm seething with rage. Still, I want to believe that one day she'll be gone, and until then, I'll keep letting it out.

The next morning, the flyer was all over school. On every bulletin board, every door, every locker.

Silently, I look at June, not knowing what to say. I was just… so angry. Out of control. Blind.

How could I have done that?

Her lower lip trembles. "Can you imagine how that felt for me?" she asks in a hoarse voice. "To be humiliated like that in front of everyone?"

"Better than you think," I reply before I can stop myself.

Being humiliated was part of my everyday life at home. Somewhere inside me, a burning pain begins to spread. I have to shut off this emotion—it doesn't belong here. And yet, it's still inside me, just like back then. I feel that uncontrollable rage taking hold of me. The sense of helplessness, the desperate urge to control at least something in my life.

June had to pay the price for that urge.

"Yes, the thing with the hamster was me, and it wasn't the only time," June repeats what she said earlier. "But if I hadn't fought back…"

"Yeah, sometimes you have to," I say, my voice cracking. "Sometimes it doesn't help, though." At least, that's how it was for me. Still, I kept going.

She stands across from me, her face filled with pain. She opens her mouth, then closes it again without saying a word.

I don't know what to think. Not about what I did, not about her reaction to it, and not about what it stirred up.

Why did this have to happen? Is June trying to help me today—or get revenge? Who were we back then, and who are we now?

These and a thousand other questions are swirling through my mind, creating too much pressure in my head.

I can't take it anymore.

It's too much.

This is where it ends.

I clear my throat. "I haven't been abroad in the past few months," I answer her earlier question, trying to escape this conversation that gets so far under my skin it hurts all the way to the deepest layers.

She stares at me, stunned. "Okay," she says a few seconds later, without taking her eyes off me.

"Don't you want to write that down?" I nod toward the medical file lying on the nightstand next to my bed.

"Write it down?"

Our conversation seems to have thrown her off just as much as it did me. "For the correct diagnosis," I mumble, unable to stop searching her unchanged expression for an answer.

Why did this have to happen?

"Right, the diagnosis." She touches her forehead, then suddenly her eyes go wide. "What time is it?"

I glance at the clock hanging above the doorframe behind her. "Eight."

She instantly goes pale. "The case review!" she exclaims, flustered, and rushes off.

Chapter Sixteen

JUNE

The others have long since left the conference room. I'm the only one still here, staring wearily at the whiteboard.

With minus five points, I'm still in last place after today's meeting, but right now, I hardly care. I'm just grateful I was even able to present my research findings from yesterday after the conversation with Ashton, even though everything inside me is in complete turmoil.

While the others were presenting their cases, my thoughts were with Ashton and all the conflicting emotions he stirred up in me earlier.

What did he mean when he said he knew what it felt like to be humiliated? He was the coolest guy in school—nobody could touch him.

None of this adds up. The image I'd held of my school years, so vivid and clear for so long, suddenly feels distorted.

Still, one thing remains true: what happened was his fault. He practically forced me to fight back. I had no choice, and it was right to stand up for myself—with every means I used. Again and again, I claimed victories, didn't see him at school for days, and drew new strength from that.

But one question remains: how are we supposed to move forward now that we've let the past resurface, even for a moment? Now that he knows I fought back then, will it change the way he treats me? Or the other way around?

I don't know. Still, he's my patient, and Dr. Young has approved my suggestions for further diagnostics.

I need to get to Ashton—the sooner I get this over with, the sooner I can refocus on what matters most to me: this job. So I turn away from the whiteboard and leave the conference room. My phone vibrates in my pocket.

A message from Mom.

Thought about it. We're celebrating your new job at The Press Gang. A special place for a special daughter. Table's reserved.

She wants to celebrate at one of the most exclusive restaurants in Halifax? "Oh, Mom…" I let out a heavy sigh and start typing a reply.

Please, Mom, let's wait and see if I actually land the job. The letters blur before my eyes, my finger hovers over the send button, but I can't bring myself to press it. The sentence sounds too negative—I revise it.

Please, Mom, let's wait until I get the job.

Yes, that's the right approach. She won't worry, and at the same time, I'm tempering her excitement a little.

That way, wc all win.

I hit send, and immediately a new message pops up.

That's not necessary. You'll get the job anyway, and it's hard to get a table at The Press Gang! Focus on the work, I'll take care of the rest ;)

A wistful feeling takes hold of me. I've longed for this kind of unconditional trust for so long. For my parents to believe in me again. What can I say now without crushing this fragile little seedling before it even grows?

I send Mom an "Okay." It's already more than enough for me. The competition for the job and Ashton—both are almost too much to handle. I don't want to risk adding problems with my parents on top of that.

Exhausted, I step out into the hallway and walk to Ashton's room. I stop in front of the door. I have no idea what kind of Ashton is waiting for me on the other side.

Because one thing is true: I ratted him out. Called him an animal abuser. Made sure the whole school hated him.

The thought that this wasn't my only attempt to get rid of him eats away at my conscience. Lost in thought, I pull my necklace out from under the hospital shirt and clutch the daisy pendant tightly in my fist. Its metal edges press into my palm and quickly grow warm.

It was right to stand up for myself.

It was right.

If I hadn't done it, I would have broken under what he did to me.

"It was right," I whisper to myself and let the pendant slip back beneath my top. I feel it close against my skin, right where it belongs, as I open the door to Ashton's room and step inside.

"Hey," I say in greeting, studying his face closely.

I wish I could read his mood from it, but it seems expressionless. Picking up the conversation from earlier now would be wrong. Completely inappropriate. His health should come first.

"We need to discuss your ongoing treatment." I approach with deliberate calm and pull the visitor's chair up to his bed.

He nods. That's a good sign. I hope.

With a drawn-out clearing of my throat, I sit down and open the medical file, needing something to hold on to. "Your persistent muscle pain worries me. It should have gone away along with the fever."

"It barely hurts anymore." He waves it off.

My gaze lingers on him longer than necessary. Is he finally ready to have a normal doctor-patient conversation with me?

When I realize I'm staring at him, I quickly lower my eyes to the documents. "Overexertion can cause muscle pain."

"Mhm," Ashton murmurs. It's not enough to gauge his mood.

"Do you work out a lot?" I continue. If that's the case, I don't need to look any further for the cause.

He shakes his head. "Not excessively."

Then trauma is the second most likely reason. "There may be sprains—those are injured joints. We'll take a few X-rays and then we'll know more."

"My joints are fine," he replies, almost too quickly.

I study him. He's tense. Why?

Yesterday, I would have asserted myself as the authoritative doctor after a comment like that. Today, I hesitate. My thoughts are on his scars, still preoccupying me. Before I discovered them, he tried to stop the treatment. Is he resisting the X-rays for the same reason? Is he afraid I'll see something else he wants to hide from me?

"I want to help you, Ashton," I hear myself say gently, because it's the truth. No matter what was—or is—between us, this is about something so much bigger than that.

To my surprise, the hardness fades from his expression. "Why?" He speaks the word so softly I can barely hear it.

"You're my patient." Even as I say it, I'm sure if that is the whole truth.

Yes, that's it, June. Don't be ridiculous.

"Your health matters to me," I add, forcing myself to focus on the one true reason. Solving his case means landing my dream job.

Exactly right, June. That's what really matters.

I look at him intently. He meets my gaze. Soft. Warm. Hesitant.

I lean forward, resting my elbows on my thighs. "Listen, I understand if it's hard for you to trust me." I have no idea if that's what is holding him back, but it is the first thing that comes to mind. "What can I do to change that?"

For several seconds, he does nothing but look at me. Sometimes I think he is about to answer, and then I am certain he never will.

It takes quite a while before he finally clears his throat. "Okay, do the X-ray."

"Thank you." I give him a tentative smile. Even though I'm not sure it is the right moment, I gather my courage. Because the right moment for this topic will probably never come. "Can I ask you something else?"

He furrows his brow but doesn't give me an answer.

"Your scars… I mean… um…" I fiddle with the edge of the medical file. "Where did you get them?"

Tensely, I watch as his expression darkens.

"I need your answer for medical reasons. It could be important for your diagnosis. The more I know about you, the better," I say quickly, even though what is going on inside me has long since gone beyond the job. Something in me wants to know. Something inside me that, more than ever today, wants to believe that behind his distant façade is a sensitive human being.

A person I want to see.

A person I want to understand.

His jaw muscles tense, as does the vein in his neck. Barely visible, but it is there. He is trying to stay in control, and on his face, he succeeds with frighteningly well. But those details tell a different story.

With forced nonchalance, he shrugs. “I was a wild kid.”

No, Ashton. Those aren’t scars from playing. That’s something else.

Shall I tell him? Or will I risk offending him?

“I understand,” I reply on instinct, trying to keep my expression neutral. “Then I’ll make sure someone takes you to get the X-ray.”

Am I imagining it, or did he just exhale in relief? “Alright,” he replies casually, and with that, everything seems to be said for now.

With a strange sense of melancholy, I return the visitor’s chair to its place and leave the hospital room. Until now, I’d always been glad to leave this place behind, but for the first time, I find myself wishing there were a reason to stay just a little longer.

But there isn’t one.

So, with a bittersweet feeling in my chest, I pull the door shut behind me.

Chapter Seventeen

JUNE

After arranging Ashton's X-ray appointment and leaving the doctors' lounge, my eyes land on Jaxon. Leaning casually against the wall, he's flirting with a nurse as if he doesn't, like the rest of us, have multiple patients to care for.

So far, I hadn't had a chance to talk to him about his case. Now, I step up to him. "We need to talk."

"Later," he says, without taking his eyes off the nurse. "And what if we had cocktails at the harbor tonight?"

"Now." I grab his arm and pull him with me—after all, this is about a human life. Something he clearly hasn't realized yet.

With a disgruntled grunt, he follows me. "No need to be jealous, Barbie. I'm man enough for more than one woman," he comments as we finally stop by the window front.

"This is about your case," I say, ignoring his idiotic remark. "I'm afraid you missed something."

An exasperated snort escapes his mouth. "Definitely not. The guy's got tendonitis, and the only reason the boss hasn't crowned me the winner yet is because it takes a few days for the treatment to be considered a success."

She said that? Seriously? When?

He grins. "Someone wasn't paying attention earlier," he says, stepping up to the window and letting his gaze drift over the Halifax skyline with a deep breath. "My deadline for making the correct diagnosis was yesterday. I already knew what the guy had by then. If my diagnosis turns out to be right—and it will, by next week at the latest, when his condition clearly improves—then yesterday's date counts, and I win."

No!

I go hot and cold at the same time. "Your diagnosis is wrong," I reply, still managing to keep my voice under control.

His pitying look hits me. "You lost, June. Deal with it." Calmly, he slips his hands into the pockets of his lab coat. "Gotta run—hot babe's waiting for me."

I gasp for air as he turns and walks away.

Did he just ignore me? And—worse—did he just ignore his patient? A father who wants nothing more than to toss his little daughter into the air again?

What an absolute idiot. He doesn't deserve this job, and yet he's ahead. It's so incredibly unfair. I rush after him and cut him off.

With a bored expression, he turns around. "So you really want it. Fine, you get your date, Barbie."

"Come with me," I say simply, ignoring his comment, and pull him toward Dr. Young's office. If he won't listen to me alone, then this is the only way.

I knock firmly. Through the glass panel, I see the boss lift her head. Frowning, she waves us in.

"Someone die?" she asks dryly, rising from her chair.

"Not yet," I reply sharply—maybe too sharply, but Jaxon just gets under my skin.

"Interesting." The boss looks back and forth between Jaxon and me. "All right, go ahead."

Agitated, I point my index finger at Jaxon. "In my opinion, his patient is suffering from anemia," I say, even though the diagnosis hasn't been confirmed yet. "It could be caused by chronic kidney disease. Autoimmune disorders, bone cancer, Crohn's disease…"

"He doesn't have anemia, just a tendonitis, nothing more," Jaxon cuts me off. "I know what you're trying to do here. But there's no lifeline left for you to grab onto. The game's been over for a while."

Dr. Young leans back against her desk and pulls a pack of gum from her pocket. She doesn't look like she has any intention of stepping into this conversation. On the contrary, she seems quite entertained by what she's witnessing.

I shake my head emphatically and list, one by one, all the symptoms I discussed with Jaxon's patient.

"Do you really want to take that risk?" I snap at Jaxon, heated. Anemias can, in the worst case, lead to heart failure. He can't possibly want that for his patient. And if not for the patient's sake, then at least for his own.

Unimpressed, Jaxon holds my gaze.

I turn to the boss. "There's something there, Dr. Young. We can't ignore it. Please…"

"Maybe," she comments, popping a piece of gum into her mouth.

"I didn't miss anything." A flash of anger sparks in Jaxon's eyes.

"Oh yes, you did. And you should be glad I'm pointing

it out to you." I would've much preferred to tell him in private, but that's not what he wanted.

The boss loudly pops a bubble with her chewing gum. "There's something to that, Number Three, don't you think?"

He bites his lower lip. "Screw it," he growls, exasperated, pushes me aside, and heads for the door. I see him wave at the nurse he was flirting with earlier. "Sweetheart, I need a full blood workup for 309. Can you check that for me?" he calls out to her.

"Thanks for the tip, June," I mutter under my breath and turn to leave as well.

A moment later, I feel Dr. Young's hand on my shoulder. "Well done, Dr. Taylor."

Wow. Praise from the boss. It's so incredible, I don't know what to say. Warmth spreads through my chest as I turn to face her. I try to play it cool, just nod at her. But even as I head for the door, a whole firework show goes off inside me.

Chapter Eighteen

ASHTON

I just want to help you, Ashton.

June's words are everywhere inside me. Ever since she left my hospital room, I haven't been able to shake them off.

This has to stop.

I pull on the gown the radiology assistant handed me earlier and step through the door into the examination room.

"Lie down, please." The assistant gestures toward the stainless steel table.

Trying not to think about June anymore, I lie down on the thin padding spread over the icy metal.

"This will protect you from scatter radiation," the assistant explains, placing a heavy blanket over my torso. Then he positions the X-ray machine above my legs. "Please don't move from now on."

With those words, he disappears. Silence settles over the sterile room. Silence that my mind quickly fills again with June's voice.

You bullied me.

She sounded so full of sorrow. So desperate.

So... anything but vengeful.

The last thing I want right now is to see June's face in my mind. And yet, it forces its way to the forefront. There she is—seventeen years old, lips pressed tightly together, fists clenched.

She hated me with an intensity I can't describe. And I made her feel that way. Because I hated her just as fiercely.

All because of one thing. One situation that, to me, so blatantly revealed June's character that I didn't doubt my judgment for even a second back then.

Absentmindedly, I stare up at the ceiling, at the neon lights. One of them is dimmer than the others—maybe it's about to go out.

Broken, the word echoes inside me.

The X-ray machine hums for a moment, then that tormenting silence returns. A hospital worker comes in, adjusts the position of the machine, and disappears again.

"You made my life a living hell," June screams at me, and once again I have no idea what to do with all the emotions her words stir up inside me.

There's so much guilt and fear.

And then there's the pain of memory, the kind she's been dragging out of me ever since we saw each other again.

"Your scars... so... um... where did you get them?"

Oh God.

I exhale sharply. If I could, I'd jump up from this table and just run away.

Away from June.

Away from what she does to me.

And away from myself.

What if the war we fought against each other—me

openly, and her seemingly in secret—took more from both of us than I've realized until now?

As if that weren't confusing enough, the June of today now looks at me in my thoughts so intensely that my pulse quickens.

She whispers gently that she only wants to help me and smiles so softly that the corners of my mouth lift in response. A lock of hair falls into her face, and I feel the urge to brush it aside.

I want to get to know her, on a deeper level. To take away the pain I caused her—regardless of whether she still holds a grudge against me. Because even if she does, she has every right to.

Out of nowhere, the assistant enters the room and swings the X-ray machine to the side. "Thank you, you can get dressed again," he says.

"Okay… um…" Still caught between my strange thoughts, the unanswered questions, and the painful memories, I get up and shuffle back to the locker room.

The thoughts of June come with me, along with all the conflicting emotions she stirs in me. And even though I'd rather not admit it, I have a feeling they'll stay with me, no matter where I go.

Chapter Nineteen

JUNE

"Alright, number one, go ahead and do that," says Dr. Young after Ben finishes presenting his case, then she shifts her focus to me. "Okay, number two, what do you have?"

Nothing. That would be the honest answer. Another day has passed, and I'm still completely in the dark.

"My patient's myalgia is ongoing, suspected sprains, but the X-ray showed no pathological findings," I summarize. "Just a few old, healed fractures were visible. I don't think they're related to the symptoms." The original bone structure has largely recovered, only a typical thickening remains visible. Ashton's fractures must be several years old.

"And that means?" Dr. Young fixes her gaze on me.

"That I'll discard this theory and focus on a new one." I pretend it doesn't bother me at all, even though the opposite is true.

"Right." At least she's not deducting points for the medical dead end—though maybe just not yet. "And that would be?"

"There could be a neurological condition behind his

symptoms," I reply, even though it's unlikely. I find it strangely difficult to say the words out loud. And imagining that Ashton might actually suffer from a neurological disorder is even harder.

It could change his life forever.

A life I realize, in this moment, I know absolutely nothing about.

"Where'd you get that crap from?" Jaxon suddenly cuts in. "The guy had a fever, stomach pain, muscle and joint aches. Nothing points to anything neurological."

The boss points her pen at Jaxon. "Aha. Very good argument, number three." Her gaze flicks to me. "Counterarguments, number two?"

His scars. If they really are from self-harm, he might be suffering from depression. Combined with the myalgia, that could be—admittedly a far-fetched—indication of Parkinson's. That's what I should say, but I can't. It feels wrong to violate his privacy like that, especially since it's just a vague idea—really less than that. It's a desperate attempt to find anything that might explain his symptoms.

"My patient reports fatigue and poor sleep," I say instead. A white lie, but a justified one, since it leads to the same result and harms no one.

Jaxon snorts dismissively. "Completely unfounded."

"Your chance, Number Three. Just keep throwing out guesses," says the boss, clearly enjoying herself.

"Pfff… well… could be lupus." He shrugs.

Yeah, right. Someone's clearly watched too much Dr. House. "Sure. Anything that seems vaguely nonspecific is automatically lupus." Once again, he's taking the easy way out. "Why not go straight for something psychological? That'd be convenient too, wouldn't it?" I sound more spiteful than I mean to. But his attitude is getting on my nerves more than usual today. No idea why I'm so thin-skinned.

"Nope, that wasn't it, Number Three." Dr. Young turns to the whiteboard and picks up the marker. "Orders, Number Two?"

"Clinical neurological exam, electromyography, MRI," I say, since extensive blood tests have already been done and I want to spare Ashton a muscle biopsy for now.

Involuntarily, I hold my breath as the boss crosses out my minus five points from yesterday and draws a neutral zero. "I'm really curious about the results."

Me too. Though not in a good way.

"How's your patient doing, Number Three?" Her expectant gaze lands on Jaxon.

"He's anemic," he admits meekly.

The boss smirks. "Well, look at that—Barbie was right after all, and things are getting interesting. Very good. Next steps?"

"Well…" he replies hesitantly, as if he hadn't prepared for this question and now has to think and speak at the same time. "The guy plays hockey, so it's quite possible he ordered some performance-enhancing drugs online that have nasty side effects. Or he came into contact with toxins."

I'd consider both possibilities likely too, but he's forgetting the second symptom. "And those would cause the muscle pain?" I blurt out.

"Why not?" he snaps, giving me a venomous look. He hates me for dragging him to the boss yesterday. But what else was I supposed to do? He didn't leave me a choice.

Dr. Young sits down on the table. "So, what's your diagnosis, number two?"

There's a cause that's far more likely than shady supplements. "I'd check the thyroid. Hypothyroidism would explain both of the patient's symptoms."

"Ohhh," Dr. Young says, clapping her hands. Then her intensely inquisitive gaze lands on Jaxon. "You're up. And… go ahead."

"Could be." His expression tells me he doesn't have the faintest clue.

"Good, then you know what to do." She nods encouragingly at Jaxon. "You shouldn't expect any points for it, though—but I'm sure you're aware of that."

A smug grin spreads across his face. "No problem. Barbie needs them more than I do anyway."

Thank you so much, how generous.

"Don't be so sure about that." With a wink, Dr. Young steps back up to the whiteboard and awards her points. "Final score for today: Ben plus one, June plus three, Jaxon plus five."

Nice. Very nice, actually.

She even deducted a point from Jaxon. No idea why, but neither he nor I ask. Ben lets out a long sigh.

"Well then, back to work." The boss quickly sets the marker aside and claps her hands. "I want to see results tomorrow."

Chapter Twenty

ASHTON

June didn't really just say that, did she?

"A neurological disorder?" I repeat in disbelief. Shit, I shouldn't have pressured her into sharing her diagnosis. But the thing with my legs and the fact that it could happen again at any moment is just too terrifying.

She raises her hands in a calming gesture. "Right now, it's just a theory. We'll run a few tests, then we'll know more."

Sure, it's easy for her to say—but not for me. I don't know much about medicine, but I'm well aware these are terrible illnesses. Just the thought that I might be suffering from something like that makes it painful to breathe. And I even forget that there's a wall I've always kept up to stop her from seeing what's really going on inside me.

"And if it is? What would that mean for me?" For the only thing that matters to me. For what I've been working toward for so long.

I already built a boat once that I was never able to finish. I already lost that one dream that was like air to me.

Now it's within reach again. And it's supposed to go up in flames all over again?

June steps to the side of my bed. For a moment, I feel like she wants to reach out to me, but she doesn't. "That depends on the results. The progression can vary greatly depending on the illness, it would be..."

"Don't give me that. Doesn't Michael J. Fox have one of those neurological things?" I snap at her so harshly she flinches. I exhale, trying to calm myself before continuing. "And what it's done to him is more than obvious."

Her gaze turns sorrowful. "Exactly," she whispers, as if the answer itself pains her. "Still. We have to wait for the results."

"How long will it take?" I look at her, questioning, and that completely idiotic part of me I can't shake is glad she's my doctor. That she's here for me, going through this with me.

"The examinations are scheduled for today, and I'm putting pressure on the lab to analyze your samples as quickly as possible." Her tone carries something soothing now, and she smiles at me warmly. "By the day after tomorrow, we'll have everything. I promise."

I don't know what to say to that. "June..." I say, my voice just as soft as hers, and a moment later, I'm overwhelmed—once again—by a heavy sense of guilt.

In school, I made her life hell. Since we met again here at Halifax Harbor Hospital, I've shown her nothing but my hatred for the world. And yet now she's standing in front of me with a caring expression, ready to do whatever it takes to help me.

No matter what she did or didn't do back then, I was the one who overreacted when I saw her with her mom.

"I..." I start again, but once more, I can't finish the sentence. I've never apologized to anyone in my entire life. Because I never gave a damn about what other people thought. But with June, it's different...

She smiles gently. "It's okay..."

No. It's not.

I want nothing more than to reach out to her, touch her fingers or her upper arm. So that she can at least feel what I just can't seem to say. But that's impossible.

"What I did back then..." I finally say.

I stop. Because I see tears welling up in her eyes. Are they tears of anger? Fear? Or memory? Whatever they hold, they make it hard for me to breathe.

"You have no idea what you did to me." Her expression adds sadly, "And how terrible it was for me."

Silently, I bite my tongue. She's right. I don't know. And until today, I didn't care either. Because I was a fucking asshole—but I don't want to be that anymore. Not with her.

"It..."

"Because of you... you... it was..." She draws in a sharp breath, turns away, and stalks to the window. Once there, she stands with her back to me. Her upper body trembles, the tips of her hair quiver. "It took years for me to get my life back on track. To believe in myself again, to think positively, to have a future."

Oh God. Why the hell was I such a fucking bastard?

"June, I..."

She turns around abruptly. "That's the past. It's nothing. Unimportant. I've long since moved on," she says firmly, but I can see in her face that our past is far from nothing to her.

Not even close.

To her, it's still everything.

Shit, I'm no good at this kind of thing. I never was. Still, I look at her intently now.

"And what's important today?" I ask. Partly to escape my own guilt. And partly to steer her thoughts toward something that might dry her tears. Something that—twisted as it may be—might make her smile again.

Chapter Twenty-One

JUNE

What's important today?

Strangely enough—him. Unbelievable. Who would've thought I'd ever end up in this situation?

I let my gaze wander across his face. The sharp features, the five-day stubble, the stormy blue-gray eyes, the black hair falling into his forehead. There's openness in his expression—maybe even genuine interest.

"This," I reply, spreading my arms. "My work, my patients." You, I add silently.

"Did you always want to be a doctor?" He sits up in his bed and adjusts his pillow.

Nodding, I run my fingers over the cool metal of the nightstand beside Ashton's bed. "My dad's a doctor too. I saw every day how much this job meant to him." He was often tired, sometimes discouraged when he couldn't help. But on the days he saved lives or reunited families, he radiated from within.

"I didn't know that." He tilts his head. "What field?"

"General medicine," I reply with a smile, thinking of

how often I visited him at the practice as a child. I can picture him clearly—his white coat and stethoscope, his warm smile, and the calm, steady way he always made the right decisions, even in chaotic situations. "He's amazing. He's received many awards and honors for his work. Mostly because he never gave up on finding the right diagnosis. So many patients with unclear symptoms fall through the cracks, suffering for years without knowing why."

Ashton's gaze drifts past me. "Sounds like the kind of father every kid would wish for." His voice suddenly sounds thick.

"He showed me what it means to be a doctor. And he was always there for me," I confirm, even though there was a time when that wasn't so easy.

A time when he stopped believing in me…

Leaning against the post of our driveway gate, I turn the folded note in my hand. The paper had already absorbed the moisture from my palms minutes ago.

I look at the red-painted wooden house with the white shutters, partially hidden behind the bushes.

Do I really have to tell them? Isn't there another way?

I feel sick.

"Do it, June," I tell myself and push off from the gatepost. I don't really have a choice.

By report card day at the latest, I'll be exposed anyway. I'd hoped I might be able to stop it. Somehow. But I'm probably not going to make it through the school year. Because of asshole Ashton.

And that's despite the fact that I've started fighting back. I yelled at him, threw things at him, reported him to the principal. I've knocked him down so many times. He should've been flat on the ground by now, but after every hit, he came back even stronger.

I have no idea how I ever could've crushed on him. And even less how I ever believed he was different from the way he pretends to be.

I hate that asshole.

With every fiber of my being.

On shaky legs, I walk up to the house and slip through the door. In the hallway, I let my backpack drop to the floor, kick off my sneakers, and shuffle toward the living room.

"What are we supposed to do?" I hear Mom ask from somewhere far off. She sounds desperate.

"Having her repeat the year is out of the question," Dad replies. He sounds tired. Tired and disappointed.

I freeze instantly.

They already know?

Damn, the school must have sent a letter.

Someone is pacing through the living room—I can hear the footsteps. It's probably Mom; the soles of her slippers squeak softly.

"She can do it, we just can't lose hope," she says.

Dad sighs. "Hope is meaningless. Only the facts matter, and they clearly speak against her."

My stomach twists into knots, my breathing quickens.

A throat clears in the living room, cutting off my thoughts. "I really thought she was smart enough, but…" Dad's voice breaks.

Fabric rustles—maybe Mom is pulling him into her arms. "I know…" she says gently. "You wanted it so badly."

"She was always so enthusiastic, she wanted it herself too," he replies in disbelief. "I was sure she'd become a great doctor."

"Your passion for the profession will live on," Mom tries to sound encouraging, but she doesn't succeed.

Nothing could cheer Dad up. His daughter is a failure who will never carry on his legacy. Everything he wishes for his patients. Everything I wish for my life. I won't pursue any of it.

"No, Emma, it won't. My fight for medical care that doesn't just scratch the surface will one day retire with me," Dad replies, and I can hear how much it pains him. "No one will continue the work I've dedicated my life to."

I know exactly what he means. All those patients who have to live with a missed or incorrect diagnosis. To Dad, no patient is just a number. People matter to him. As a doctor, he's an incredible role model. A role model I can no longer follow.

"Did we fail with June?" Dad now wants to know from Mom.

A heavy mix of guilt and disappointment over how far I've let my life spiral out of control settles on my chest.

I quickly reach for my daisy earrings beneath my loose hair—earrings I still wear every day, even though the luck they brought me for so long abandoned me months ago. It will come back. Someday.

"I'm afraid we did," Mom says now, to make matters worse. "But let's not show it to June, okay? She shouldn't think we don't love her—after all, it's not her fault."

"Yeah," Dad replies wearily.

My knees threaten to give out. I brace myself against the wall beside the door and fight against the despair rising inside me.

Suddenly, I feel a hand on my shoulder. A pleasant warmth seeps through my T-shirt, yet I still flinch.

"June, are you okay?" There's nothing but wistfulness in Dad's expression, disguised as a friendly smile.

I nod. "I'll be in my room."

"Alright." He pats my shoulder wearily.

I can't bear his disappointment for another second. I tear myself away from the sight, rush up the stairs to my room, and let the door slam shut behind me.

Leaning against the door, I sink to the floor.

I feel like an old piece of chewing gum—chewed out, colorless, and flavorless. That's how I stick to Dad's soles, a stain that'll never come off.

It's all Ashton's fault. If he didn't keep making me doubt myself more and more, there wouldn't be a problem.

I'm smart, and that's exactly what I need to prove. But first, I have to start believing in myself again—and I can only do that if I finally get Ashton to leave me alone for more than just a few days.

But how am I supposed to do that?

What could finally stop him?

"June?"

Ashton's voice pulls me out of the memory.

"Doesn't that hurt?" He nods toward my hands.

My gaze drops instinctively.

My fists are clenched, the knuckles stark white and sharp. And suddenly I feel a burning pain where my fingernails have dug into my palms.

"Are you okay?" I hear Ashton ask gently.

With a distracted motion, I tuck a strand of hair behind my ear. "I'm fine."

He studies me for a noticeably long time. "Your father seems like a great man," he says then, in a tone far too tender. "And you're his daughter, so..."

He shouldn't be doing that. And he shouldn't be looking at me like that.

So... admiringly.

I'm not perfect. At least not in the way I wish I were. Back then, I did things I'm not proud of. Even though I had no choice and I know it was the right thing to do, it still feels awful.

Now the corners of his mouth lift, and the image of Ashton on the first day of school flashes in my mind. That smile. It was the exact same one he wore back then.

It was one of a million reasons why I fell in love with him.

And right now, in this moment, they're all sneaking back into my thoughts.

What is happening right now?

He's nice to me once, and suddenly that same warmth from back then spreads through me?

Am I crazy?

Yes, June, you are.

Abort!

Frantically, I smooth down my lab coat. "Thanks. I'll just..." I gesture toward the door.

A questioning look dominates his face, and I avert my eyes. "I just wanted to..." he begins, but I raise my hand to stop him.

This is too confusing.

"Your tests... you know... they're important..." I stammer, stumbling toward the door.

Chapter Twenty-Two

ASHTON

On her way out, June stumbles, nearly falling.

Did she have this completely ridiculous fluttering in her chest too?

Definitely not. And I must have imagined it as well.

I should let her go. That would be for the best. But just now, when she stared absentmindedly at my blanket, I saw something in her expression that I can't shake.

That melancholy. The pain.

She must have been thinking about our school days, remembering what happened back then.

I have to do it, even if I don't know how. I can't just leave what I did to her uncommented.

"Please don't go yet," I call after her.

With her hand on the doorknob, she pauses without turning to face me. "Why?"

I quickly throw back the blanket and get up to walk toward her. "Please, stay."

"What for?" she whispers tonelessly.

"Because there's something I need to tell you." I'm

almost close enough to touch her. Her delicate scent drifts into my nose. "Something important."

She turns her head and looks at me questioningly over her shoulder.

I swallow against the tightness in my throat, feel my pulse quicken.

"June, I knew I was being mean, but at the same time, I was too much of an idiot to realize what I was actually doing. What I was really putting you through..." The words leave my mouth soundlessly, even though I tried to force them out with all my strength.

I hear her strained breathing, feel her tension. Her hand slips from the door handle, and she turns to face me. "Why did you do it?"

How am I supposed to explain that to her?

"Bad friends?" June offers as an answer. Maybe because that's what she wants to believe most.

Thoughtfully, I dig through my memories. "Maybe that too." My group was pretty intense, but I couldn't say for sure who dragged whom down in the end.

"Why were you even friends with them?" There's something in her voice. Maybe a hint of doubt about whether she really wants to hear the answer. She leans back against the door behind her, as if she needs the support.

I step next to her—keeping a safe distance—and let myself slide down against the wall. My fingers trace the small bumps in the paint, probably left behind during the painting.

I know the answer to her question. And there's only one reason I'm going to say it out loud, even though it will tear open a wound inside me whose pain I never wanted to feel again.

And that reason is June—just June.

"I didn't really like the guys all that much," I begin, my eyes fixed on the ceiling tiles of the hospital room. "But they were my friends." In a new world where I had no one else, I add silently.

In that new world I never wanted to be part of. If it had been up to me, we would never have left Toronto. But Dad was determined to move to Halifax, and as much as we both might have wished he'd go alone—I was underage and had to go with him.

"Anyone would've wanted to be friends with you," I hear June whisper in the midst of the memory that's raging painfully inside me.

I turn my head toward her with a questioning look. "Why would you think that?"

She bites her lower lip, as if trying to stop herself from answering. What's going through her mind? I try to read it in her expression but fail.

"The guys were the first people I met in Halifax. They were cool. We had a lot of fun." And every minute I didn't have to spend at home with Dad was worth its weight in gold.

Her hurt expression hits me. "Fun?"

I move a little closer to her.

Wait a second. What am I doing?

I quickly put some space between us again. "Fun isn't the right word," I admit. "You distracted me, and I really needed that."

"Distracted you from what?" A tiny crease forms between her eyebrows.

I've always answered, *That's none of your business*, no matter who asked me.

All my life, I thought I didn't owe anyone anything. But this is different. I feel like I owe June an explanation.

The truth about me. And my story.

"There was a reason we moved to Halifax." I feel my shoulders grow heavy. "Back home in Toronto, everything had fallen apart."

She reaches out her hand to me but stops when she sees me pull back. "What do you mean?"

I take a deep breath, but still feel like I'm not getting enough air. "Jeremy was about to move to the U.S. Stanford had accepted him." Dad had a constant grin on his face—one I haven't seen on him since. "I convinced Mom to come with me to get him a going-away gift."

Just a little something from the mall. Nothing big. Less than ten kilometers away.

"A drunk driver crashed into her car." Holding my breath, I stare at the gray linoleum floor of the hospital room. "She died instantly," I say tonelessly.

And if I had gone with her, as originally planned, maybe I'd be dead too.

A mix of sympathy and shock crosses June's face. "That's awful."

I try to shrug, but there's too much memory weighing on my shoulders. "Sometimes a single moment can change everything."

She nods. "Especially when you don't see it coming."

Yeah. We weren't prepared. Dad, Jeremy, and I. None of us could believe Mom was really dead, but unlike me, the two of them got used to her absence quickly.

I don't want to think back to that time. It's tied to too much pain, too much darkness. But now, as I tell June about it, I sense that maybe that was the problem. I always kept my anger and fear, my grief and pain to myself. Because there was no one I could share it with.

But here's June, sitting so close that I'd only have to

reach out to touch her. And she's looking at me with that intense gaze of hers, the one that tells me everything's okay.

That I'm okay—even with this dark rage inside me.

"My brother left for the U.S. less than a week after Mom's funeral." All he cared about was his damn studies, his own life, and the career he wanted to build. Mom's death didn't mean a damn thing to him.

"And you?" June asks gently.

No idea. "I had my buddies." Whom Dad took away from me a few months later, as if things hadn't already been hard enough. I clench my fists and press them against the wall behind me. "When Dad forced me to move to Halifax with him, I lost them too."

She nods understandingly. "Mhm," she murmurs. "But you still had your dad." There's hope in her voice.

A tired snort escapes my lips. "Dad… he was… not the same after Mom died. Work was the only thing he cared about anymore."

I turn my head toward her and see tears glistening in the corners of her eyes.

Because of me. Because of my story. And she hasn't even heard all of it yet.

"He didn't want me. I was a burden to him," I say, admitting something no one else knows.

"You were completely alone," she breathes, her voice trembling. Is she thinking about how safe her own childhood home was? How lucky she was with her dad? And her mom?

"Yeah. I was." Alone. And searching for something to hold on to. I've never seen it this clearly before. "The guys were my family." I would've walked through fire for them. And they would've done the same for me.

June blinks rapidly, then takes a deep breath. "Sometimes a single moment can change everything," she repeats my words from earlier, with an expression on her face I can't quite read. All I know is that it puts a strange feeling in my chest.

It's warm. Pleasant.

Yeah, it feels like, for the first time since back then, I can finally breathe again—even if it hurts to do so.

Chapter Twenty-Three

JUNE

A thousand different emotions are racing through me like a roller coaster. Regret, disbelief, confusion.

And somehow, guilt too.

Oh God.

You didn't do anything wrong, I tell myself, and yet one thought keeps rising in me, unstoppable.

If I had known back then what was hiding behind his façade… would I have fought back against his attacks with the same vehemence? Would I have gone so far as to even destroy the cabin…

You couldn't have known that, June!

Yes, for a while I hoped he was different. But only because I was in love. Not once did I see what he's showing me now.

Nothing about Ashton is the way I thought it was back then. He was the coolest guy at school, always seemed untouchable.

Now he's leaning against the wall beside me, a wistful look on his face, surrounded by pain.

The image I had of him for years started to crack the moment I saw his scars. But what I've learned now turns those cracks into deep fissures. And from those fissures, flames rise, devouring the image of Asshole Ashton West in seconds.

Unable to grasp what it all means, I look at him. "I don't know…"

He lifts his hand wearily. "It was a long time ago."

Still, it hits him right in the heart. So much so that his eyes glisten with tears.

"What I did to you wasn't okay, and I'm incredibly sorry." With a distracted motion, he runs a hand through his hair. "Whatever was going on with me doesn't matter. It was wrong. No matter how you look at it," he says, resting his head against the wall.

That's true. Maybe. I don't know.

"Yeah," I reply, trying to get a grip on the mess of emotions swirling inside me. I don't stand a chance. "Why me, of all people?"

"Your mom," he answers hesitantly. "You… you sent her away."

Suddenly, I clap my hands over my mouth. "The day everything began."

He nods. "I couldn't bear it. The way you sent her away…"

"…while you missed your mom so desperately," I finish his sentence.

Until now, I was sure I knew the line between right and wrong. But now I no longer know where it lies—or if it even exists.

Even if I didn't realize it at the time, a part of it was my fault too. It all started with me—and with my infatuation with Ashton, which had driven me back then.

Lost in thought, I suddenly hear Ashton groan.

I turn to him immediately. "What…?"

He doubles over, pressing his hands to his chest. "It burns."

"Where?" I close the distance between us, but before I can support him, he steps aside in a panic.

His cheeks are flushed—the fever is back.

Damn.

"Lungs," he gasps.

"Always or only when you breathe?" I watch helplessly as he struggles toward his bed, one hand stretched out toward me to keep me at a distance. I follow him and press the emergency button by his bed as he sinks into the pillow with a groan.

"When I breathe," he replies, his face contorted in pain. At least a six out of ten on the Visual Analogue Scale.

"What about your stomach? Does that hurt too?" His fever had always been accompanied by abdominal pain before.

Ashton nods.

Damn it, what the hell is going on here?

I take my stethoscope, put the earpieces in, and reach for Ashton's T-shirt to lift it up.

"Don't touch," he protests loudly, then yanks the shirt off himself.

I study him, puzzled. He just opened up his heart to me, and now he's putting up walls again. Shutting me out. Why?

He lets out a pained groan. Helping him is more important right now than my question.

"Just the metal." I show him the chest piece of the stethoscope, and he nods. "Please turn slightly to the side."

I begin my examination next to his shoulder blade.

The sound of his breathing gives me pause.

"It could be pleurisy," I say as calmly as I can and take his temperature.

Just under one hundred and four degrees.

Why?

At that moment, a nurse bursts into the hospital room.

"We need ibuprofen, four hundred milligrams IV," I call out to her. "Would you also bring me the portable ultrasound machine, please?" Luckily, the ward has one.

She nods and heads off immediately, while I turn back to Ashton to do what I'd forgotten in my earlier panic. "It's pleurisy," I explain to him. "Don't worry, we'll get it under control."

He grimaces in pain.

The nurse is already back. I grab the portable ultrasound machine as she steps toward Ashton with the oxygen mask.

"I'll do it myself," he gasps before she can put the mask on him, even though it clearly takes a lot out of him.

Whatever works—as long as the mask is in place and his brain is getting enough oxygen.

"Would you sit up, please?" I coat the ultrasound probe with gel and place it on Ashton's chest. Keeping my eyes on the monitor, I move the probe up and down. Pleurisy—definitely. But there's something else.

I squint. Is that…?

I quickly adjust the angle and press the probe more firmly against Ashton's chest.

Oh God, this can't be happening.

"There's fluid between the layers of your pleura." Probably a result of the inflammation. How could the pleural effusion have developed so quickly? "How long have you had pain when breathing?"

He shrugs. "A little while, but it wasn't bad."

"You should've told me." I look at him seriously, then turn to the nurse. "I'm going to perform a thoracentesis."

"Shouldn't a surgeon handle that?" she asks cautiously.

Definitely not. "Please take him to an available treatment room. I'll discuss it with Dr. Young in the meantime," I say, to avoid starting a debate in front of Ashton.

"All right," she replies, hooking up the ibuprofen drip.

I smile at her. "Thank you." Then I turn back to Ashton. "I'll see you in the treatment room."

His expression is still contorted with pain, but at least he nods.

As hard as it is to leave him alone right now, I urgently need to speak with Dr. Young. Hopefully, I can convince her to let me handle the procedure.

Chapter Twenty-Four

JUNE

Nyla hands me the zucchini. "And then?" she asks breathlessly, fixing me with her doe eyes.

"Then I went to the boss." I place the vegetable on my cutting board and pull a knife from the knife block. "I wanted to do the puncture myself." How could I have let Ashton suffer any longer than necessary?

Just a moment ago, my roommate had opened the pantry to grab a pack of pasta—now she pauses. "That's always done by the surgeons in the ER." She tugs at her short haircut.

First the nurse, now her too. I can do this—why doesn't anyone trust me? "Oh please, you don't need a surgeon for that," I reply, shaking my head as I cut the stem off the zucchini.

She reaches for the spaghetti, her charm bracelet jingling softly. "True. They already think they're gods in white coats—could do with a little reality check." She wrinkles her nose briefly. "Just today, I requested a surgical consult in the ER. The new senior physician showed up himself. Dr. Stone." She pushes out her lower lip. "What a guy."

I watch as she peers into the pot to see if the water's boiling yet. "His reputation definitely precedes him," I say —after all, he's Sonora's boss, and she's heard enough about him to fill an entire tabloid. It's going to be interesting when they meet for the first time tomorrow.

Carefully, Nyla lets the lid sink back onto the pot and leans against the counter. "But aside from that—why was it so important to you to do the puncture yourself?"

That same confusing feeling from this afternoon spreads inside me again. I quickly lower my gaze to the zucchini and position the knife. "I don't know."

"You wanted to impress the boss," my roommate says with a knowing tone. "I would've done the same."

No, that wasn't it. Or not only that. Of course I want this job—more than anything—but there was something else.

Something that had to do with Ashton. I wanted to help him. Desperately.

Thoughtfully, I slice the zucchini into rounds. "His mom died before he came to Halifax."

"Oh," Nyla says, and in the same moment, I realize how inappropriate that was of me.

"I'm sorry, that was wrong…" My God, how stupid can I be? Not so long ago, Nyla's own life was hanging by a thread. It's hard enough for her to move past that, and here I am, bringing up the topic so carelessly.

She waves it off. "Don't worry. Death has no power over me." As if she urgently needs something to do, she looks around. "We still need a pan for the vegetables," she says with purpose and walks past me to the kitchen cabinet. "So you think his mom's death has something to do with Ashton's illness? Something genetic?"

"No, not because of his illness." Shaking my head, I turn the knife in my hand. "I think he's not as much of an asshole as I always thought," I say, pensive, because that's been weighing on me ever since the conversation with Ashton.

"Excuse me?" Nyla walks toward me, frying pan in hand. "We're still talking about the same patient, right? The guy who bullied you in school."

Yes. That's exactly who we're talking about. By now, all the girls in my flatshare know about him. Nothing stays secret around here anyway.

"It's not that simple." I shrug as I slide the zucchini slices onto a plate and turn my attention to the bell pepper.

Out of the corner of my eye, I see my roommate eyeing me closely. "Mhm. So tell me. Does he get your blood pumping?" There's a mischievous lilt in her voice.

"Pfft, he's anything but hot," I say quickly, even though a tingling sensation rushes through my whole body.

Because Ashton is insanely hot. He was back then, and he still is. But that's not the point, and anyway, Nyla really needs to stop staring holes into me.

"Oh yes, he is…" she replies with a grin. "Well, well… June, June, June…"

"Cut it out." I attack the bell pepper like I'm trying to dice it into microscopic pieces. The red vegetable juice seeps into the fine cracks of the cutting board. "It's not like that."

She sets the pan on the stove and turns it on. "Okay, enlighten me. What is it like, then?"

Sighing in exhaustion, I set the knife aside and turn to her. "I don't know either."

"That's not a lot." She pouts, holding the bottle of oil in her hand.

No, it's actually less than that. It's nothing at all. So why the hell does it feel like it's… everything, somehow.

Nyla steps toward me and places her hand on my shoulder. "He bullied you, June." There's a hint of sympathy in her voice. "And as much as I want you to fall in love…"

She doesn't need to tell me that—I know it better than anyone. "I'm not saying I've forgiven him."

She nods with a gentle smile. "Dead mother or not, I'm afraid Ashton was still responsible for his actions."

That's true. "But what if…"

"People don't change." Her expression turns sad. "Unfortunately."

"Never?" Suddenly overcome with fatigue, I nudge the bell pepper onto the plate beside the zucchini slices.

Instead of answering, she just lifts her shoulders in apology, the palm-sized hoops in her ears jingling softly. The boiling water makes the pot lid dance. While Nyla slides the pasta into the water, I stare out the window, lost in thought.

Only a small patch of sky is visible; the rest is hidden beneath a thick blanket of clouds.

If people don't change, then not only is Ashton still the same as he was back then—I am too.

But can that really be true?

Am I still who I used to be? And who was I, anyway? Was everything I did back then really the right thing?

Self-defense or not. In the new light I see Ashton in now, some of my comebacks seem pretty harsh.

Too harsh.

Leaning casually against the wall, I peer toward the door.

Ashton is with the principal. I made sure he had to show up there after class. Right now, he has to explain why he recently got pushy with a tenth grader out on the fire escape.

Oh yeah, take that, asshole Ashton!

Of course it's not true. All I actually know is that he smokes out there. But it could be true, and besides, I don't have much of a choice anyway.

I've been spying on him for weeks now, trying to find something I can use against him. And it's not even hard.

An asshole like him does fifty things a day he should be held accountable for.

Watch, report, and at least get a few days of peace. It's a good strategy. And it comes with an unexpected bonus I didn't see coming: I no longer feel like his helpless victim.

I'm not running from him anymore. On the contrary, I'm following him. Sure, I make sure he doesn't notice me. Still, it feels good—it makes me feel strong. And I can even focus on studying again.

Maybe I'll actually make it through the school year. Maybe things can go back to the way they were. If I stick with it now.

I glance at the door again. He's been in there so long—he's probably getting a serious talking-to.

Perfect.

I feel a satisfied grin creeping onto my lips.

The door handle moves downward.

He's coming!

I quickly hide behind a pillar, brush my hair into my face, and peek in his direction.

At that moment, he steps out of the door. With a resigned tone, he says goodbye to the principal, then walks down the hallway straight toward me. His eyelids are lowered, his jaw clenched.

I hope you learned your lesson, asshole. It's not so funny when you're the one getting trampled on for no reason, is it?

Now he passes me, his hair trembling with rage, his muscles tense. A furious growl rumbles in his throat, like a wolf preparing for battle.

I turn my head to watch him go.

His hands curl into fists. Suddenly, he steps toward the wall, pulls back, and punches the masonry with all his strength.

The crash makes me flinch. And when I see the blood streaming from the wounds on his fingers down his hand, I feel sick.

He deserves this, June, I remind myself, because pity is starting to rise inside me.

He just needs to stop with his crap, then I'll stop too.

That wasn't the only thing I did—and maybe not even the worst. With each act, I became bolder. Stronger.

Meaner.

Was it really the right thing to do?

Back then, it felt like it. But wasn't there another way? How was I supposed to know…

"Pass me the vegetables."

Lost in thought, I look up and see Nyla standing at the stove with a spatula. "Hm?"

"Come on, the oil's hot," she says, motioning for me to hurry.

I hand her the plate.

"Everything okay?" she asks, studying me as she takes the vegetables and lets them slide into the pan.

It sizzles softly. I place the knife and cutting board in the sink. "Yeah, all good."

No idea if she believes me. "Alright, then back to the pleural effusion puncture. Did you perform it?"

Right, that's a much better topic than my confused feelings for Ashton. "Sure did. And with flying colors." Ashton's breathing pain eased quickly, and he looked at me with a gratitude that hit me way too hard. "Dr. Young gave me three points for it. Whether that's enough to catch up to Jaxon, I'll find out the day after tomorrow during the case review," I add quickly, hoping to chase away the image of Ashton from my mind.

Nyla raises her hand for a high five. "Very cool."

I high-five her. "But the case itself is still a mystery, unfortunately."

"You'll crack it too." With a confident nod, she stirs the vegetables in the pan.

"In addition to the ongoing tests, I've ordered further exams because of the pleuritis," I tell Nyla. One of them just has to yield results—otherwise, I'm running out of ideas. "By the time I'm back at the clinic the day after tomorrow, all the test results should be in." Jaxon offered to keep an eye on it for me. Probably just a way to score extra points with the boss. He's definitely not doing it out of kindness.

"That's right, you've got the day off tomorrow!" She grins. "Then we absolutely shouldn't talk about work any longer."

I grunt in agreement. It's hard to leave the hospital and everything that happens there behind after a shift. Not to take the cases home, to stop overthinking, and to just be a normal person for a few hours.

"Okay, work's on mute." I grab a dish towel and dry my hands. "I should focus on setting up my room anyway." It's still total chaos in there. "You're our style queen. Will you help me?"

"I've got the afternoon shift tomorrow—we can hit the furniture stores in the morning," she replies brightly.

"Perfect, thanks." If I get up a little earlier, I can even squeeze in my run before we start. Once again, I'm glad we decided to start this shared apartment. Everything's easier together.

"Can you set the table?" She stirs the vegetable mix in the pan.

"Sure." And I'm also going to put on some Italian music. Because that's exactly what I need right now—to unwind a little and kick off my day off.

A day when I won't run into Ashton. A day after which, hopefully, things will be clearer.

I pull open the cutlery drawer and can't help but grin at the sight of all the different forks, spoons, and knives. Each of us brought our own utensils when we moved in—this drawer is just like us: a colorful mix. "Who's coming over for dinner?"

Chapter Twenty-Five

JUNE

Frowning, I look at Jaxon, who casually opens his locker with a flick of his hand. "Excuse me?"

"Chill out, June, they'll show up," he says, pops a piece of gum into his mouth, and reaches for the stethoscope in his locker.

I check the battery level on my pager. "But you promised me you'd keep an eye on things while I was off duty." And now, a day and a half after the tests, Ashton's results still haven't come in.

Damn it. I shouldn't have trusted him when he offered to help. I should've asked one of the colleagues whose patients I'm covering while they're away.

"Had a lot going on." Jaxon stares at something inside his locker door. Does he have a mirror in there?

"Is your patient getting worse?" Hopefully not.

He runs his hands through his hair. "No idea, haven't checked on him yet."

Is there anyone he doesn't let down? His patient. Me. And most of all, Ashton.

Immediately, I picture Ashton's angular face, the black strands of hair falling across his forehead, and those eyes filled with fear. Whether I want to or not, my heart grows heavy. Even though I still don't know how to process everything that's come to light lately—despite having the day off—I do know one thing: it's not fair that Ashton has to wait this long for his test results.

"Whatever. Thanks for nothing, Jaxon," I say, clip my pager to my waistband, and hurry out of the changing room.

"No problem, happy to help," he calls sweetly after me.

He's completely lost it. Rage simmered inside me as I stepped up to the elevator and pressed the call button. I glanced at my smartwatch.

It was three o'clock. Even though my shift had just started, the lab would only be fully staffed for another two hours. After that, only the emergency team would be on duty. If they hadn't already started processing the samples, we'd be cutting it close on getting results. The only thing I had was the electromyography analysis, and that wasn't enough.

Tomorrow, at the next case conference, I'd have to answer to Dr. Young. Even though Ben was still groping in the dark and Jaxon's diagnosis had vanished into thin air, I had to stay on it.

I didn't wait for the elevator any longer and instead ran to the stairs, sprinting up to the first floor where the lab was located. As I reached the glass swing door, I nearly collided with Olive.

"Where are you off to in such a rush?" she asked, smiling at me with her perfectly defined lips.

Immediately, I felt the urge to undo my messy ponytail and shake out my hair. How did she do it? She didn't seem to be doing anything special—just standing there opposite me. And yet she radiated the glamorous aura of a celebrity.

"Oh, you know how it is. Miss one day and…"

She nodded sympathetically. "Oh yes, I know that feeling. I've got a tip for you."

I couldn't shake the feeling that she didn't believe I could handle this on my own.

"I always bribe the lab lady with chocolate from the vending machine—it works like a charm." A mischievous grin flashed across her face.

"Really? She does that?" I ask, appalled. "Even if it means emergencies have to wait?"

"Oh, they'll figure it out." She shrugs.

"Thanks, but I'll find another way," I reply quickly. A proper way, more importantly. Smiling, I squeeze past her.

"Suit yourself." She tucks her wavy, shoulder-length hair behind her ear. "I've got to get going anyway, before my resident kills someone."

And I have to put pressure on the lab—somehow. "Good luck," I say with a smirk, since she already told me about that resident yesterday when we were at Pilates together. He really does sound like a public menace.

She thanks me with an unreadable expression, we say goodbye, and I step into the lab.

An elderly lady sits behind the counter. The delicate gold chains on her glasses sway back and forth as she looks up at me over the rim. "Yes, dear?"

With a friendly smile, I lean on the counter. "When will the test results for patient P010424-060 be ready?" I ask politely, despite still being furious with Jaxon. After all, it's not her fault he left me hanging.

"Let me check, sweetheart." She turns to her computer. "What was that number again?"

I repeat Ashton's identification code and lean forward to sneak a look at the screen myself.

The woman types his ID number into the search field, and immediately all the tests I requested appear on the screen. The tests for Parkinson's and MS, as well as the ones added because of the pleuritis. Some have green checkmarks next to them, but the result for the ordered antibody test for MS doesn't. Damn. Of all tests, it had to be that one. "The antibody test is really urgent," I say quickly.

"I'm sorry, it's still processing." She pushes her glasses up. "The results will definitely be in by tomorrow."

"That's too late," I reply, a bit too emotionally. "Unfortunately," I add quickly, apologetically.

She props her elbows on the counter, resting her chin in her hands. "If only I got a dollar every time I heard that sentence…"

"Then you wouldn't be here anymore, and that would be a real shame." I smile as I notice the corners of her mouth lift. "Can you bump the test up in the queue?"

"That's against protocol." She bites her lower lip.

Really? What's that even supposed to be good for?

Whatever. I definitely don't want to encourage her to break the rules. On the other hand, I promised Ashton the day before yesterday that he'd find out today whether he has a neurological disorder. If I were him, I'd be climbing the walls with worry. I can't show up without answers. That's just not an option.

"What if I talk to someone? Explain the situation?" I suggest. That way, she doesn't have to do anything and won't bother her colleagues. "Look, my patient might have a life-changing illness…" There's a pleading note in my voice, so intense that for a split second I wonder if I'd do this for every patient.

Yes. I would. People are all that matter—Dad taught me that.

"Hm." She taps her chin with her index finger. "Give me a moment."

Tense, I raise my eyebrows.

She picks up the phone and dials a number. "Tom, can you do me a favor?" she asks a few seconds later. "Mhm… yeah… could you let me know how far along you are with the antibody test for patient P010424-060?"

My pulse quickens involuntarily. At the same moment, my phone vibrates.

I check the message. It's from Mom.

Warning: Your dad got a gift for your party. Might've gone a little overboard…

My stomach twists into a knot. I quickly shove the phone back into my pocket and look at the lab technician with hopeful eyes.

She winks at me, then focuses back on her conversation partner. "Okay, thanks, Tom, you're the best."

Fidgety, I shift from one foot to the other.

As soon as she hangs up the phone, she beams at me. "The test just finished. The results should appear in the portal shortly."

Only now do I realize that I've been holding my breath for far too long. Relieved, I let myself sink against the counter.

"Thank you so much," I whisper, freed.

Chapter Twenty-Six

ASHTON

Where is she? She said she'd be here at the start of her shift, and now it's already 3:30 PM and June still hasn't shown up.

Restless, I stare up at the ceiling tiles in my room. By now, I know every single one by heart—where the stains are, which ones hang slightly crooked, and where the beams have scratches.

I've been here for almost a week and a half. Far too long.

I take a deep breath and savor the fact that it doesn't hurt. My thoughts drift to June and the way she smiled at me after the puncture. The gentle tone in her voice when she explained that all that was left was a final X-ray to complete the treatment for that fluid buildup in my lung. Several strands of hair had come loose from her ponytail during the procedure and framed her face.

She looked so beautiful that I wasn't sure whether this was reality or just a fever dream.

We didn't see each other yesterday. It's absurd, but I missed her.

Somehow.

I don't know.

Maybe I'm just slowly going insane in here and imagining the whole thing.

My phone buzzes on the nightstand. I reach for it.

Jeremy. Again. Ever since he got back to New York, he's been calling at exactly the same time every other day. He probably has a reminder in his calendar—otherwise, he'd forget.

I decline the call and sink back into my pillow.

"Where are you, June?" I ask longingly into the silence of the room, unsure whether I miss her or the test results she promised me.

No, it's the test results. Nothing more.

Five agonizing minutes later, June finally walks into my hospital room.

"You look better," she says after a brief greeting. Her smile warms me from the inside out. "And the fever has gone down, too." She furrows her brow. "That was fast."

"I feel much better." If it hadn't already happened twice before—getting better, then worse again—I'd assume I'd be out of here by tomorrow at the latest.

"I'm glad to hear that." She tilts her head, and her ponytail swings to the side.

"Thank you, June, for… you know… for helping me." That pain when I breathed—it felt like I was going to die. And June was the one who pulled me out of it.

Suddenly, her cheeks turn pink. She looks away and clears her throat. "It's my job."

Right. For her, it wasn't anything special. She does this kind of thing every day. But for me, it was.

"I have your results." Her expression is neutral. Is that

good or bad? "Shall we go through them?" She steps over to the small table and pulls out one of the chairs.

For almost two days, I couldn't wait to finally find out whether my life was about to change forever. Now that the moment has come, I'm not so sure I want to know.

Besides, it would be nice to see something other than this sterile room. The nurse told me I'm not allowed to go out alone, but if June comes with me, it might be possible. "Can we go outside for a bit?"

She freezes mid-movement, confused. "Where to?"

"Anywhere. As long as it's out of here," I reply.

She purses her lips in thought. "Okay, I'll get you a wheelchair."

I don't even try to argue. Honestly, I don't care—getting out is worth it either way.

Less than ten minutes later, June wheels me out of a side exit of the hospital. Even though the sky is overcast, I feel as if everything around me is getting brighter. I inhale the salty sea air with pleasure.

"We can talk over here." June points to a small park, pushes my wheelchair up to a wooden bench, and sits down next to me. "Ready?"

Oh God. When she asks like that, it can only mean something bad. I nod hesitantly.

"Let's start with the good news." She turns to face me directly. "The follow-up X-ray was clear, so we can consider the pleural effusion successfully treated."

That is great, but not what I want to hear. "And the tests? About..." The words neurological and disease won't come out.

A tender look appears on her face. "They were negative."

Only now do I realize that I've been holding my breath

the entire time. "Oh God…" I gasp, exhaling in exhaustion. I feel myself collapsing into my wheelchair.

"That's great news, but…" She trails off, biting her lower lip.

"But?" I ask, probing, because I don't like her tone.

"Let me see your forearm," she asks. "The spot where you got the injection the day before yesterday."

I roll up the sleeve of my sweater. She reaches her fingers toward me.

Everything inside me tenses up.

She mustn't touch me.

I can't let that happen.

Quickly, I run my own hand over my skin before she has the chance to touch me. "No idea where it was. I don't see the injection site anymore."

"Hm." With a hum, she pulls her hand back.

What does "hm" mean? "Is that good or bad?"

"The injection was a test for tuberculosis—a possible cause of the pain you felt when breathing," she explains with a troubled expression. "A positive result would be accompanied by more or less noticeable swelling."

"So that means I don't have tuberculosis?"

"Exactly," she confirms.

That's good news—so why does she still look so frustrated? "Well, that sounds like a good thing to me." I study her, waiting. "What's wrong, June?"

She looks at me so intensely that my stomach turns. "Everything we've tested for so far, we've been able to rule out. That's great, but at the same time…"

"…it doesn't get us anywhere," I finish her sentence.

With a sigh, she breaks off a splinter from the wooden bench with her thumb. "Something's wrong with you. The recurring fever and the abdominal pain are the constants.

But every time, there are different accompanying symptoms."

Suddenly, she seems helpless—so much so that I want to place my hand on her upper arm to comfort her, even though I'm the patient here. Still, my arm remains motionless on the armrest of the wheelchair.

Touching her… that's unthinkable.

And even though I search for them stubbornly, I can't find any words within me to lift June up. All I can do is look at her with understanding.

She clenches her fists. "I can do this," she murmurs so quietly that I can barely hear her over the rustling leaves in the wind.

"Of course you can," I reply with absolute conviction. I have no idea where it comes from, but I just know. "You're an amazing doctor." Just look at how much you're doing for me—far more than you have to.

She jerks her head toward me, her eyes shining. For a moment that lasts far too long, she looks at me with that strange mix of disbelief and relief. "Do you really believe that?"

Why wouldn't I? "Since I got here, you've been fighting for me. You've spent more time with me than any other doctor ever has. You want to dig deeper, to really help me." And that, even though I didn't want to let her in at first. Despite everything that happened between us back at Halifax High. Once again, guilt gnaws at me.

Why the hell couldn't I control myself? How could I have been such an asshole and taken my anger out on her so harshly?

Once again, I'm on the verge of reaching out to her. Maybe to stroke her cheek. Or to find her fingers, touch her knee, gently nudge her forearm.

And for the first time, I wonder what would have happened back then if I hadn't acted like the biggest idiot.

Would we have grown closer? Could we have been friends? Maybe even the kind of friends I so desperately needed back then?

Or could there have been something more? Something that went beyond friendship?

"I'm doing my best to help you," June confirms, pulling my thoughts back to the present. "But what if that's not enough?"

No. She can't think like that. "I trust you. You can do this." No sooner have I spoken the words than I freeze.

Did I really just say that?

Yes.

And it's true. I do trust her.

She blinks rapidly. "Thank you," she whispers, then turns her gaze to the sky.

I follow her lead, watching silver gulls glide through the air and the wind shaping new cloud formations again and again. A tiny gap opens, and bit by bit, the blue sky peeks through the white clouds.

"What happens now?" I ask her, without taking my eyes off that spot above.

"We talk." June's tone is steadier now, as if she were drawing new strength. "I need to know everything about you, Ashton. And I mean everything. Every detail could be a clue."

A ray of sunlight breaks through the hole in the clouds. "That might take a while."

"Let's start with your medical history," she suggests.

I tear my gaze away from the sky to look at her. "I'm afraid there's nothing interesting there."

She smiles. "Let me be the judge of that."

"All right. I need to think." I nibble on my lower lip as I try to figure out where to begin.

"Were you sick a lot as a child?" she asks, probably trying to help me along.

"No more than other kids." I sift through my memories. "I basically had all the usual childhood illnesses. Although, now that I think about it…"

"Yeah?" She sits up straighter and pulls one leg toward her.

"My stomach was probably always my weak spot," I reply, thinking of the countless stomach bugs that have plagued me all my life. "Mom always put a hot water bottle on me and made peppermint tea."

She used to stroke my hair, look at me lovingly, and tell me that I'd feel better soon.

A deep sadness washes over me. Because I can't help but think about how that changed after she died.

How, little by little, all the light in my life had to give way to darkness.

I'm doubled over with stomach pain, the beads of sweat on my forehead feel icy cold. Still, I force myself through our new house in Halifax to Dad's study and knock on the door. "Dad?"

"Not now," comes the curt reply through the closed door.

My stomach tightens. "It's important."

He doesn't answer. I wait in uncertainty outside the door, then hear footsteps growing louder.

Angry footsteps.

The door is flung open, and I step back.

"Didn't I tell you not to bother me?" he snaps.

I lean against the wall. "It's an emergency."

As if he hadn't noticed my condition, he raises his eyebrows. "What have you done this time?"

Nothing at all. Why does he always assume I've done something wrong?

"I'm sick," I reply, even though it's probably pretty obvious.

"Oh, not that too," Dad grumbles irritably. "Did you eat something bad? Can't you be more careful?"

"Mom always used to…"

"Be quiet," he snaps at me, his voice sharp. Anger rules his face. Anger and pain. "I don't want to hear a word about it."

"But…"

"Ashton. You're seventeen years old. Don't be such a wimp." He rolls his eyes toward the ceiling. "Get some pills, go to the doctor, make yourself some tea. It's not that hard."

No. It's not. In theory. Still, it would be nice not to be alone. To have someone who takes care of me.

Someone who actually cares about me.

Someone like Mom.

"Why are you still standing there like an idiot?" Dad snaps at me. "Get out of my sight."

Another cramp grips my stomach, and I don't know what hurts more—my belly or the fact that no one cares how I'm doing.

"How often did you have stomach pains?" I hear June ask in the middle of my memory. "Were they always accompanied by a fever?"

I'm not exactly sure. "Maybe once every few months? Three times a year?" I guess.

"Were you ever tested for intolerances or other digestive disorders?" She pulls a notepad from the pocket of her lab coat and clicks a pen.

"It was never anything serious, usually gone after two days." Nobody thought much of it, not even me. "Kids pick up all sorts of things."

She taps the pen against her chin. "And how was it in the past few years?"

"Well, it did happen now and then," I answer truthfully. I guess I got so used to it that I started thinking it was normal. Maybe it is. I look at her doubtfully. "Do you really think it could be a clue?"

"It's certainly interesting." A gentle smile plays at the corners of her mouth. "Thank you for telling me."

I stare at her lips, transfixed. They look soft.

Gladly, I almost reply, and in a rather sheepish tone at that. "No big deal," I force myself to say instead.

She turns further toward me and rests her elbow on the back of the seat. "What about your work?"

I wish I could offer something helpful, but there is nothing. With an apologetic expression, I shrug. "Just odd jobs, mostly manual labor, sometimes gardening."

Thoughtfully, she chews on her lower lip. "Are you in contact with paints, solvents, asbestos, or pesticides?"

"I always wear protective gear," I reply, feeling the urge to apologize again for not giving her any leads.

Her intense gaze meets mine. She gnaws on the end of her pen, looking as if she were wrestling with herself.

"What about the scars on your thigh?" she finally asks, her voice so cautious it suddenly makes me afraid.

It is a kind of fear I have never felt before. The fear that not only *I* might break under the weight of the answer to that question.

But *her*, too.

Chapter Twenty-Seven

JUNE

Holding my breath, I wait for his answer. Was it right to ask about his scars? Or should I have held back, now that he's finally starting to trust me?

He lowers his eyelids, his shoulders slumping forward.

"Whatever it is, you can tell me," I add. When I reached out to him earlier, he recoiled with a look of sheer panic in his eyes. Should I try again?

Pain flickers across his face. "I don't know…"

"What?" Again, I inch a little closer to him.

He shakes his head. "The way I…"

The way he what? It must be something that's eating him up inside. Just knowing that is enough to make my heart heavy. Still, we have to talk about it. It could be important. "Exactly the way you're thinking it."

He stays silent for a while. I can see his jaw tightening more and more.

"I told you that after Mom died, Dad wasn't the same anymore," he says eventually, his gaze lowered to the gravel path.

A dark suspicion spreads inside me.

What if…?

No. Please, no.

Swallowing hard, I nod. "Did he…"

Ashton's jaw muscles tense. "With every day she wasn't with us anymore, it got worse." His voice sounds dull. Distant, even though he's so close I'd only have to move my hand a few inches to touch him.

I don't want to ask what exactly he means by got worse. I'm afraid of his answer—and of the possibility that it might break my heart. But I have to.

Just as I'm about to speak, he looks at me with those stormy blue-gray eyes, full of anguish. "I couldn't do anything right for him. He buried himself in his work and wished I would just disappear."

How can a father treat his child like that?

"Jeremy was gone, Mom was gone. It was just him and me," he continued in a rough voice. "He blamed me for everything that went wrong. And then there were all those letters from the principal. Every single one of them…"

Oh God.

It's hard to breathe. And once again, I see that time at Halifax High in a new light.

You made my life a living hell, I had thrown at him just a few days ago.

And I wasn't the only one who messed up, was I?, was his response.

Only now am I beginning to understand how far those words go. How deep they run, and how much pain they carry for him.

That was me. I poured oil on a fire that was already raging, by ratting him out again and again. "Because of me," I say tonelessly.

Instead of answering, he gives a barely perceptible nod.

And slowly I realize that I hurt him far more than I thought at the time.

Should I have looked more closely instead of stubbornly and blindly dedicating myself to fighting him? Should I not have given up so quickly on him—and on my hope of finding something beautiful inside him?

He tries to smile, but it doesn't work. "They were just more drops in a glass that was already overflowing."

Drops that I added. Every time I complained about him. Every time I made sure he got into trouble and was suspended from school for at least a few days.

I can't look at him anymore. Too many emotions crash over me all at once like a tidal wave. I feel like I'm drowning, gasping for air.

"It wasn't your fault." The sound of his voice makes my whole body tremble.

Staring at the white blossoms planted throughout the park, I pull both legs up and wrap my arms around them. "I… it…"

"Look at me, June," he pleads, his voice urgent.

"I can't," I say, my voice choked, and in that same moment, I know it's not enough.

This changes so much. Maybe even everything.

Out of the corner of my eye, I see his fingers clutching the armrests of the wheelchair. "You were just trying to defend yourself. I was the problem."

He only says that because he doesn't know everything I did.

But now I do it anyway. I turn my head and look directly into his eyes, which are so full of emotion that I feel as if they might pull me under. "No, Ashton, that's not true. It was your father. It all started with him."

It was a vicious cycle, and we were both trapped in it. We lashed out—he and I—helplessly, because we didn't know how to escape.

He leans toward me. "I let go of Father a long time ago," he says weakly. "No matter what he did, it doesn't excuse the way I treated you."

I shake my head thoughtfully, a tear slipping from the corner of my eye. If only I had known back then what lay behind his behavior: a desperate cry for love and security.

With a softened expression, he tilts his head. His right hand releases the wheelchair's armrest. He lifts his arm.

"I shouldn't have hurt you even more. I should have…" My voice breaks, not least because of the way he's looking at me now.

With a mix of panic and sorrow on his face, he stares at the tear trailing down my cheek. "You are…"

My heart skips a beat as he reaches out his fingers toward me. He doesn't touch me—not yet—but even so, I inhale sharply.

Against all reason, I silently show him what I long for most in this moment: his closeness.

I want his fingers to keep moving to my hair, to pull my face toward his. I want to breathe in his scent, to feel his breath on my lips.

I want to kiss him.

Then it happens. His thumb touches my cheek, right where a single tear rests. He brushes it away, infinitely gently, never taking his eyes off me.

A whimper escapes my lips.

"It's not your fault, June," he says hoarsely.

I twist my lips into a pained smile. Because deep down, I know it's not that simple.

"Are the scars on your thigh from him? Did he…" I begin, but I can't finish the sentence.

He pulls his hand back. "Only once."

Chapter Twenty-Eight

ASHTON

She shouldn't look at me like that. So full of horror and regret. Her eyes wide open, she touches the exact spot where I just touched her. And I lower my gaze to my hand in disbelief.

I touched her. And it didn't sting. On the contrary, it felt right.

"Even once is already too much." June's breathing is shallow.

That's exactly it. And that's why, just under a year after Mom's death, my life completely changed once again.

A hiss escapes my lips, my eyes burn. Still, I don't stop applying the ointment to my burns. Maybe because I don't know what else to do.

Through the bathroom door, I can hear Father talking to the police.

"No, I don't want that," he says, exhausted.

"Sir, we've detected traces of accelerants. This is clearly a case of arson."

"Still." Dad clears his throat. "I'll handle this myself."

I snort derisively and turn my gaze to my wounds. And what a job he did of it.

"As you wish, sir. If you change your mind, you know where to find us."

"Thank you." How polite Dad sounds, even though it's been less than ten minutes since he completely lost it.

Asshole.

I take the box of bandages from the drawer. Downstairs, the front door closes, Dad's footsteps head into his study, the door slams shut.

With my lips pressed together, I stick bandages over my burns and pull up my sweatpants. Then I shuffle downstairs. At the bottom of the stairs, I hesitate. At one end of the hallway is his office, at the other, the exit.

Today, he crossed a line. Even though I'd felt for months that this moment would come eventually, I didn't want to believe it.

I clench my fists and march to his study. Without knocking, I walk in.

"I'm moving out. With or without your approval," I say, deliberately calm, even though a storm is raging inside me.

He lifts his eyes from his papers. To my surprise, there's no anger on his face. Just pain. "Pick a boarding school. I'll take care of the rest," he replies, resigned.

I've never seen him like this before. So... broken. Is he trying to play the pitiful one now or what?

Asshole.

"Fine." That's all I can get out. Not after what happened in this house just minutes ago.

I turn on my heel, head back to my room, and start looking for a boarding school. I find one quickly, because only two things matter to me.

That it's at least a thousand kilometers from Halifax. And just as far from Stanford.

"After what happened, I finished school in Vancouver," I tell June, who's slowly sinking into the wooden bench, even though I haven't given her any details. "It was the best thing for everyone." And maybe it even saved me. The distance from my father was liberating, yet I still haven't managed to process what happened.

"So that's why you suddenly disappeared," June whispers, so relieved it's as if she'd been afraid she was the reason. "Not because of…"

"I told you, you had nothing to do with any of it," I repeat what I said earlier. She shouldn't feel guilty.

Thoughtfully, she furrows her brow. "If I'd known, I would've helped you. Instead…"

"No." Without thinking, I reach for her hand.

I touch her. Again. And this time, it feels even more intense than before.

"It's no use. We should leave it behind." Forget what happened, whose fault it was, and who could've helped whom, and when.

Gently, I let my thumb glide over the back of her hand. Again and again, until her breathing begins to calm.

"But I…"

I shake my head, not looking away from her. "How about we start over?" I ask, trying to stop her from tormenting herself with the past.

I register the tenderness in my voice, I'm aware that I'm caressing her hand, and I feel that wild tingling all through me.

I know how messed up this is.

Still, it's there.

All of it. In this very moment.

June blinks rapidly. "Can we do that?"

"We should at least try." Who knows, maybe we're better at it now than we were back then? Maybe she can help me become a real person again. Someone who can open his heart to others. Someone who isn't an asshole.

I look into her deep blue eyes, waiting. They lock onto mine so intensely that I lose all sense of what's happening around me.

Suddenly, I feel something.

Her fingers.

On the back of my hand.

She touches me. Gently, her index finger traces along my tendon and circles the knuckle of my pinky finger.

Panic should crash down on me like a hurricane. My throat should tighten. The fire of the past should blaze high.

But none of that happens.

She touches me. Gently. With great care. And breathes a silent "Okay" that feels like it fills the darkness inside me with light.

Chapter Twenty-Nine

JUNE

I said goodbye to Ashton hours ago, and yet it still feels like he's with me. I can't shake what he told me today in the hospital park. The way he looked at me. The tenderness of our touch. The emotional chaos he stirred up inside me.

All of it is still within me.

"Cheers, girls." Olive raises her cocktail.

Absentmindedly, I follow her lead. Nyla, Sonora, Autumn, and I clink our glasses against hers at the same time.

"So great that we finally made it happen." Sonora shakes her curls out of her face and takes a sip of her white wine.

We've been living together for almost two weeks now, but until today, we hadn't had a single free evening together. That made it all the more important to enjoy tonight—sitting with all of them in the cozy bar at the Halifax Harbor Waterfront. With a view of the colorful wooden cottages on the pier and the city lights shimmering across the canal. Surrounded by the vibrant, upbeat energy of the other guests, the sea breeze in our hair, and the sound of the waves in our ears.

"Okay, guys, I've got a suggestion." Nyla pulls the little umbrella out of the pineapple that decorates her Malibu Beach and sets it on her napkin. "Tonight, we're not doctors. Halifax Harbor Hospital doesn't exist. We're just here to have fun."

Olive nods in agreement. "Girls' night? I'm in." Her gaze sweeps around the table. "So, who's got something exciting going on in their personal life?"

Autumn lowers her eyelids, Nyla shakes her head emphatically.

"Personal life? What's that?" Sonora shrugs with a grin, her dimples flashing. "Do any of you even do anything besides work?"

Not really. Though today in the park with Ashton didn't feel like work at all.

Quite the opposite.

It was... I have no idea what it was.

Beautiful? Confusing?

Crazy?

Yes. Crazy. Clearly.

Excited chatter starts up around me, but I don't listen. My thoughts are once again with Ashton as I let my gaze drift across the water, which glimmers softly in the light of the setting sun.

Someone laughs—maybe Sonora.

I should have apologized for every single thing I did to him back then. Yes, that would've been the right thing to do. Wouldn't it?

Right. What does that even mean?

Until two weeks ago, I thought I knew exactly what was right and wrong. But after everything I've learned about

Ashton since then, there's only one thing I'm sure of: that I don't know anything at all.

Lost in thought, I take a sip of my Aperol Spritz.

"June?" Someone nudges me from the side. "It's your turn."

"With what?" I look into four curious faces.

Nyla's doe eyes sparkle with amusement. "An experience that recently made your heart race."

Sonora props herself up on her elbows, her mane of curls brushing the tablecloth. "We can hardly wait."

My roommates fix their eyes on me expectantly. I pretend to think hard for a moment. "Hauling the moving boxes."

Nyla tilts her head, her long golden earrings brushing against her neck. "Not your patient?"

Tattletale. I shoot her a mockingly venomous look.

"Ooh." Olive leans across the table toward me. "Now it's getting interesting."

"No. Not my patient." I tug at my napkin until one of the layers peels away, trying to stay cool. But I can feel my face burning.

Just the thought of Ashton is enough. Of how he suggested we could start over. And how good that felt inside me.

It was as if we'd gone back to our first meeting and decided to choose new paths from there.

Better Ways.

"Does anyone here believe our little tomato?" Sonora asks the group.

A collective shake of heads is the answer.

"Every word, of course—not." Autumn blows her bangs out of her face, the strands glowing deep red in the evening light.

"Alright." I raise my hands in mock surrender. "You got me. It was Ashton. He made my heart skip a beat." And how he did.

Nyla gestures for me to elaborate. "How'd he pull that off?"

Good question. "I don't know," I admit. He was just there, and everything about him felt so real.

Olive reaches for the straw in her cocktail. "I'd say infatuation level five, wouldn't you, ladies?" she asks, glancing at the others before taking a sip.

Sonora studies me intently. "At least. But I don't get it."

Well, she's not alone in that. "He's completely different from what I thought." I trace the rim of my glass thoughtfully. "What happened between us back then… there were probably a lot of misunderstandings." Yeah, that's one way to put it without saying too much. "We talked things through. And then… well… one thing led to another, and…" I let out a heavy sigh.

I would have loved to kiss him in the park, but I didn't dare. And he didn't make a move either. We touched each other far too briefly, looked up at the sky together, breathed together, stayed silent and savored what we had—whatever it was—before I had to turn to my substitute duties.

"Was that wrong?" I ask the group, mostly so they can reassure me that it wasn't. The feeling is too beautiful to ruin. Much too beautiful.

"Why? I don't see a problem." Sonora shrugs, the wide neckline of her top slipping off to one side. "Flings with patients aren't forbidden, after all."

"That's true," Nyla chimes in, then turns to me. "If you two really cleared things up back then, then…"

"…we can start over and see where it takes us," I finish her sentence. Really get to know one another.

And maybe fall in love. Perhaps.

A pleasant warmth rises in me. It carries a tingling sensation I feel everywhere. In my mind, I trace Ashton's attractive features with my index finger until I reach his lips. He breathes a kiss onto my fingertip. My skin tingles, as if he'd set off a tiny firework there.

"Looking at you like this, I'd say you're already well on your way to finding that out." It's Autumn's voice that pulls me back to reality once again.

I feel a blissful smile creeping across my face. "That might be true," I admit, and in that moment, I can hardly wait to see him again tomorrow. "Now I just have to figure out what's making him sick." I want that—more than ever before.

Chapter Thirty

ASHTON

Since June left my room yesterday, I've been waiting for her to walk through that door again. Every time I hear footsteps in the hallway, my heart beats a little faster. Every time someone walks past my room without coming in, my pulse settles again.

I know the day hasn't started yet and her shift doesn't begin for another two hours. Still, there's this ridiculous hope inside me that she'll stop by early. Not as my doctor, but as the woman who showed me a new world yesterday.

A world where nothing has to be lost forever. A world where things are possible that I once thought impossible.

We touched each other.

And it wasn't painful memories that filled me, but a warm tingling sensation.

A metallic sound catches my attention. The door handle—it's moving downward.

June tiptoes into the room. Despite the dim light, I can see the loving smile on her lips. And I see that she's not wearing her lab coat.

"Hey," she whispers, padding over to me. When she reaches my bed, she stops and tugs at her sweater.

"Hey." All of a sudden, I feel like a schoolboy who has no idea how to behave. My gut tells me I should take her hand, pull her onto the bed with me, and wrap her in my arms.

"How are you?" To my disappointment, she turns to the visitor chairs and pulls one over to the bed.

"No fever—at least not when the nurse checked last night, no pain," I reply, sitting up. I feel a bit weak, but after so many days in bed, that's probably normal. I really need to get out of here.

She shakes her head thoughtfully. "What on earth is wrong with you?"

Maybe nothing at all. Maybe this time it's really over. "Just one thing right now," I reply, looking at her intently.

I see her chest stop moving, as if she's holding her breath. "And that would be?"

You. In a world that isn't the hospital. That's the right answer. "I want to see the ocean," I say instead, because the other words scare even me.

She wrinkles her nose. "As long as you haven't been discharged, you're only allowed to stay on hospital grounds."

"If that's the case, you should discharge me immediately." I grin at her and don't even think the idea is that bad. "Then you take the day off on short notice, and we'll spend it together on the coast."

"That sounds wonderful." There's a deep longing in her voice, and for a moment, I see her eyes light up. "But I can't. I can't take time off."

"Then just say you've got a terrible migraine," I suggest.

She immediately raises her hands. "I don't do things like

that." She gets up from my bed and paces a few steps through the dimly lit room. Suddenly, she spins around. "I've got an idea."

"I'm in." Whatever it is. If it makes her light up like that, it must be something beautiful.

Ten minutes later, the elevator doors open with a bright ding in front of us, and we step out. Despite my protests, June has once again put me in a wheelchair.

"Where are we?" This doesn't look like a hospital—it looks more like a basement. Bare concrete walls, exposed piping, no windows.

"My roommate Sonora told me about this place." June grins mysteriously and looks around. "It must be over there."

With determination, she pushes my wheelchair to an emergency exit door, behind which lies a plain rooftop. The surface is dotted with ventilation shafts. It's anything but pretty, but when the wind picks up and the salty sea air drifts our way, I no longer care. And when we reach the railing at the front, everything behind me is already forgotten.

"Wow." I get up from my wheelchair, step up to the metal railing, and gaze out at the endless sea. The first rays of sunlight pierce the thin layer of clouds, and the peaceful silence is broken only by the cries of the seagulls.

Out of the corner of my eye, I notice June stepping up beside me. The wind blows a few strands of her blonde hair across her face. She brushes them back, closes her eyes, and takes a deep breath. The way the warm light touches her skin and makes it glow. The way she turns toward the new day with such delight. The way her lips curl slightly when she smiles. All of it forces me to ignore the water and look only at her.

"Didn't you want to see the ocean?" she asks with a smirk, without opening her eyes. As if she can feel me staring at her.

"Sorry, what?" I frown in confusion.

She points toward the horizon with her index finger. "The ocean—that's why you're here."

"I am," I reply, still confused, because I can't quite follow her. My gaze clings to her. Cautiously, I take a step closer, my upper arm brushing against hers.

She rests her head on my shoulder. The scent of her hair mingles with the salty sea air. "Do you like it?"

"Very much." My heart pounds hard against my chest. It would love to pick up right where we left off yesterday. I wonder if hers wants that too.

"Tell me something about you that I don't know yet," she says gently. "Something beautiful."

There's not much, unfortunately. Since Mom died, nothing in my life has really been beautiful. Except for one thing. "From where I sleep, I can look straight out at the sea."

She slips under my arm and moves in front of me, resting her head against my chest. "Why do you love the ocean so much?"

I gently pull her toward me. Everywhere our bodies touch, a comforting warmth spreads through me. "It's wild and free and untamed," I reply.

"Like you." It's not a question—June believes she knows, but she's wrong.

"Like I always wanted to be," I say wistfully. "When things got worse at home, all I wanted was to disappear. To sail out to sea and never come back. To see the world. To be free."

That was my big dream—and it still is. I never stopped breathing for it, even though so many times I wished I could. I held on for that dream, came back here after school, scraping by with odd jobs ever since, and started building my boat.

June nods against my chest. "To be free. I wished for that too, sometimes," she whispers softly.

Because of me. And because of what I did. My throat tightens.

"Tell me more about you." She looks at me intently.

I hold her tighter as a heavy weight settles on my chest. It's not the first time since we reunited that I've felt guilty. No—it's more than that. I'm the reason June—maybe even now—is still hurting. I broke something inside her.

And yet she's here. With me. In my arms. And she's willing to leave our past behind. She forgives me for my mistakes.

"You're so much stronger than I am," I blurt out. So much braver, so much greater. So much more human.

"What do you mean by that?" Her hand strokes across my chest.

The sea breeze tugs at my shirt as I gaze out toward the horizon. Until today, I never would've dreamed of forgiving anyone for anything. Not Jeremy, and especially not my asshole of a father—because I couldn't care less about either of them. And that's not going to change.

But things with June and me are different.

"Just because," I reply absentmindedly, swaying her gently from side to side. "Now it's your turn. Tell me something about yourself that I don't know yet."

June looks up at me with a meaningful expression. "Last

night, I dreamed about kissing you," she whispers, barely audible.

Her words send a sharp tingling sensation through my stomach. I place my hands on her hips and turn her so she's standing directly in front of me. "Really?"

Behind June, the sun climbs over the horizon, but it doesn't come close to matching the glow on her face. Without taking her eyes off me, she rises up onto her tiptoes.

I lean in toward her, feeling the gentle tremble that runs through her body and her hot breath against my skin.

My heart pounds wildly in my chest, the world around us blurs. There's only June and me, drawing closer to each other, piece by piece. My hands gently gripping her hips. Her fluttering eyelids. Her lips.

Our noses touch, and instantly it feels like that spot is on fire.

A soft sigh escapes her lips as she slightly parts them.

This woman takes my breath away. So much so that I feel dizzy. My legs suddenly feel weak.

"Oh June…" I murmur hoarsely.

Only a few millimeters separate us. One small movement, a single word, a gust of wind—that's all it would take.

"Yes?" she breathes, and for a split second, I feel her lips on mine.

I don't know if this is right. Only that I want it more than anything. "If we now…"

She lifts her eyelids and looks at me with her deep blue eyes. "Maybe it would be better if we…"

Yes.

No.

Maybe.

"Or we could…" Oh God, what is this woman doing to

me? Two weeks ago, I hated her, and now I'm about to kiss her.

She bites her lower lip. "This is crazy, isn't it?"

Definitely. "I don't know…" How to deal with this. What it all means. Who we are—both of us—standing here together in the sunrise.

"You're right." Her breathing is heavy. "Right now it's… um… complicated."

She pulls away from me, but I don't let her go. "You know what?" I ask quietly.

"What?"

"Right now, I don't give a damn," I reply, and finally do what every part of me has been longing for.

I kiss her—as intensely as I've never kissed a woman before.

Chapter Thirty-One

JUNE

Joy and sorrow. Fortune and misfortune. Hope and fate.

Nowhere do these things collide more violently than in a hospital.

Even though I had to help with an emergency this morning and didn't see Ashton, I still felt like I was floating. Somewhere above the clouds, where sky and infinity meet. A place where there is only joy, happiness, and hope.

But just seconds ago, I was ripped from that place. Now I'm where sorrow, misfortune, and fate reign.

A heavy silence hangs over the library, which we use as a meeting room. Dr. Young turns to the whiteboard and removes the cap from her marker. Without a word, she touches it to the surface and draws a single line across the entire column labeled number one. The squeak the marker makes on the plastic cuts straight through me.

"Oh man," I hear Ben whisper wearily beside me.

The boss pauses with her back still turned to us. For several seconds, I wait for her to come up with some sarcastic remark about Ben's failure, but so far, she's only left that one line on the whiteboard. Now she turns around.

"You may go, Number One," she says, her voice hoarse. "All the best to you."

Ben rises from his chair. "Thank you," he mutters, turning to leave.

I have no idea what the others are thinking, but to me, Dr. Young's little "game" has just taken on a seriously nasty aftertaste. None of us sitting here together for the case discussion can truly win or lose.

Our patients do.

Ben's patient lost last night.

"Dr. Miller?" the boss says as Ben opens the door. He turns back to us with a sorrowful expression, and I can see he has to force himself to meet Dr. Young's eyes. "It wasn't your fault."

Ben forces the corners of his mouth upward. "I know."

We all know it. None of us would have treated his patient any differently. Sometimes life does things we're powerless against.

Sometimes life is just plain shitty.

I glance at Ben in a way that's meant to say I'm so, so sorry. He nods, unable to manage a smile. Then he disappears through the door.

"And now to you." Dr. Young fixes her gaze on me, passing the whiteboard marker from one hand to the other. Deep furrows crease her forehead.

If there's one thing you have to master perfectly as a doctor, it's the ability to flip the switch in an instant. Whatever just happened—no matter how devastating, sad, or alarming—you have to keep going. Not just a little, but at two hundred percent.

"My patient is on the road to recovery," I say, incredibly

relieved to finally have something positive to report. Even though Ashton's illness remains a mystery, at least he's doing well.

"Wrong," my boss corrects me. "Your patient's kidneys failed last night."

The news hits me like a thunderclap.

That can't be.

That's...

Why?

Yesterday on the roof, everything was fine—no, more than that: he was better than he'd ever been! How could his kidneys suddenly fail? And why didn't anyone tell me?

Under the table, I dig my fingernails into my thighs to keep my emotions in check. It doesn't work.

Not even close.

I have to get to him. Right now.

"None of the previous symptoms indicated that," I say, doing everything I can to sound professional. But the truth is, Ashton's condition hits too close to home for me to think clearly.

Out of the corner of my eye, I see Jaxon. He seems entirely focused on flicking his pen just far enough that it doesn't leave his notepad.

"I'm gone for one day and your patient's already in danger." Waving her hands through the air, the boss paces back and forth. There's no trace left of her dark humor or her usual playful demeanor. She hastily slams the lab tests down on the table in front of me. "These were ordered by the attending physician."

I lower my gaze to the results. "The tests show an abnormally high concentration of light chain proteins." I wish I could focus, but I have no idea what that means. "That indicates... um..."

"Amyloidosis. Which in turn caused the kidney failure," Jaxon cuts in loudly.

"At the last meeting, you were still planning to let Barbie take some of the credit," the boss snaps at Jaxon. "What happened? Got cold feet?"

He grins at her with smug confidence. "Not even close."

"Good. Then zip it and wait your turn." With that, she turns to me expectantly. "Go on."

Sure. No problem. It's not like the ground just got ripped out from under my feet or anything.

No, June, you're a professional. Show her that! And the sooner you get this over with, the sooner you can check on Ashton.

"The tests also revealed that it's a case of AA amyloidosis," I continue reading. I sit up as straight as possible and try to relax my shoulders while I dig through my knowledge of this disease. "Possible causes: secondary to chronic inflammation or infection, as well as hereditary fever syndromes," I recite, textbook-style.

My boss responds with an impatient tapping of her foot. Jaxon scribbles something in his case file.

I place my hands on the table and rise from my chair because I just can't sit still any longer.

To them, this isn't about Ashton. He's patient P010424-060. Male with abdominal pain and pyrexia. Room 320. But to me, he's more than that. So much more.

I want to help him—desperately. Still, I don't understand. I have no idea how this new development fits into his clinical picture, don't know what I'm supposed to do next.

Distressed, I search for a connection. "The main cause of amyloidosis is usually arthritis, but we were able to…"

Fuck.

"Notice anything, Number Two?" Now it's the boss herself who cuts me off. "You're going in circles."

I know that myself, for fuck's sake. I already ruled out arthritis last week. And I'm well aware that none of this adds up.

More than that.

It's driving me crazy.

"Looks like this one's a bit too much for our blondie," Jaxon murmurs conspiratorially to the boss.

She, in turn, nods toward the whiteboard. "Can you read, number three?"

Jaxon grumbles something under his breath that probably means yes.

"Good. Now, if you also know your basic arithmetic, you'll quickly realize that your colleague Taylor is currently ahead of you by six points. Because…?"

Colleague? She's never called me that before. Normally, I'd be bursting with joy on the inside, but given Ashton's uncertain medical condition, it means surprisingly little right now.

Jaxon rolls his eyes toward the ceiling. "Because six is more than five."

"Excellent," the boss exclaims with exaggerated enthusiasm, momentarily sounding like her usual self before her expression turns serious again. "Continue, Barbie."

Well, I'd love to. If only I knew how. "I suspect an underlying condition—most likely inflammatory—that primarily causes abdominal pain and fever, but also leads to a wide range of secondary symptoms," I summarize, because that's the only thing I'm truly sure of. Also, based on what I learned in the park, I should keep the ACE score in mind. Traumatic childhood experiences can be linked to health issues in adulthood. But I'll keep that to myself for now.

The boss neither agrees nor corrects me. And Jaxon is already back to scribbling in his notebook.

I step away from the table and take a few steps through the conference room. "So the question is, what's triggering the underlying inflammation," I continue, struggling to keep my words from sounding like a question.

"What are you testing for?" the boss wants to know.

No idea. I'll have to research that to give a reliable answer. Still, I have to say something now. Something that doesn't sound completely idiotic.

"Crohn's disease." That could make sense. Maybe. "It fits with both the amyloidosis and the recurring abdominal pain."

"And what about the muscle pain?" Jaxon chimes in again. "Didn't think of that, did you, Barbie?"

I turn to him with what I hope is a confident smile. "Well, there are patients who suffer from more than one illness at a time. It's called comorbidity—look it up if you like," I snap back, and immediately regret it. Lashing out at him wasn't right. I should act professionally, no matter the turmoil raging inside me. I'm a doctor—I need to keep my emotions in check.

Jaxon shakes his head at me in disdain. "Last meeting, you tore me apart for suggesting lupus—which I still stand by, by the way—and now you come up with something even less likely?" He kicks his pen aside. "You're so screwed."

No, I'm not!, I want to scream. But I won't give him that satisfaction. Instead, I turn to the boss, who has apparently been watching our exchange with amusement.

"Endoscopy, abdominal ultrasound, as well as X-ray and a repeat test of inflammatory markers. Also, preventive treatment with glucocorticoids," I suggest firmly, steering the conversation back to what really matters.

Ashton.

The only thing that matters is that he gets better as soon as possible. I want to learn so much more about him, spend so much more time with him. I want to find out what makes his heart beat faster, what makes him smile, what makes him sad.

I want him to get well.

The boss studies me for a moment, then shrugs one shoulder. "Approved."

"Thank you." I exhale the breath that had built up inside me over the past few minutes and return to my seat.

"But, Number Two," I hear Dr. Young say with a sharp undertone as I pull my chair back, "I strongly advise you to get your symptom carousel under control. You can't afford too many more special rides, understood?"

As if I enjoyed being wrong all the time. My fingers dig into the back of the chair. "Understood."

Jaxon chuckles in amusement, though quietly enough that the boss, now turning to the whiteboard, doesn't hear it.

"Well, let's not be too harsh," she says, picking up the marker to adjust the score. "Technically zero, since you're still pretty much in the dark, aren't you? But since number three kindly created more difficult conditions, you get a point for perseverance."

She updates my plus six to a plus seven and immediately turns to Jaxon, who sheepishly admits that the hypothyroidism I suspected in his patient last time was, in fact, confirmed.

"What now?" At least the boss is taking the same demanding tone with him as she did with me earlier.

"Obviously, we treat them with thyroxine, schedule follow-ups, give advice on lifestyle and nutrition. The usual," he replies smugly, while my thoughts drift to Ashton. I need to get to him, as soon as possible.

Dr. Young leans against the bookshelf and tucks the whiteboard marker behind her ear. "You're quite the problem solver, number three. Impressive." Her words drip with sarcasm—clearly, she's back to her old self.

"Thank you," Jaxon replies, as if he hasn't noticed her tone, and once again I wonder how he even made it to the shortlist. "That gives us another deadline. If the treatment works, I've solved the case as of today."

Of course. Just what we needed.

"Only if the pain in his leg subsides for good," the boss replies with a forced smile.

"It will." Jaxon's chest swells with pride.

"There are no points for such a basic treatment plan, though." Dr. Young strolls back to the whiteboard and places the marker in the holder.

"No problem, I don't need them anyway."

The boss shrugs one shoulder. "If you're that sure, I'm sure it'll be just like that."

I study her, unable to shake the feeling that she's up to something. Does she know more about Jaxon's patient than she's letting on? Does she suspect—or even know for sure—that the diagnosis is wrong?

No. That's impossible. It would mean she's playing with people's lives, and no doctor—no matter how grotesquely they behave—would ever do that.

"All right then, off to your patients," I hear Dr. Young call out in the middle of my thoughts.

Relieved to finally check on Ashton, I stack my papers

and stand up. Jaxon is long gone by the time I reach the door.

Suddenly, I feel a hand on my shoulder. I whirl around and find myself looking into Dr. Young's troubled face.

"You do realize your performance today wasn't exactly glorious, don't you?" she asks in a tone my dad always used when he was trying to figure out what was going on with me.

Is she actually worried about me? And here I thought I had her all figured out.

"Of course." I nod quickly, mostly to hide my confusion about her behavior.

"Good. Your patient is counting on you, Dr. Taylor."

Did she just call me Dr. Taylor?

"And I… will… be there for him," I stammer, perplexed, under my breath.

A warm smile softens the tension usually etched around her mouth. "I would never doubt that," she replies, giving my shoulder a pat.

I don't dare move. I stand rooted between the conference table and the door, a cramp tightening in my stomach, growing more intense by the second.

What is she trying to tell me?

What exactly is it that she doubts?

If it's not my willingness to be there for my patients, then what is it? My competence, maybe? Does she think I'm not up to the job?

Fantastic. That's exactly what I don't need right now. Not when Ashton's health is on the line.

"Today I'll accompany you to your patient." Dr. Young lifts her chin. "I want to see for myself."

That's anything but a vote of confidence, isn't it?

I force a smile onto my face. "Of course."

Chapter Thirty-Two

ASHTON

The door to my room bursts open so forcefully that I jolt awake from my light sleep.

The doctor I complained to about June on my first day sweeps into the room. What was her name again? "Good morning, Mr. West."

Behind her, I spot June, who somehow looks smaller than usual today. Her hands are buried in the pockets of her lab coat. Her fingers fidget nervously beneath the fabric, yet she gives me a tentative smile. I smile back, if only for a moment, because I notice how June's boss is staring at me.

Why did she come along?

"Is there a problem?" I ask, glancing back and forth between the two of them.

"I'm Dr. Victoria Young, and I'll be overseeing your care today along with Dr. Taylor." The dark-haired woman raises her hand and wiggles her fingers. "Medical chart?"

June immediately steps forward and hands her my documents. While Dr. Young immerses herself in the file, I try to catch June's gaze. It takes a while before she looks at me. I furrow my brows questioningly. She wrinkles her nose, lowers her eyelids, and bites her lower lip.

A strange queasiness comes over me, even though, strictly speaking, there's no real reason for it. I slowly push myself up in bed. The electrolyte drip I've been hooked up to since my kidney failure last night is working. I feel better, even though I have to admit that what happened is worrying me.

Deeply worrying.

"I should've given point three for the lupus suspicion," June's boss murmurs as she flips through the file.

What is point three? And what points?

"Lupus?" I ask, because that's clearly the most important thing. Isn't that a kind of cancer? Or am I confusing it with something else?

Dr. Young fixes her gaze on June. "Abdominal pain, fever, breathing difficulties, kidney failure, chest pain."

June squares her shoulders. "No hair loss, no rash."

The dark-haired woman turns to me, raising her index finger. "Excuse us for a moment, Mr. West. We'll be right back."

I nod, bewildered, and the two of them disappear out the door.

"Back to the rash," I hear June's boss say out in the hallway. Her voice is muffled, but loud enough to understand. "Did you really check everywhere?"

No. She didn't. Because I didn't let her touch me for far too long.

"Of course," June replies with a certainty that makes me suspicious.

When did she do that? During a fever spike when I was barely conscious?

Either that—or she's lying to her boss.

But why would she do that? What would she gain from it?

I throw back the blanket, get up, and sneak toward the door with the IV stand. Whatever the two of them are discussing, I want to hear every word.

"Besides, the medical history didn't show any headaches or fatigue," June says now.

Paper rustles. "Last week, when you were focused on neurological disorders, fatigue and poor sleep were your main arguments for that."

Fatigue? Poor sleep? What is this woman talking about?

"Listen." That's June's boss again. "Just because you don't want Number Three to solve your case doesn't mean you can ignore his diagnosis. That's not how you win."

Solve the case? What is this, CSI?

More and more questions are rising inside me, while I understand less and less of what's going on here.

Do I have lupus?

Did June make up symptoms for me?

To win? And if so, win what? What kind of trophy is my health worth?

"It's not lupus," June insists stubbornly.

"Ten points off." Dr. Young snorts disdainfully. "Now order an ANA test."

June is silent for a moment. "Right away," she replies at last, sounding utterly miserable—defenseless and in need of help in the middle of the storm.

I feel for her.

"I'll make sure the results are ready for the team meeting tomorrow," I hear June say.

I drag myself back, collapse onto the bed, and stare at the scratch in the ceiling tile.

The feeling that something isn't right won't let go of me. But what is it?

Hopefully June comes back alone soon so I can ask her about it.

Chapter Thirty-Three

JUNE

Autumn's green eyes widen. "Oh. My. God. Seriously?"

Together, we enter the farmer's market. The first vendors are setting up their stalls, and the scent of freshly baked bread and spiced coffee fills my nose. "It's never been this bad."

After the reprimand, Dr. Young didn't take her eyes off me all day yesterday, no matter which patient I was attending to, so I didn't get to spend any time with Ashton. And today, I have the day off. If I show up at the hospital, she'll dock points—at best.

"It's not over yet. You can still get the job. Just don't give up." She pulls a canvas tote bag from her purse and slings it over her shoulder. "Veggies?" she asks, nodding toward the stall with wooden crates overflowing with bright red tomatoes, basketball-sized pumpkins, and juicy heads of lettuce.

I nod, and we start strolling. We pass the herb stall and the flower kiosk, which fills the air with a sweet, fresh scent.

Autumn's right—I shouldn't give up. But she doesn't know that Jaxon is nearly finished with his case.

If she did know, she'd start doubting me. Just like my parents did back then. And the confidence I've worked so hard to build over the years would vanish in an instant.

But even worse would be if Ashton thought I was a failure too.

We reach the vegetable stand. I grab a bunch of leeks, sniff them, and drop them into my shopping bag. "Let's talk about something else. It is my day off, after all." Besides, I have to solve my problem on my own anyway.

"Gladly." She nods empathetically. "How's it going with Ashton—the guy?" With a flourish, she grabs a shopping basket from the stack next to the stand.

"Good." I lean against the post supporting the striped awning of the vegetable stand and take in the colorful selection. "He's… sweet."

Very sweet, actually. The look he gave me when I walked into the room with Dr. Young was pure sugar. I could tell he wanted to help me—maybe even protect me.

A bulb of garlic disappears into Autumn's shopping basket. "And?"

I let my fingernails glide over the wood grain of the post. Just thinking about Ashton sends a tingle through me. "Nothing and," I say, and at the same time feel a pretty lovestruck grin creeping onto my lips.

"Did you kiss him?" She was just about to reach for the beefsteak tomatoes, but now she pauses to study me.

Heat flares up inside me. "A little..."

She grins. "So you forgave him."

There's nothing to forgive. But there's a lot to understand. "We both made mistakes."

Autumn sets her shopping basket down. "What exactly happened back then? I know he bullied you. But what did you do? Something that also had serious consequences?"

Oh God, yes. And "serious" doesn't even begin to cover it. "Disastrous" is more like it. I nod, guilt-ridden.

"So serious that he's still suffering because of it?" she asks, picking up a few potatoes.

That's a question I've never asked myself before. But now that she's brought it up, I realize I should have.

I know far too little about him.

Where does he live? Who are his friends? How does he spend his free time? And what about his brother? When Ashton was admitted, he didn't seem to care about Jeremy being there. On the contrary, he seemed full of hatred toward his brother.

"What if the answer is yes?" I ask, troubled. What if what happened back then still controls his life today?

From his medical file, I know he lives out in Peggy's Cove. It's pretty remote. He hasn't mentioned any friends, and as far as I can tell, he hasn't had any visitors so far.

How could I, of all people, be someone he—however that may look—actually likes?

There's no rational reason for that. Right?

The thought makes me feel a little sick.

"What if he's playing me?" I ask, worried. Maybe he thinks he needs me to get better and wants to keep me happy until then.

Suddenly Autumn is beside me, pulling me into her arms. "Oh, honey…" she whispers lovingly in my ear. "Do you really think that?"

No. That's absurd.

It can't be.

Still, I'm not entirely sure. All I know is that I hate the thought itself. Until now, I never once doubted that Ashton's behavior was genuine. Was that a mistake?

"It wouldn't be the first time I fell for him blindly," I reply, worried.

Can I trust myself on this?

Something inside me aches. The part that hates that I'm even worried about this. The part that wants to fall into Ashton's arms and listen to his heartbeat. The one that saw a whole new world in his eyes—a world that has to be real.

But there's another part, too. The one that warns me not to trust Ashton. The one that whispers he might still be the same angry boy he once was, just waiting for the right moment to strike back. Especially now that he knows I wasn't exactly kind to him back then either.

No.

That's not who Ashton is. Not anymore. And as long as he doesn't give me a reason to think otherwise, I shouldn't. Period.

"Let me know if I can help." Autumn lets go of me and gives me a warm smile.

I nod gratefully, then turn to the vegetable stand in search of a distraction. "What else do we need?"

Chapter Thirty-Four

JUNE

Agitated, I stroll down the hospital corridor. I haven't been to see Ashton since Dr. Young tore into me the day before yesterday. Even though she had the decency to reprimand me in the hallway, Ashton has surely noticed in his hospital room that she's not pleased with me.

What if he now thinks he was wrong to entrust me with his health? What if he no longer looks at me the way he did over the past few days? What if he's disappointed in me?

Those questions kept me up again last night. I spent half the night out on our apartment balcony, staring up at the sky. Mom's message, telling me that the party is apparently going to be a little bigger than originally planned, only made things worse.

Was Dr. Young right? Did I only rule out lupus because the suggestion came from Jaxon and I wanted to do everything I could to stop him from snatching my dream job right out from under me?

Did I treat Ashton unfairly? Did I put his health at risk? Out of sheer selfishness?

Instinctively, I reach for my necklace to pull the pendant out from under my shirt.

My lucky little daisy.

I let my fingers glide over the rounded petals. This pendant helped me stay strong back then. It helped me get through my studies. It was with me when I slowly regained my parents' trust, piece by piece.

It might seem ridiculous, but without this pendant, I would have fallen apart. It held the fragments of my soul together until they could heal again.

Even now, it should give me strength and courage to get through this grueling job application marathon. But today, it only reminds me that the victories I once celebrated over Ashton weren't victories at all. That the strength I drew from this pendant may have helped me, but at the same time, it hurt Ashton.

Is it happening again? Am I trying so hard to be strong that I don't see how it's weakening him?

That's wrong. It has to stop now.

As I walk, I pull the chain over my head and slip it into one of my lab coat pockets. My neck feels bare, as if I've lost my shield, but I don't put it back on. Instead, I head straight for Ashton's room.

I knock gently on the door, wipe my hands on my coat, and step into his room.

He smiles at me, and immediately I feel better.

"Hey," I greet him warmly. My heart beats faster as I reach him and gesture toward the edge of the bed. "May I?"

He shifts to the side to make room for me. "Sure."

"How are you today?" I place my hand on his, savoring the warmth of his skin.

"Better." His fingers brush over mine.

"Sorry you had to see that the day before yesterday. My boss can be a bit…" I shrug, searching for the right word. "Blunt."

He stares at me so intently, it's as if he's searching my face for something very specific. "Do I have lupus?"

Admittedly, many of his symptoms fit. Still… "Lupus is a very difficult autoimmune disease to diagnose," I explain to him. "It's the first thing less dedicated doctors think of when they can't clearly assign symptoms to a specific illness."

"But that doesn't mean I couldn't have it." A barely visible crease forms on his forehead.

It's hard for me to admit, but he deserves the truth. "That's true." Gently, I let my thumb glide over the back of his hand. "The results will be in soon. But even if the test comes back positive, that still doesn't necessarily mean you actually have lupus."

"I don't understand." He gives a barely noticeable shake of his head.

I explain to him that even healthy people sometimes show positive ANA test results. And that other autoimmune diseases can also be behind such a result. I tell him every detail, and it even makes me feel a bit better myself.

There's so much knowledge in my head. I'm not a bad doctor.

When I finish, he exhales slowly. "Okay."

No, that's not it. I can see it in his expression, feel it in his hand, which still lies motionless beneath mine and doesn't return any of my tenderness.

"What's wrong, Ashton?" I ask, and immediately my pulse quickens. "Are you disappointed in me? Because I didn't consider lupus as a possible diagnosis?"

Please say no, Ashton. Please!

He presses his lips together and looks at me intently. "Why did you tell your boss I have trouble sleeping?"

"You heard that?" I ask, ashamed.

He nods. "Well?"

"When I was applying the cold packs, I saw your scars and thought maybe you were hurting yourself," I admit, even though I'm embarrassed. I was wrong back then, and Dr. Taylor can't afford to be wrong. She always has to do what's right—for her patients.

His mouth opens. I gesture for him to let me finish speaking first.

"Self-harm is often associated with depression, which, along with the other symptoms, reinforced the suspicion of a neurological disorder." I look at him intently.

"And?" His expression softens. Ashton probably knows I had to make those assumptions because he never gave me an explanation for the scars.

"Self-harm and depression are heavy burdens. Diagnoses that quickly lead to stigma." I clear my throat. "I wanted to spare you that, Ashton. Especially because I wasn't sure. So I made something up to support my theory —something that wouldn't brand you."

His eyes widen. "You helped me."

I nod. At that moment, I feel his fingers gently weaving through mine. Slowly, our hands entwine, his thumb caressing my skin.

"Thank you," he says in a husky voice, and once again I'm caught. I see the Ashton who makes my heart race. The Ashton who has the power to flood my world with golden light, just by being there.

This is real.

Nothing stands between us—because we're being honest with each other. It's not like it was back then; we're not like we were back then. Ashton doesn't want to hurt me—I can feel it deep down.

Smiling, I lean down toward him. "I was happy to do it."

He places his hand on my upper arm and pulls me closer. His warmth surrounds me, and instantly I feel like I'm high.

Ever since we kissed on the rooftop, I've been longing to do just that all day long. And even now, I catch myself staring at his lips. Imagining how soft they are. How they taste. And what they make me feel when they touch mine.

Just the thought of it is enough to make heat rise inside me. It builds up beneath my lab coat, so I shrug it off and toss it over the visitor's chair.

Ashton gives me a crooked grin, as if he knows exactly what's happening to me. Then he slowly lets his fingers glide over my bare forearm.

I melt—into his presence and into this moment. Nothing else seems to matter; the hospital feels far away. My fear that he might not feel the same way about this as I do no longer exists. And what Dr. Young thinks of me? I couldn't care less.

He matters. He and this moment, in which I feel deep inside that this is the beginning of something wonderful. Because the way he's looking at me now—intensely and full of longing—I'm certain he's thinking the exact same thing.

I lean closer to him, his hand moves upward, first brushing my shoulder, then my neck. Now he places it at the nape of my neck.

We're about to kiss.

The loud beeping of my pager makes me flinch.

No. Not now!

"Duty calls." Ashton gestures toward the pager at my waistband, his expression less than thrilled.

Sighing, I reach for the nuisance to read the message, and it takes only a fraction of a second before I crash hard into reality. "Your test results are in," I manage to say.

His gaze is once again filled with worry. "And what if it's lupus?"

It's not lupus! Can someone finally believe me?

Gently, I stroke his forearm. "Then we'll find a way to manage your illness so you can live an amazing life."

His smile doesn't reach his eyes. "Okay."

"Do you trust me?" I hold my breath, because the answer to my question means the world to me.

He nods. "I trust you and I believe in you."

Hearing that feels like every light in the world is turning on at once to brighten my life. Along with Ashton's thousand-watt smile, which he now gives me too.

I rise from his bed without letting go of his hand. "See you soon," I say.

"See you soon." There's a warm affection in his voice. His fingers tighten around mine.

"Okay." I take a step to the side, but I can't bring myself to let go of his hand.

"Okay," he replies, as his thumb brushes across the palm of my hand.

"I'm going now," I murmur, rocking back and forth on my shoes.

"Go ahead." His thumb traces circles around mine.

My chest rises and falls faster than it should. "Then…"

He nods toward the door and loosens his grip.

Our hands slip apart. I feel a little colder instantly. One last air-kiss, then I tear myself away and leave his room.

Out in the hallway, I bump into Jaxon, who's leaning

next to the door of the nurses' station. "Well, well, your cheeks are practically glowing." His gaze trails down the length of my body. "And I guess you didn't have time to put your coat back on, huh?"

My smile freezes. "Are you waiting for me?" I ask, ignoring his stupid comment. It has no place here anyway.

That knowing nod of his rubs me the wrong way. "Wanted to make up for the lab test mix-up from last week." I watch in disbelief as he pulls folded printouts from the pocket of his coat. "So I picked up the ANA test results from the lab myself."

So he could hardly wait either. "That's very sweet of you," I say calmly, even though my pulse is racing, and reach out for the test results. "Let's see."

"First, I need to get something off my chest." The corners of his mouth turn downward.

I cross my arms. "Yeah?"

"You're a great doctor. Much better than I am."

Excuse me? This is a trap. Isn't it? "Thanks," I stammer, confused. "Can I see the results now?"

With a guilty look, he hands me the papers, and that's when it hits me—what's behind his odd behavior.

The test was negative. He was wrong, and I was right. Thank God.

"No lupus, right?" I ask, taking the results from him.

He shrugs and nods toward the papers. I lower my gaze and unfold them. "What?" That can't be! "This is…"

"Positive for ANA," I hear Jaxon announce gleefully. "Congratulations, June, your patient has lupus."

No! "That's hardly proof." He knows it just as well as I do. It might be a clue—one I never would've considered—but nothing more than that.

He leans casually against the wall again. "Order the special tests, then you'll see."

I will—and right now. Furious, I crumple the papers in my hand.

"That's at least five points for me. And for you?" He taps his chin, pretending to think. "What do you think the boss will deduct from your score?"

Who the hell cares? Ashton could have lupus!

"Minus eight. At least." He adjusts the stethoscope around his neck. "But that's not all."

What? How could it get any worse? I signal to him urgently to get to the point.

"My patient doesn't have any more pain in his leg. Soon, we'll have the thyroxine dosage perfectly adjusted too." Calmly, he pushes off the wall, steps closer, and locks eyes with me. "Then it's bye-bye for you."

He can forget that! There's no way I'm leaving this hospital before Ashton. "We'll see about that," I snap, glaring at him.

"You're damn hot when you're this wild, Barbie," he murmurs, then turns and shuffles away. I'm left standing in the middle of the hallway, gasping for air, feeling like my whole body is on fire.

And with the knowledge that I have to do more than just wait for the lab results to finally diagnose Ashton's illness properly. Because that's exactly how I can save us both.

But what else could I do?

Chapter Thirty-Five

ASHTON

I stroll leisurely down the hospital corridor. I'm heading to the bay window at the far end, where a few chairs and green plants glow in the sunlight streaming in. I can hardly stand being in my room any longer.

It's cramped. And filled with emotions I can't make sense of.

There's June, and the way she looks at me in her thoughts. The warmth and reassurance she gives me. The feeling her touch leaves on my skin.

I reach the bay window and step up to the glass. On the right, I catch a glimpse of part of Halifax Harbor. The boats gently rocking in the water stir a familiar longing in me. But there's something else, too. I let my gaze drift across the horizon, trying to grasp what it is. The conversation I had with June yesterday changed something.

I realized I wouldn't be leaving this hospital anytime soon.

Clouds drift across the sky like thin veils, constantly shifting into different shapes, growing denser, then dissolving again. No matter how many times I try to predict how they'll change in the next few seconds, I'm always wrong.

Lost in thought, I pull my phone out of my pocket and unlock the screen. Since I was admitted nearly two weeks ago, Jeremy has called repeatedly. I haven't picked up once. I only responded to his messages, in which he asked how I was feeling and if there was anything he could do for me.

Everything's fine. Don't need anything.

Was it okay to brush him off like that? Or was it finally time to be honest with him? Just like June and I had been?

What if he has a story too? A pain that made him act the way he did back then?

The thought scares me. Too much to follow it any further. I quickly tuck the phone away again. A moment later, I feel a hand on my arm.

"Hey." That's June's chocolate-smooth voice. "So this is where you are."

Even though I was just lost in heavy thoughts, I can't help but smile now. I turn to her. "Hey," I reply—admittedly a little dumbly—but the sight of her makes me forget every word I knew.

She looks at me so intensely that a warm tingling runs down my spine. I can't help but reach for her hand.

"There's news." Her gaze drifts for a moment to the medical file in her hand.

"And what if I don't want to know?" What if I'd much rather run away with her and drive to the coast? If we could leave the clinic and my shitty illness behind, even if just for a single day, to be free together?

She gives a gentle smile. "The ANA test came back positive, but fortunately, further testing allowed us to rule out lupus."

That's great—so why does she still seem tense? "How disappointing," I reply jokingly, trying to cheer her up a little.

With a sigh, she places the file on one of the visitor chairs. "No. It's good news, I'm sorry."

I feel the urge to step closer, until we're so near I can hear her breathing. "What's wrong?" I ask, just like she did with me yesterday.

She leans against the windowsill. "We're back at the beginning. What if I can't figure out what's wrong with you?" she asks in a flat voice, staring outside, then immediately presses her lips together.

I stand beside her, rest my hands on the windowsill too, and reach out my pinky finger toward hers. "You will, I know it," I say, trying to comfort her. "I'm feeling better..."

She inhales sharply. "It's just a phase—like so many times before. The symptoms will come back. And they might have even worse cons—"

"No." I place my hand protectively over hers. The thought that I might have to stay here for weeks, maybe even months, already drove me crazy earlier. But if she's now trying to tell me that I might not leave this clinic alive, then I don't want to hear it.

She turns her head toward me with an intense look. "We don't know. Anything is possible." She swallows hard. "Even the unthinkable."

Three weeks ago, that news wouldn't have affected me much. My life was empty. Worthless. But now there's June, and what she stirs in me. "I don't want to die," I hear myself croak.

I want to live, and I want to be healthy, so I can enjoy what's beginning to grow between us for as long as possible. So I can breathe and laugh with her. So I can wake up next to her every morning, every day, until eternity swallows us whole.

Wow. Did I really just think that?

June intertwines her fingers with mine. "I'll do everything I can." I read the rest in her expression— even if it costs me my own life.

That's the moment when I no longer have any doubts. There's only June and me and this moment in which I want to show her how much she means to me.

What we both need now is something to give us hope. Something to work toward. A dream we'll make come true.

I let go of her hand to pull her into my arms. "One day, all of this will be behind us. Then we'll stand out on the cliffs," I whisper into her ear as an image forms in my mind. There's the sea, crashing against the rocks below us, making the air tremble. There's the wind tugging at our clothes. And there's a new day, just beginning. "We'll hold hands and watch the first of countless sunrises—each one belonging to us."

I have no idea where those words came from. But the thought that June and I might get a second chance at life is so beautiful, it overwhelms me effortlessly.

She looks up at me. "We will," she breathes, as a single tear catches in her lashes. The drop glistens in the slanting sunlight.

I lean toward her, stroke her back, feel her heartbeat. Her breath brushes against my lips. Slowly, I tilt my head, never breaking eye contact. Her eyes are like a mirror, reflecting my own emotions.

The longing. The racing heart. The hope.

I press my lips to hers, and we sink into a kiss that makes me forget everything I ever thought I knew.

Chapter Thirty-Six

JUNE

We kiss. Passionately and intensely, so completely entwined that it feels like we're one, inseparable by anything or anyone.

With both hands, I cradle his face and feel his warmth as we dive deeper into the kiss. It's surreal. A dream I dreamed so many years ago, now coming true in a way that's far better than anything I ever imagined.

Standing here, kissing Ashton, with this tingling sensation coursing through me. Smelling the scent of his skin, tasting him, inhaling his nearness.

It makes me forget everything. Nothing else matters. Not this job, not my parents, not even what Dr. Young thinks of me.

Only the two of us matter. Just us and the bond we share.

"June," Ashton breathes against my lips.

My knees go weak.

"I…" Suddenly, it feels like he's losing his balance too. "I feel…"

Instinctively, I open my eyes. His cheeks are flushed bright red, sweat covers his forehead. Oh no. Please, no.

"You have a fever." I sound just as panicked as I feel.

"My legs…" he stammers, and a second later he collapses with a painful cry. He clutches his arms around his stomach. "Fuck."

Nausea hits me like a wave. Not just the fever—other symptoms he'd had before are back. "I need help!" I shout into the hallway, then turn to Ashton. "Try to breathe slowly," I urge him, catching a glimpse of my colleagues already rushing toward us.

Two nurses lift Ashton onto a stretcher. On the way to his room, I quickly arrange everything that had helped during his previous episodes. By the time we arrive, a nurse is already there. While she hooks up the IV, I place cooling pads on Ashton's joints. Then I check the flow rate of the pain medication.

"You'll feel better soon," I promise, doing my best to suppress the worry in my voice.

Ashton groans in pain.

I thank my assistants as they file out of the room one by one. Then I pull a chair closer for myself. I won't take my eyes off him for a single second. Gently, I take his burning hot hand. "I'm here," I assure him, even though his eyelids have already closed.

At the end of the shift, I lean against my locker in the changing room and sink to the floor.

Despair threatens to overwhelm me.

Ashton is stable, yet he's worse off than he's ever been since his admission.

Damn it, why?

I rub my eyes harshly. I need his diagnosis. Immediately. Because the truth is, no one knows how much time Ashton has left. With each fever spike, his symptoms have become more alarming.

What's coming next?

No, I don't even want to think about that. Fate has given us a second chance, and I'm not going to mess it up. The correct diagnosis has to be in the data I already have. It has to be hidden in there somewhere—there's just no other way.

My laptop is on the top shelf, along with my phone, which lights up as I touch it.

A message from Mom.

We should go shopping together before the party. There will be a lot of guests who haven't seen you in a long time, and you'll want to look nice, right? And besides…

My eyes start to burn again—I can't keep reading. In a flash, I put it back in its place.

I'm going to disappoint them all.

Especially Ashton.

"Think, June. Think. Finally. Think." I press my fist against my forehead and close my eyes to help myself focus.

But as soon as the doors close, all I can see is Ashton's face in my mind. He looks at me, silently pleading for help. Then the corners of his mouth lift into a smile that throws my heart offbeat.

I already lost him once because I didn't understand anything.

That can't happen again.

I rush into the washroom and rinse the tears from my skin. In the mirror, a June with bloodshot eyes and a swollen nose stares back at me. Her cheeks are sunken, yet I still recognize the June from back then.

She's helpless. And desperate.

And that's exactly what's wrong. Fear and despair have no place here. Only one thing matters: Ashton's life.

Chapter Thirty-Seven

ASHTON

"So this diagnosis doesn't make any sense either." June has been pacing up and down in front of my bed for minutes. Words like differential diagnosis, asymptomatic progression, and names of various diseases pour out of her at lightning speed. I don't even remotely understand what she was trying to tell me. Her face is as pale as the wall, deep shadows lie under her eyes. Her cheeks look sunken.

She probably hasn't slept last night. Because of me.

"Don't be so hard on yourself, June," I say, weakened by the many problems my body is currently battling. "Come on, sit with me."

She stops at the opposite wall, where she leans against it. "There must be something I've missed. But what is it?" She massages her temples with effort. "Are there things you haven't told me yet?"

Why so accusatory? "Hey, easy with the accusations," I blurt out.

She studies me, pressing her lips together. "These aren't

accusations, I just want to help you," she replies in a pleading tone.

Something is wrong with her. I have never seen her this panicked. "What's going on?" I ask, because her behavior is scaring me.

"Nothing," she answers far too quickly. "I want to get to the bottom of your problem before…"

That sounds so final. Why? Does she know more about my illness than she is letting on? "Before what?"

"Let's start over," she says, gesturing wildly, then rattles off all kinds of medical terms I don't understand. "Genetic disorders. What about those?" she asks at the end.

She already knows that. Shaking my head, I look at her. "I'm sorry, but there haven't been any new ones in the past two weeks."

"Damn." She growls irritably and presses her fingers to the bridge of her nose. "Okay, this is getting us nowhere. I need to keep researching."

With that, she storms out of the room.

Should I go after her and at least try to calm her down a little?

Yes, I should. After all, the medication I got yesterday is already working. My life isn't in danger—at least not immediately. Hopefully. Of course, I can't know for sure. Still, June shouldn't torment herself so much over my diagnosis. She's overreacting.

With effort, I peel myself out of bed, drag myself to the door leaning on the IV stand, and slip out into the hallway. There I see June with another doctor, who's pointedly tapping his wristwatch.

"Don't you have your own patients to take care of, Jaxon?" she snaps at him, hurrying past without waiting for his response.

This Jaxon watches her go, shaking his head. So I'm not the only one wondering what's gotten into June. Maybe he knows how to calm her down? After all, they're colleagues.

"Hey," I call out to him on impulse, raising my hand.

His gaze lands on me. "Yeah?"

I motion for him to come over, because in my condition, the walk to him feels insurmountable. "The doctor…" I begin as he stops in front of me.

"Career-obsessed bitch," he cuts me off. "What do you need from her?" he then asks with a professionally polite smile.

"Did you just say 'career-obsessed bitch'?" About June? The woman who only cares about her patients?

A worn-out expression flashes across his face. When he glances at the door behind me, he nods knowingly. "Ahh, room 320." His hand lands on my shoulder. "My condolences, man."

Because of June? Is he out of his mind? "Why?"

He waves it off. "Doesn't matter, won't be relevant for much longer anyway."

Now I'm completely lost. Tired, I lean against the wall. "What do you mean?"

"Our dearly beloved Barbie," he gestures with his thumb in the direction June disappeared earlier, "will soon have to admit she's not up to the job."

"Why?" What makes him so sure she won't be able to diagnose my illness?

He grins at me. "Because she's about to get fired."

"From the clinic?" Wow, that's intense.

"From the game," he replies.

June is playing a game? What kind of game? Before I can ask the question, I suddenly remember what June's boss said to her outside my door the other day.

Ten points deducted.

In my mind, puzzle pieces I didn't even know existed suddenly start falling into place. The determined way June initially refused to be brushed off. The gentle tone she used to coax information out of me—things I never would have told her otherwise. Her panic earlier, because she couldn't figure out what was wrong with me.

"What's the game about?" I ask, growing increasingly uneasy.

"The specialist position, of course." He furrows his brows, giving me a puzzled look. "Oh," he says suddenly, "June didn't tell you?"

I shake my head, confused.

"Doesn't really matter anyway—I've already won." His chest puffs out. "And as for you," he lowers his voice, "don't worry. As soon as June's out of the picture, you'll get a real doctor."

"How reassuring," I reply dryly, though my thoughts are already elsewhere.

So June has to solve my case to get a job. One that means a hell of a lot to her. Why did she keep that from me?

"Hang in there a little longer," Jaxon says, turning to leave. "You've got this."

Without saying a word, I drag myself back to bed, where a thousand questions come crashing down on me all at once.

Has June been pretending? Am I nothing more to her than the key to her career?

And for this job as a specialist, did she really go so far as to fake forgiving me for what happened back then?

Is she only pretending to have feelings for me?

I don't know. All I know is that the thought of it makes my chest feel unbearably tight.

Chapter Thirty-Eight

JUNE

"Without his permission?" Olive grabs her handbag from the coat rack. "That's trespassing."

"Maybe so, but what else am I supposed to do?" Leaning against the kitchen doorway, I take a sip from my jumbo mug of coffee. The test results have been nothing but dead ends so far. Even the Crohn's disease theory didn't hold up.

The truth is, I've spent the last two nights buried in research, and I still have no idea what's wrong with Ashton. Meanwhile, the accompanying symptoms have only gotten worse with each new fever spike.

What's next? A stroke? Liver failure? Heart attack? Pulmonary embolism? Just thinking about all those possibilities makes my stomach turn.

Desperately, I look to Nyla, who's slipping into her sneakers. "What do you think?"

"It's about his health," she replies thoughtfully. "That always has to come first—and in this case, it definitely does."

"Still, June needs permission to search his house for possible causes of his symptoms." Olive casts a critical glance at the mirror and adjusts her wavy hair, even though it already looks perfect.

"I'm sure Ashton wouldn't mind," I say, stepping aside to let Nyla pass as she heads toward the apartment door.

"I think so too," she says with a grin. "Ashton never minds anything June does."

I stick my tongue out at her briefly. "Doesn't your shift start in fifteen minutes?"

"Yup." Out of nowhere, Nyla's cheeks turn a glowing red. "And I have to be on time, otherwise the ambulance will leave without me."

Right, Nyla isn't assigned to the emergency room today. I study her flushed cheeks, and she lowers her eyes. "Something special happening in the ambulance?" I ask curiously.

She shakes her head quickly. "Not that I know of."

"Mhm." Grinning, I take a sip of coffee. "Then I'm curious to hear what you'll have to tell us tonight."

"Not just you," Olive adds, throwing me a conspiratorial glance. "But I've got to go now." She checks the fit of her blouse, then turns to me while slipping into her high heels. "Get the approval, okay?"

How am I supposed to do that? I'm not allowed to show up at Halifax Harbor Hospital outside my working hours, and with the way Dr. Young feels about me right now, I really shouldn't take any risks.

But I could do something else. "I'll call Ashton."

"Do that." Nyla opens the door. "Bye, June, enjoy your morning." She blows me an air kiss. "Coming, Olive?"

"Just a sec." Olive digs a lipstick out of her bag and touches up her lips.

The way she puckers her lips right after makes me

pause. She looks like she stepped out of a glossy magazine —as usual, really—but today she seems to care even more about her appearance than she normally does.

"Let's go," she says before I can ask her about it, then rushes out the apartment door.

"See you later," I call after the two of them and pull my phone from the pocket of my sweatpants to call Ashton.

An hour later, I flick on the turn signal of the rental car to turn onto Peggys Point Road. I hadn't been able to reach Ashton, which isn't all that surprising. After all, he's going through a real marathon of tests today, since in my desperation yesterday I ordered every remotely reasonable examination I could think of.

Still, I'm sure he won't mind me checking in on him. Olive's warning is still ringing in my ears, and just a few weeks ago, I would've agreed with her a hundred percent.

Gaining access to private property without permission is definitely wrong. But today, I'm no longer so sure. Right doesn't always feel right, and wrong doesn't always feel wrong. Where exactly the line lies is a mystery to me.

No. Nyla's arguments carry more weight. This is about Ashton's health, and that has to come before everything else.

I steer the car onto Church Road, where his house is supposed to be, and slow down to check the house numbers as I drive by. But when I reach the end of the street, I only get to house number 25.

Ashton lives at number 27. At least, that's what he stated when he was admitted.

Confused, I look around. To my right, a narrow path

winds further toward the sea. It's barely visible on the stone-covered ground—only the absence of moss hints at tire tracks. It seems to be the only option, so I guide the car off the asphalt onto the unpaved road and putter along the winding path.

It actually ends at a dark red-painted cabin. Next to it stands a trailer, surrounded by grasses and low shrubs that seem to cling to the rocky ground. I stop and get out. A sharp breeze blows my hair into my face, and the surf crashes loudly against the rocky coastline at the edge of the property. The thunder echoes inside me as I walk over to the mailbox mounted on a wooden post in front of the trailer.

Church Road 27.

Perfect!

Quickly, I grab the Tupperware containers I took from the shared kitchen in case I wanted to collect samples and pull on my gloves. As I start searching for a spare key next to the makeshift steps leading to the trailer door, I feel like a burglar.

Why didn't I think to come here yesterday? I was on duty and could've easily asked Ashton for permission.

"That's not helping you now," I scold myself, reach for the work shoes on the step, and turn them upside down.

No key, so I place them back the way I found them and feel along the underside of the steps. I come across a raised section, trace the edge, and find a button, which I press. With a sharp click, a lid pops open and the key falls to the ground.

Silvery and gleaming, it lies before me. I should take it and have a look around the trailer. Still, I hesitate.

In just a moment, I'm going to break into Ashton's place. Is that right or wrong?

Right.

With determination, I grab the key and unlock the door. Stale air hits me as I step inside the trailer and take in my surroundings. There's the kitchen, with a folding door leading off from it, a dining area, a sleeping area, and a workspace with a laptop.

So this is where he lives. This is the air he breathes every day. His bed, where he sleeps night after night. All the things that matter to him.

Why did he choose to live in a trailer, I wonder?

Tomorrow, I'll ask him. And a thousand other things I want to know about him, because even though he's told me so much about his past, we still clearly don't know each other well enough.

The only thing I do know is that he stirs this crazy feeling inside me. And that I have to help him.

The metal handles of the miniature kitchen gleam in the incoming light, just like the sink, next to which I spot an overturned cup on a dish towel. Beside it, a water canister—this is the first thing I check. It looks new, and the spout seems to have been recently replaced. I inspect the fridge, but it's spotless too. No old food, no potential hazards like mold or bacteria. There are no pipes here that could leach heavy metals and endanger Ashton's health either, so I move on to the tiny bathroom, which consists only of a sink, a toilet, and a showerhead. I open the cabinet above the washbasin.

One by one, I go through everything I find in the shelves—tubes, jars, and utensils. Toothpaste, mouthwash, skin cream, mild painkillers, band-aids.

Nothing is expired, nothing could explain his symptoms.

It goes on like this until I've searched the entire trailer. Just to be sure, I take samples of every possible material, but my hope for any useful result is rapidly approaching zero. At last, feeling helpless, I start pulling open the drawers of his desk one by one.

Batteries, pens, cables. A notepad, paper, a metal tin.

I push the notepad aside, pick up the metal tin, and flip open the latch. My eyes fall on the contents.

That's my earring!

The second daisy I've been missing for years.

Confused, I sink down onto the bed right next to the desk and let my fingers glide over the metal petals. "How did you get here?"

Has it been with Ashton all these years?

What does that mean?

My hand moves instinctively to the back of my neck. A split second later, I remember that I took the necklace off yesterday—because I thought I wouldn't need it. Now, without it, I feel vulnerable all over again.

I turn the earring in my hands.

How did Ashton get his hands on it? Did he steal it? Did he somehow find out how important my earrings were to me, even though they were always hidden beneath my hair?

Even though this daisy is really nothing more than shaped and painted metal, the thought of it still hurts deep inside me.

"That was back then," I remind myself. "And back then, everything was different." Ashton was different, just like I was. If I hadn't constantly tried to get back at him, he wouldn't have stolen my earring.

With a deep breath, I close the metal tin and put it back where I found it. That past doesn't matter anymore. Only the present counts—and Ashton's health. So I push myself up from the sleeping spot and take one last look around.

There's nothing here. No clues. No leads. That just

leaves the wooden shed next to the trailer. If I don't find anything there either, I'll need a new plan. A better one—whatever that might look like. Maybe I should investigate the substances he comes into contact with during his odd jobs. Even if Ashton wears protective gear, something could still be endangering his health—though it's highly unlikely.

"Let's go." I slap my thighs with determination and step out of the trailer.

The shed is unlocked. As soon as I slip through the door, the resinous scent of wood hits my nose. In the dim light, I fumble for a switch and find two, pressing them both at once.

Neon lights flicker on, illuminating the scene for a split second. I spot pieces of wood resting on some kind of framework.

Another flash of light reveals blueprints pinned to the walls.

With a hum, the lights flicker on for good, and in that moment, I understand what Ashton uses the shed for.

He's building a boat here.

When things got worse at home, all I wanted was to disappear. Sail out to sea and never come back. See the world. Be free.

Ashton told me that just a few days ago on the hospital roof.

"Sail out and never come back..." I whisper, and even though I wish I didn't believe it, I feel deep down that it's true.

It wasn't just a simple dream—it was so much more than that. It was everything he had.

My God, what have I done?

I freeze. I can't breathe.

I gasp for air, the shed with the half-finished boat blurring before my eyes. My surroundings grow hazy, while inside me, everything becomes clearer than ever.

The acrid smell of gasoline, which I just poured over the walls and floor, burns in my nose. Determined, I reach into the back pocket of my jeans.

I fumble for the lighter and pull it out. The gasoline fumes are dizzying, but I can't forget why I came here.

This will be the end.

"Take that, asshole Ashton West," I growl with conviction, even though I'm completely alone here, then I flick the lighter to life.

More than once over the past few days, I nearly called off this carefully planned revenge. And every single time, Ashton himself gave me the perfect reason to stick with the plan.

He spends most of his free time in this shed, as I now know thanks to my surveillance. Among garden tools and a dilapidated boat, he plots how to make my life hell next. It has to be that way—this is the place he enters with a grim expression and leaves with a smile, right before he calls me a useless failure, a fat cow, or a coward the next chance he gets. Today, I'm going to take this place away from him.

This will be the end—because it simply has to be.

I stare into the flame. Gather my courage.

Is this really the right thing to do?

Can I actually go through with it?

Isn't there a better way?

Uncertain, I shift my weight from one foot to the other. The fire dances before my eyes, and the metal wheel of the lighter grows hot.

Ashton will never stop putting spiders in my locker, stealing my pants during gym class, and shoving me against the wall. Never. I have to fight back.

If I don't, I'll lose everything that matters to me. Mom and Dad already lost faith in me, just like the teachers did. Only if I stop Ashton now can I get my old life back.

Everyone will think he started the fire. Hopefully, that'll be enough to finally get him expelled from Halifax High.

Then I'll retake the exams, earn extra credit. I'll turn things around and pass this class. But it'll only work if I start catching up right now.

This is the end—because I can't let that asshole steal my dreams.

Still, I just stand there, frozen, staring into the flame that's supposed to save my life, while the lighter's head grows hotter and threatens to burn my thumb. And I can feel all too clearly that I might not be able to go through with this.

"Fuck," I hiss as the tension of the past few hours drains from my body, my muscles growing heavy.

So incredibly heavy.

Without my doing, my arms drop to my sides, and the lighter slips from my hand.

I hate myself. For not being able to do it.

And I hate Ashton. For being perfectly capable of doing things like that.

A split second later, a flame flares up. It races along the trail of gasoline toward the shelf at the back wall, climbing up the wooden posts.

With eyes wide open, I watch the spectacle. An invisible wall of heat forces me to stumble backward, and I slam into the doorframe.

I scream uncontrollably, but all I hear is the explosion as the canisters on the shelf blow up at the same time. Pressing my hands over my ears, I hold my breath. A wall of fire shoots up before my eyes, the shelves come crashing down. The sea of flames rolls along the ceiling toward me. My lungs feel like they're being pierced by a thousand needles.

I have to get out of here. Now.

Frantically, I rip my hands from my ears and stumble outside.

Then I start running. As fast as I can.

Oh God.

Everything around me spins as I sink to the wooden floor strewn with sawdust. Tears stream down my cheeks, my muscles feel heavy.

Because right now, I'm realizing something I didn't understand back then.

That was Ashton's boat in the shed I set on fire!

I didn't just destroy the place I believed was the source of all the pain I had to endure. I set his greatest dream—the only hope he had to cling to at the time—ablaze.

That one dream that, clearly, still hasn't let him go to this day.

Once again, boundaries within me shift—boundaries I thought were unshakable.

Ashton wasn't the asshole between the two of us.

I was!

Chapter Thirty-Nine

ASHTON

June walks into my hospital room with slumped shoulders. She tries to lift the corners of her mouth, but she can't manage a smile.

I was planning to confront her about the game as soon as we saw each other again. And I still will. But right now, the sight of her hits me straight in the heart.

Something has happened.

Something bad.

Without thinking, I make room so June can sit next to me. "What's going on?"

Her eyelids flutter as she sinks onto my bed. "I have to tell you something."

Oh man, this doesn't sound good at all. "You've got a diagnosis," I guess. A devastating one. One that's going to turn my life upside down.

She avoids looking at me. "No," she replies with a pained expression.

"You'll figure out the cause of my illness eventually." I have no idea why I say that. I should really be confronting her with what I found out from that Jaxon guy. "We should…"

I fall silent when I see her jaw tighten. Her fingers dig into the bedsheet. What's tormenting her? The fact that she can't help me—or rather, that she might lose her dream job because of it?

"Spit it out, June. What's going on?" I demand, feeling a wall rise inside me at the same time. What my mind has pieced together over the past few hours isn't nonsense. It could have been true from the very beginning.

She twists her mouth into something that's probably meant to be a smile. "I was at your place today."

Instinctively, I put some distance between us. She was at my trailer? What was she doing there? Going through my stuff? Why?

"I wanted to ask for your permission, but you weren't reachable and I only had that one free morning," she quickly adds. "Leaving you a message would've been pointless."

Did she? Maybe. I haven't looked at my phone all day.

She clears her throat. "After all the theories turned out to be wrong, I wanted to explore other possibilities. Environmental toxins can cause a range of symp…"

"Okay," I say quickly, finally noticing how guilty she feels.

She doesn't look relieved. On the contrary, she shifts nervously back and forth on the bed.

"Did you find something?" Her rapid blinking makes me suspicious. Is she struggling with herself? Why? "Is it something bad?"

Shit, I feel sick. And her shrug doesn't help.

"I was in the shed and… well, there was…" she whispers.

She was in my workshop too?

"...the boat," I finish her sentence. "You found my boat."

She lowers her eyelids, her lips trembling as she nods.

Suddenly it hits me what she might be thinking. She saw the half-finished boat and put two and two together. She knows I still want to leave. And that I won't be coming back.

Back here, where she is.

"Listen..." I begin, but don't go on, because I don't know what to say. Yes, this boat means everything to me, just like the dream that comes with it.

But by now, she means something to me too. Something I can't put into words but feel all the more intensely. Something that quietly gnaws at my heart when I imagine she's only making such an effort because of the residency position.

I take a deep breath to tell her exactly that, but she raises her hand to stop me.

"Please, Ashton, let me fini..." Her voice breaks. She shoots up from the bed and walks to the window with clenched fists. "I have to..."

"What?" Alarmed, I sit up. What the hell is she trying to tell me?

With her upper body trembling, she leans on the windowsill. "Oh God..." I hear her whisper in despair.

I leave the bed and step up behind her. So close that my chest touches her back. So close that I could pull her into my arms if I wanted to.

"I'm sorry," I whisper in her ear, because no matter what her reasons were for not telling me about the game, I didn't want to accuse her of anything before hearing her side. Back at Halifax High, we never spoke openly with each other. That was our problem. I don't want to fall into that same vicious cycle again, so now I'm taking the first step. "I should've told you about the boat and what I was planning to do with it."

Sniffling, she shakes her head. Her ponytail brushes against my neck. She doesn't respond, so I say what I should've said long ago.

"You probably remember how badly I wanted to get away from home, right?" I feel the urge to pull her into my arms, but I hold back. The moment feels too fragile. "The boat I was building back then was destroyed in a fire," I add, and immediately the same emotions from back then flood over me.

Anger. Frustration. Hopelessness.

I don't want to feel any of this, and I know I wouldn't have to if I just stayed silent. But I have to tell June. It's the only way she'll understand what this new boat means to me.

"Father blamed me for the fire." I draw in a sharp breath as the memory of his furious face flashes through my mind. That deep crease between his brows, his eyes narrowed to slits. The tiny droplets of spit that landed on my face as he screamed at me with all his might.

The burning sensation his first slap left on my cheek.

The uncontrolled tone in which he told me that those who won't listen will have to feel. The metallic click of the lighter's flint wheel.

The flame that made me recoil.

The smell of my burned skin.

Now it's not just June who's trembling—I am too. "He lost it, completely lost his mind."

June lets out a sob. "That was the night he hit you that one time," she says, her voice choked with tears. "The night I never saw you again."

The way she feels this with me makes warmth spread through me, despite the awful memory.

"When I left Halifax, I knew only three things: that the shit was finally over. That Father was dead to me. And that one day I'd have my boat, the one I'd sail out into the world with." To defy Father. To show him he didn't break me. That he has no power over me or my life.

June weeps against my chest, shedding all the tears I haven't carried inside me for a long time.

"I'm sorry I didn't tell you much sooner," I repeat the words I said earlier and hold her gently.

"No." She sniffles. "I'm sorry, Ashton. So incredibly sorry."

She doesn't have to be. It's not her fault. "Shhh," I murmur tenderly, because she won't stop crying so bitterly. I slide my index finger under her chin to lift it. I look into her tear-streaked face, her swollen eyes, and red nose. "There's nothing you need to apologize for," I say, brushing her damp cheeks gently.

She looks at me, swallowing hard. She opens her mouth, inhales sharply, then closes it again.

"But maybe there's something else you want to tell me?" I ask, because there's something beyond this past that matters so much more. This would be the right moment to tell me about thc game.

She looks at me, and in her eyes, I see pain. "I have to... Oh God, I can't do this," she gasps, breaks free from my arms, and runs out of the room.

Frozen, I remain standing by the window. Why didn't she take the chance I just gave her? And what is that supposed to mean— I can't do this?

Chapter Forty

JUNE

I slam Ashton's bedroom door behind me as if a monster were chasing me—one that absolutely must not catch me.

Which is completely insane. Because the damn monster is me!

That truth weighs heavily on my chest, in my stomach, on my shoulders.

When I entered that room earlier, I intended to confess that I had set his boat on fire and to tell him how deeply sorry I am.

But what Ashton just told me knocked the ground right out from under my feet.

It's my fault his father got violent.

It. Is. My. Fault.

The hospital corridor spins around me, nausea rises in my throat. I stumble, bump into the wall, and swallow hard against the acid creeping up my esophagus.

I have to go back. Tell Ashton. Right now.

"Number Two, there you are." The woman's voice reaches my ear, distorted. "To my office."

With effort, I lift my eyelids and recognize Dr. Young, who signals for me to follow her. I stumble after her, trying to clear my head, but the chaos inside me is overwhelming.

Nothing is as it should be. Everything I ever thought I knew no longer applies.

I don't know how I manage to follow the boss into her office and sit down in the seat she indicates. I have no idea where I find the strength to lift my head and listen to her either.

"We need to talk," she says, folding her hands into a triangle. "You've been treating Mr. West for two weeks now and…"

"He doesn't have lupus," I interrupt her far too impulsively. What's wrong with me? As a doctor, I should be in control at all times.

"Do you think I don't know that?" she says, adjusting a chair. "Honestly, I didn't expect that test result."

Of course not. She had already written me off in her mind. I bite my tongue and meet her gaze.

"That's exactly the problem," she says, sinking into her chair.

Why is that supposed to be a problem? Did she wish he had lupus or something? Is anyone even thinking about Ashton here? "Well, I'm sorry this isn't going the way you want it to."

"Slow down, Barbie." She raises her hand with a warning look. "I'm afraid you don't understand the gravity of your problem."

"Of course I do," I reply, far too emotionally. "This is about a human life." Nothing could be more at stake. Why does she think I don't know that?

She gives a barely noticeable shake of her head. "No, this is about more than just a human life."

Sure, it's also about my dream job, but on the one hand, those things are connected, and on the other, that's no longer the top priority. Especially not now, now that I've realized I already ruined Ashton's life once before.

"This is about the life of Ashton West," she continues, leaning her arms on the conference table.

I frown, completely lost. "Thanks, I know my patient's name," I snap, unable to get a handle on the storm of emotions inside me.

She studies me for a moment. There's something probing in her expression. "Good, then it seems you're well informed."

Something's off here. Is this conversation a test to see if she can drive me so crazy I'll quit on my own? Is this one of her stupid jokes? Does she think this is funny somehow?

I lean forward. "What about Ashton?"

Is that pity I see flickering across her face now? "Oh dear, you really don't know."

"What?"

"He's Paul West's son." She raises her eyebrows expectantly.

What is she trying to tell me? "And Paul West is…?" By now, I'm sitting on the edge of my chair.

"Come on, Dr. Taylor. Did you do no preparation at all for this job?" She throws her hands into the air.

I did. I devoured every bit of specialist literature, not just on medical topics, but also on ethical and social issues. I dreamed of differential diagnoses, rattled off symptoms faster than most people can speak, completed internships. What more was I supposed to do?

She fixes me with such intensity that I instinctively hold my breath. "Paul West is the CEO of Halifax Harbor Hospital."

Suddenly, my world stops spinning.

"You can probably imagine what that means for your aimless—and unfortunately completely unsuccessful—probing into his son's symptoms."

I can barely hear the boss's voice.

A cold shiver runs down my spine. Ashton's father decides everything that happens in this hospital? Does Ashton know about this?

No. He cut ties with his father years ago. Besides, Ashton would never agree to be treated in a hospital run by that man.

Dr. Young clears her throat repeatedly until she has my attention. "I wanted to give you the chance to shine. That's the only reason you got the case. But it's been two weeks now, and you still haven't come up with a proper diagnosis. You're completely in the dark."

Oh yes, I am. Absolutely. I have no idea who I am, what I'm even doing here, or where the damn light switch is.

"Listen." Dr. Young sounds softer than usual, almost yielding.

Am I fired?

Yes, I'm fired.

Oh no. No, no, no, this can't be happening.

"I can't keep Mr. West in the dark any longer, do you understand? I won't be able to protect you much longer," the chief says urgently.

I lift my eyelids. Why protect me?

"Don't look at me like that. Who do you think I am? The evil boss who enjoys tormenting everyone?"

Admittedly, that's exactly who I think she is. Most of the time, anyway.

Her expression takes on something maternal, something I've never seen in her before. Still, I immediately sense that this might be her true face. "Solve the case by tomorrow, or there's nothing more I can do for you."

Because Ashton's father will personally throw me out. Which he would do anyway if he knew I set his shed on fire —which is a criminal offense.

He wouldn't just fire me; he'd have me thrown in jail. My parents wouldn't understand the world anymore. Everything I've fought to reclaim would slip through my fingers. Ashton might…

Damn.

Damn. Damn. Damn.

"And if I may give you a piece of advice." She gives me an easy smile. "Don't let yourself get distracted. Anything that doesn't lead to an accurate diagnosis has no place in your head right now."

I suppose I should nod, so I lift and lower my head, which feels heavier each time. "I understand," I reply, even though I have no idea how I'm supposed to get this emotional chaos under control.

Chapter Forty-One

ASHTON

I have no idea what to do. When I gave June the chance to tell me about the game earlier, she stormed out of the room. I really want to understand her. I do. But it's hard.

The day June's colleague warned me about yesterday might be fast approaching—the day her shot at the job she wants so badly will die because she still doesn't have a diagnosis.

Of course it's weighing on her. It's been her dream for as long as she can remember. Still… something doesn't feel right. Why does she still want to keep it a secret from me? What does she gain from that?

The ringing phone pulls me out of my thoughts.

It's Jeremy. I stare at his name on the display. Two days ago, I almost reached out to him. To give him the chance to tell me his side of the story.

Something that clearly didn't work with June. And that just feels like crap. Can I do better with him?

I bite my lip and answer the call.

"Ashton?"

"Hey," I say, instantly feeling awkward. I've pushed him away for so long. It's the only role I know.

"I didn't think you'd pick up." I hear a jumble of voices in the background. "I'm at court right now and soon my…"

Of course. He didn't actually want to talk to me—just play the concerned brother. And like an idiot, I fell for it.

"Can we talk another time?" he asks. "I could come visit next week."

Like hell we can.

"No need. I'm getting discharged from the hospital today," I lie, just to get rid of him. "So you don't need to come anymore."

"Oh," he says, and I can't tell if he's surprised or relieved. "Yeah, um, good, that's great. Really, Ashton, I'm glad. So it really was your appendix?"

Yeah. Exactly. The appendix. That's why I've been in the hospital for over two weeks. Totally normal for something like that. "Mhm," I grunt, because anything else wouldn't be worth it.

"Too bad—I was hoping to see that hot doctor again when I visited," Jeremy says with a joking laugh, and I already regret picking up the call for the second time.

"Why don't you call her? Her number is 666—go to hell," I snap back hoarsely.

He stays silent for a while, the voices behind him falling quiet. "Why are you like this, Ashton?" He actually sounds like he has no idea. Even though he can't see it, I shake my head. He doesn't get it at all. "Why do you hate me so deeply?" he adds.

It's not the first time he's asked that. Until now, I've never answered, convinced it wouldn't make a difference. "You weren't there for me when I needed you the most," I hear myself say accusingly, because it finally needs to be said.

"When was that?" he asks, confused. "Honestly, Ashton, I don't know what you mean." He's not lying—on the contrary, there's a pleading note in his voice.

"You really don't?" Is that even possible?

"Please, explain it to me. When wasn't I there for you?" he presses, and in that moment, I start to realize that what happened back then might look very different from his perspective.

How could he have known how much I needed him? He was thousands of miles away, and all he had from me were a few messages asking if he had time to talk.

Despite how distant he acted, I should have told Jeremy what was going on at home. I should have confided in him instead of pretending to be the cool one with him too.

I guess it's time to change that.

"Your first year at Stanford," I answer. "Back when you didn't give a damn about Mom's death. Just like you didn't care about anything else."

Fabric rustles, followed by a dull thud. Did he just sit down and set his papers aside? "You wrote to me often, but… I couldn't," he says apologetically. "Mom's death… the memories… I didn't want to think about any of it. I had to push it away, or I wouldn't have survived a single day at Stanford."

"So you had a hard time after Mom died too," I blurt out. I never once wondered back then how Jeremy was doing or what was behind his behavior. Just like with June. I only saw the world through my own eyes—blind to everything else.

"What was going on back then?" Jeremy's tone carries concern. As if he senses that things weren't easy for me at home. And when I tell him what really happened, he falls silent. "Oh man, Ashton. I'm so sorry," he says hoarsely. "If I'd known what..."

"I should've told you much sooner," I cut him off, because in a way, it was just as much my fault as his.

"Listen, I'll move some things around. I'll be with you by the day after tomorrow at the latest, and we'll talk about everything," he offers.

"Okay." I notice a smile creeping onto my face. "Please don't freak out, but I lied to you earlier. I'm still at Halifax Harbor Hospital."

Jeremy laughs. "Well then, I might even get a chance to see that hot doctor again."

Smiling, I shake my head. "You will," I say, and end the call. But that won't do you any good, I add silently, because suddenly everything is clearer than ever before.

What's happening between June and me right now—I don't want that. We need to talk, even if it's hard.

Yes, she should've told me about the game. Still—or maybe because of that—I should go find her and do what I should've done back then: show her openly what's been going on inside me since I found out. Let her see that I'm hurt. Tell her that we're in danger of falling into that same crazy downward spiral again if we don't.

Back then, neither of us was wise enough to back down. Today, I'm the one who's going to take that step. For what has developed between us over the past few days. The thing that, for the first time in years, has given me a sense of hope.

Because this is what's worth fighting for.

I sit up in bed. I still feel weak, and my circulation protests as I set my feet on the floor. Still, I get up and take a few steps toward the door. As I reach for the handle, I lose control of my body for a moment and slam hard into the wall.

I blink and realize I've crashed into June's lab coat, which is hanging on the wall. The other day, when we were so close, she took it off and forgot to take it with her—probably thanks to her obsession with diagnosing my illness.

I wedge my hands between the coat and my body to push myself away.

Something hard digs into my palm. A dull pain spreads instantly.

"Fuck," I mutter.

I slump against the wall again to find the culprit. There's something in the coat pocket. I reach in and feel a metallic object with a rounded edge. Puzzled, I pull out the thing, which appears to be attached to a chain.

A split second later, I'm staring at a daisy pendant.

Stunned. Disbelieving. Shocked.

"This can't be happening…"

My jeans chafe against my burns despite the bandages. It stings with every step, but that doesn't stop me. Yesterday, Father forced me to stay in my room, but now, at dawn, I've snuck out.

I have to get to the shed. I need to see how much of my boat survived. Find out if I can still save it, and how long it will take.

With clenched teeth, I weave my way through the trees. The smell of charred wood hits my nose.

I take the shortcut through the bushes. The branches crack loudly as I push them aside and step through.

My eyes land on what's left of the shed.

A pile of ash. Nothing else.

No!

Panicked, I run toward the heap of ash. I no longer feel my wounds as my gaze sweeps over the black-gray dust that covers the entire ground here.

The dust that, just yesterday, had been my nearly finished boat.

Just a few more weeks, and it would've been ready. I could've packed my shit and finally gotten the hell out of here.

Screaming in rage, I drop to my knees. In disbelief, I plunge my hands into the ashes and let them sift through my fingers. My skin turns black instantly.

A dull sound reaches my ears. Something shiny catches the light in the darkness around me. I reach for it.

An earring.

Shaped like a daisy.

How did that get here?

And who does it belong to?

I close my fist around the thing and squeeze so hard the metal digs painfully into my palm.

Because at least one answer to my questions is obvious.

The firestarter left it behind here.

No, the firestarter is a woman—this was done by her.

"I'll find you and make you pay," I hisd angrily. She would pay for what she did to me. "Even if it's the last thing I do."

"It was June," I hear myself whisper tonelessly in the here and now, unable to grasp the meaning of my own words.

Because I left Halifax a few days after the incident, I couldn't search for the culprit anymore. Still, I kept the earring—as a reminder.

Now the time has come—the firestarter has been unmasked.

I shake my head, which feels heavier with each passing second. My heart clenches painfully. And no matter how much I wish this were just a terrible nightmare, it is, and remains, real.

It was June.

She was the one who set my life ablaze back then.

Chapter Forty-Two

JUNE

"Anything that doesn't lead to a correct diagnosis has no place in your head right now." The boss's words echo in my mind as I close the door to her office behind me.

My head feels heavy. Too heavy to form a coherent thought.

Ashton West is Paul West's son.

The hallway, along with my colleagues, blurs before my eyes. I sway.

Someone grabs my upper arms.

"Are you okay?" asks a distorted voice.

I manage to nod. Nothing more.

Paul West is the CEO of Halifax Harbor Hospital.

That means I didn't just destroy Ashton's life with the fire—I ruined my own as well.

If Paul West finds out what I did, I'll never set foot in Halifax Harbor Hospital again. Maybe not in any hospital across Canada, because in his position, Ashton's father probably has connections everywhere. He could make me disappear without a trace.

Forever.

My phone vibrates. Mechanically, I pull it out of my pocket. It shows a new message from Mom—this time without any text.

It's a picture. Of a newspaper ad scheduled for the day of the celebration in the Chronicle Herald, congratulating me on my new job.

Oh God. That's just what I needed.

I lean back against the wall, put the phone away, and rub my temples.

Come on, June. Focus. What's the right thing to do now?

A throbbing pain pulses through my head, and I squeeze my eyes shut.

Diagnosing Ashton's illness is the right thing to do.

And what about the boat?

A wave of intense nausea washes over me.

What if I confess everything to Ashton? Could he forgive me for this unbelievably horrific act? Or would he throw the truth in his father's face—the truth that will destroy me—just to finally prove he had nothing to do with the fire?

He would have every right to do so, because for him, this means something far more significant than it does for me.

I have to do it. I owe him that.

Taking a deep breath, I push away from the wall and head for Ashton's room. My legs feel weak, as if they can barely carry me. I search feverishly for the right words but find none—because there's no excuse for what I've done, and I know it.

When I enter, my heart pounding, he's standing with his back to me at the window.

"Hey," I say, relieved to see he's well enough to be up. "I need to tell you something."

He slowly shakes his head. "I don't think so."

He's hurt, and that's more than understandable. "I'm sorry I ran off earlier." I take a few unsteady steps toward him, but something in his posture makes me keep my distance.

Tense shoulders, clenched fists.

No, more than that: clenched fists that are trembling.

Oh God, it hit him even harder than I thought. How am I supposed to start this conversation if he's already mad at me? Hesitantly, I shift my weight from one foot to the other. "I…"

Suddenly, he turns around and fixes me with an accusatory stare. His cheeks are flushed. "What, June?"

"I… well… I." Damn it, just tell him, June!

He looks at me, shaking his head, while my damn lips refuse to cooperate. A tired snort escapes his mouth. Then he lifts his right hand, opens his fist, and reveals my necklace with the daisy pendant.

"You know what's funny?" he says dryly, pointing at the delicate flower with his index finger. "I've got one of these too."

Right. The earring I found in Ashton's trailer. I thought he'd stolen it, but now I can't believe that anymore. Not when he's looking at me with that mix of disappointment and surprise.

But if he didn't steal it, then how…?

"Want to know where it came from?" He walks toward me, his eyes narrowing to slits.

His expression terrifies me. My breathing grows shallow. I want to say something, but once again, no words come out. I can only stare at him, instinctively shaking my head. What a pathetic coward I am.

"Oh?" He twists the necklace in his hand. "Why not?" His lower lip trembles, sweat covering his face. "Is it because you already know?"

Every detail about him—the way he stares me down, the disgust in his voice, the threatening posture—brings tears to my eyes.

"You lost it when you set my boat on fire," he says, his voice so cold it makes me shiver.

Oh God.

I gasp for air, but it's not enough. "I'm so sorry. I was young and stupid and didn't understand anything," I try to explain, stammering. "And I was full of self-doubt and panic. The situation with my mom, how it all started—you misunderstood it. I didn't send her away because I didn't love her, but…"

"You always twist everything to suit yourself, don't you?" he snaps venomously.

I press my lips together to keep them from trembling. "If I'd known back then what was going on with you…" I try again. "If I'd had any idea what I was doing to you with that fire…" My God, I never would've gone that far. Never!

"Forget it, June." That hatred in his expression. That unrelenting resentment. "I've known for a long time what you're really after. What the only thing is that actually matters to you."

What is he talking about? "That was thirteen years ago," I say pleadingly. "We wanted a fresh start. You wanted a fresh start. I only realized during our conversation earlier how…"

"Get out, June. I don't want to see you here anymore." He snorts with effort.

No! Please don't.

"I'm not leaving. Not until you're better," I reply firmly, because it's the least I can do for him. I won't abandon him again. Not. Again. "Let me help you."

"Help, my ass." Pure disappointment clouds his gaze. "You never wanted that."

How can he think that? Hasn't he felt over the past few weeks how much he's come to mean to me?

"Your damn game for the specialist position ends here. You've lost." His gaze cuts through me, ice-cold.

I have no idea how he found out about that, but it doesn't matter. "There hasn't been a game for me. Not for a long time."

His expression suddenly turns sad. So unbearably sad. "Why should I believe you?"

Tears stream relentlessly down my cheeks as I step toward him. "Because of this." I touch his heart with my index finger, then my own.

He silently shakes his head. "Cards on the table, June. What else did you do?"

Chapter Forty-Three

ASHTON

June looks at me with a mix of panic and despair. Tears shimmer in her eyes, her cheeks flushing red. "I'm sorry. If I could undo it, I would. Right now."

No. She wouldn't. What happened back then is one thing. But unlike me, she clearly never stopped hurting me. Who even knows what part of everything that's happened in the past few weeks was fake?

"What else did you do?" I repeat my earlier question. "Did you treat me wrong on purpose?"

She clearly stops breathing at my words. Her eyes fly open in disbelief.

How perfectly she plays the innocent. That shouldn't surprise me—she's always been excellent at it.

"What?" Her deep blue doll eyes wide open, she looks at me. "The school mascot?"

I shove the ungrateful fat cow back into the alcove. "Don't lie to me, bitch."

She raises her hands. "I really don't know what you're talking about."

Rage boils up inside me. Sure, there's no proof she spread that shit about me. And she's not the first I've confronted over it. But I'm not giving up that easily. That spoiled brat with her stupid perfect family is going to find out who I am. "At least admit it, you fucking coward."

"It wasn't me," she says again, without even blinking.

Fuck, it really wasn't her—and that only makes me even angrier than I already am.

"You know what you are? A useless piece of shit who'll never amount to anything in life." That's the truth, plain and simple.

"But..."

"Did I give you permission to speak?" I snap at her, showing her my clenched fist.

She swallows hard, pretending to be afraid of me. But at least she keeps her damn mouth shut.

"There we go, that's better," I say dryly and give her a shove. "Don't you dare do that again," I warn her, then turn to leave.

"It wasn't me," she calls after me, pleading.

In response, I flip her off.

Back then, I believed her, even though she lied to my face without batting an eye.

And she's doing it again now.

She lies every time she opens her mouth, only ever looking out for herself.

"You can drop the act—I've seen right through you." I square up to her. "Now tell me, did you enjoy playing with me?" With my feelings and my fucked-up life. Just so she could get her damn job!

She presses her index finger against her chest. "I played you?" Her voice cracks.

Unbelievable. I can't think of anything else to say. How devious can a person possibly be?

"How can you even think something like that?" she continues bitterly.

I cross my arms, but immediately uncross them again because too much heat is building up in my chest.

"I would never risk a patient's health." She looks at me intently. "Least of all yours."

"And there's the next lie," I throw at the woman, whose face suddenly looks strangely contorted. I touch my forehead, feeling clammy sweat and searing heat at the same time.

Damn it. The fever.

"That's what you think of me? That I don't care about my patients?" she replies, desperate.

I can't suppress a snort. She doesn't give a damn how I'm doing. Why else would she pretend not to notice my condition?

Congratulations, June Taylor. Must feel good to finally let the mask drop.

"If you really believe I'm such a terrible doctor, then do it. One call to your father is all it takes." Her tone grows more agonized, her gestures more desperate.

A call to my father?

What does she mean?

"Tell him what I did. Clear your conscience." Her breathing is labored. "Destroy everything I've fought for my entire life." Her voice breaks; her lips tremble as she fixes her gaze on me.

My eyelids feel heavy, just like my arms. My legs are growing weaker, the hospital room blurs. Still, I gather the last bit of strength and lock eyes with her. "What are you tal—?" I manage to say, before everything begins to spin.

"Ashton?" Arms catch me. "Damn it, what's going on?"

Someone maneuvers me onto a bed, which only worsens the pain in my abdomen. I groan in agony. June's feigned concern flickers in her blue eyes above me every time I manage to open mine.

She starts fumbling with my shirt.

"Get away." I meant to shout the words, but they come out as a weak whisper. "Don't touch me," I add, louder this time.

But she doesn't care. I feel her lift my shirt. Her fingers touch my stomach, which continues to cramp more and more.

"Damn," I hear June cry out in panic a few seconds later.

Chapter Forty-Four

JUNE

I press my thumb down on the emergency button so hard it hurts. Then I turn back to Ashton, who's lying in bed in front of me with a pained expression. His face is nearly the same color as the white pillow beneath him.

Once again, I focus on the greenish-brown discoloration around his belly button that I just noticed.

This can't be happening. Another new symptom. And one he hasn't had before.

If that's the Cullen sign…

Oh God.

"Where does it hurt?" I ask him, but all I get in response is a gruff grunt, followed by a piercing scream. At least his hand points to his stomach.

Okay, the stomach. As always. He has a fever too—that's more than obvious. He's also shaking with chills.

"Can you breathe?" With trembling fingers, I reach for my stethoscope.

At that moment, the door bursts open, two nurses and

—of all people—Dr. Young herself storm into the room. She's going to think I've lost control of the situation.

And damn it, she's right. The situation is slipping through my fingers.

Ashton is slipping through my fingers!

Sometimes a single moment can change everything.

Those were his words, the ones that turned the world I knew upside down just a few days ago. And deep inside, I know this is another one of those moments.

Because everything I ever cared about is falling apart right now.

"Suspected acute pancreatitis," I inform my boss. Even if I tried to control the turmoil inside me, I wouldn't succeed. Why is Ashton's pancreas suddenly inflamed? "Treatment with 50 micrograms of fentanyl IV. Fluid management to balance electrolytes."

"Step aside, Dr. Taylor." Dr. Young steps up beside me and gives me a look that sends a chill down my spine.

I immediately raise my hands and step back. Now, all I can do is watch as she bends over Ashton, palpates his abdomen while he groans in pain, and listens to his lungs. One of the nurses calls out his vital signs, the other prepares the fentanyl drip I ordered. Dr. Young gives a confirming nod, and the nurse connects the drip.

Powerless, I stand at the edge of the scene, feeling more useless than ever before. Instead of helping Ashton, I shouted at him in my desperation. Instead of recognizing what was wrong with him, I only saw my own despair.

Now he lies in bed, tormented by pain.

It doesn't matter what just happened. It doesn't matter how much he hates me or how little he trusts me. I'm his doctor—it's my job to treat him.

Still, he has yet another new symptom, making every

one of my previous theories seem even more unlikely than they already were.

My thoughts are spinning. My heart pounds against my chest. Beads of sweat cover my forehead. My hands begin to tremble uncontrollably.

"What can I do?" I ask anyway, turning to my boss, because just standing around doing nothing isn't an option.

I have to help.

I want to help!

Dr. Young pulls the earpieces of her stethoscope from her ears and turns toward me. Suddenly, her eyes widen, though she isn't looking at me. There's something behind me she wasn't expecting.

Or someone.

"Mr. West," she says, forcing a smile onto her face. "This is a bad time."

Mr. West? Ashton's father?

I freeze, not daring to turn around. For just a moment, I catch a glimpse of Ashton, his brows furrowed.

"What are you doing here?" he asks his father, followed by a groan filled with pain.

"Who is the attending physician?" a deep male voice growls behind me, so loud it makes my ears ring.

Me.

That's the only right answer.

Ashton's condition is my damn fault.

Dr. Young raises her hands. "We can sort that out later. Right now, what matters is your son…"

Before she can finish her sentence, I turn around. From his dark eyes, Ashton's father glares accusingly at my boss, completely ignoring me.

His black hair trembles slightly, and despite his tanned

complexion, his cheeks look pale. "I want to know what's going on here right now and who screwed up."

Me.

That's what I should say. I should square my shoulders, step forward, and look him in the eyes. But I can't. He's so… terrifying. I feel far too small, too weak, too helpless.

"Well?" His jet-black eyebrows lift.

"Mr. West. Your son may be suffering from pancreatitis. We're currently trying to determine whether a bleed beneath his peritoneum requires surgery," Dr. Young explains with remarkable composure.

She's defending me, even though she doesn't have to, which only makes me feel worse than I already do.

"His health is the most important thing right now. This is not the time for assigning blame," my boss continues, and once again I sense that behind her dark humor and sometimes harsh exterior hides a warm and kind heart.

Still. This is wrong. She shouldn't be standing in front of me, taking the wrath that's meant for me.

"I… well…" There's nothing I want more than to own up to my mistakes, but the words I'm responsible just won't come out. I don't want to be that weak, yet I can't fight it.

Out of nowhere, Mr. West turns his gaze from the chief and fixes it on me. "And who are you?"

Come on, June, say something already!

"June Taylor, your son's attending physician." I wish I sounded more confident. At the same time, I'm just glad I managed to say anything at all.

"Why are you just standing there? My son's life is at stake," he snaps at me, visibly shaken. "Do something!"

I wipe my sweaty hands on my coat. "O-Of course." My mind is blank. I look around, searching. What still needs to be done? Has Ashton already received his medication? And if so, at what dosage? "Your s-s-son has…"

His expression darkens further, a frighteningly deep crease forming on his forehead, the vein in his neck bulging. "Did I give you permission to speak?"

The moment the words leave his mouth, I freeze again. Because suddenly, memories of the degrading things Ashton used to throw at me come flooding back.

They sounded just like his father's. Every time he tore me down, it was his father speaking through him.

"Well, finally," Mr. West grumbles irritably, and not even a split second later, panic floods his face again. "Now help my son already."

All I can manage is a nod. I know I shouldn't let him speak to me like that, but I'm paralyzed.

So that's how he treated Ashton too—maybe even worse. Day after day, he called him an idiot, crushed him, stripped away his self-worth.

Hearing it from Ashton was one thing. But experiencing it firsthand—feeling it in my own body—is something else entirely.

"Good God, are you mentally deficient or what?" Mr. West rants, locking eyes with Dr. Young. "How can some useless runway Barbie be my son's attending physician?" he hisses, outraged.

I should stand up to his judgment of me, confront him, show him what I'm made of. But I'm nothing more than a miserable wreck.

"We'll discuss this calmly later," my boss replies, making a calming gesture with her hand.

She's still defending me. Me—little, foolish June, who can't get anything right.

Guilt and my old familiar self-doubt—the kind I swore

I'd never feel again—flood over me faster than I can hold them back.

"Dr. Taylor, we need you here," I hear my boss say, her voice muffled as though through cotton. Someone grabs my arm, pulls me aside. "We'll talk later, Mr. West."

"Not so fast," he snaps, without taking his eyes off me. "You." He points his index finger at me. "I don't want to see you here again. Get out."

I gasp for air.

"Now!" he adds, so agitated his whole body trembles. "And you can hand in your staff key at administration. We don't need you here."

Bullseye. Straight to where it hurts more than anywhere else. A pain I know all too well shoots through my chest, right to my heart.

I stagger try to breathe but can't get any air.

"Go," a woman's voice whispers warmly to me—maybe my boss.

Someone nudges me, and I stumble toward the exit. When I get there, I cling to the door handle and turn around one last time.

I look at Ashton; our eyes meet.

I never want to see you again, his expression says.

Exhausted, I hold his gaze. *Don't worry, you won't,* I reply silently, fully aware that this is the end of all my dreams.

Chapter Forty-Five

ASHTON

The door clicks shut behind June. I still don't know whether this is really happening or if it is just my fevered imagination tricking me into believing my father is here, tearing down everyone who is trying to help me.

Leaning against the wall, he waits until the doctors—drifting around me like wisps of fog—finish their work.

June's boss leans over me. "A surgeon will be here soon. Then we'll know whether we need to operate." Her gaze shifts to the thin tube through which pure relief is dripping into my body. "How's your stomach?"

"Better." My mouth is dry, and I glance sideways at my father.

Is he really here?

He pushes off from the wall. "Are you finished?" he asks Dr. Young, suddenly looking exhausted.

She nods. "He's stable."

"Can I talk to him?"

She nods again. "Five minutes."

This feels way too real.

Wait a minute. What if this is it?

Then he just fired June. No, he can't do that. He has no authority here. And why would the staff do what he says? If this were real, someone would call security. Instead, in my dream, the doctors and nurses are leaving the hospital room.

My head is pounding, and it's hard to breathe. I close my eyes, wanting to wake up from this hallucination.

"And now to you," I hear Father say in a tone I can't quite place. Is he nervous? "Look at me when I'm talking to you, Ashton."

Oh God, please make this stop.

I blink and see Father's massive figure at the foot of the bed. "Forget it. I'm not talking to you," I say to my fake dad. Maybe that'll make him disappear. Or maybe I just need to wait a little longer for the meds to kick in and end this nightmare. Hopefully.

"If I'd known you were here earlier…" His fingers clutch the bed frame, as if he'd lose his balance otherwise.

"Sorry you're not on my emergency contact list," I reply dryly. My stomach knots up again, but it's not as bad as before. The stuff in the plastic bag above me is pretty good. Way better than anything I've had so far.

"You should have told me." His face contorts into a grimace. Is that supposed to be concern?

I snort with disdain. "I don't have to tell you anything."

Is he walking around the bed now to stand beside me? The image in front of my eyes wavers, but I think he really is. Yes, he's standing here, right next to me. "I would've made sure only the best doctors treated you."

Sure, with his fortune, he could've pulled all the strings. I can do without that. "Save it."

"I won't." Is that a worried crease on his forehead? Is he sweating? "Dr. Young said you might be seriously ill."

Yeah, I am. And that's exactly why he should leave now. Can't he see I need rest?

Wait a second.

Something's not right here.

"What gives you the right to talk to the doctors about my condition?" Has this Dr. Young ever heard of doctor–patient confidentiality?

He tilts his head, his brows drawing together. "Why shouldn't I?"

"Because it's none of your damn business!" Can't he just disappear already?

Suddenly, I feel his hand on my arm, and that's when I know this isn't a hallucination.

He's really here.

Thirteen goddamn years have passed—years in which we didn't see each other for a single second and avoided all contact.

And now he actually dares to touch me?

I pull away from his touch, even though I barely have the strength to do it. "What the hell do you think you're doing…"

A hardness settles over his face. "Don't be so childish, boy. I'm worried about you…"

Now I don't understand anything at all. Who is this man standing by my bed, acting like he suddenly cares about me?

"Just get the hell out." My voice sounds hoarse.

Instead of leaving, he grabs one of the visitor's chairs and sits down. "I won't."

I cross my arms. "I don't care what you want." If he says one more word, I'll explode. "Get lost, asshole."

He can shove that remorseful look wherever he likes. He's just as much of a liar as June.

I meet his fake, concerned gaze with defiance. For a few seconds, he refuses to give up—then finally, he stands and walks out of my life, just as another sharp pain shoots through me.

I double over, press my arms against my stomach, and gasp for air. Gasping, I grope for the cord with the emergency button, but I can't reach it.

Everything in me grows heavy. And heavier still.

So.

Endlessly.

Heavy.

Chapter Forty-Six

JUNE

The salty breeze brushes my face as I approach the Dartmouth Ferry dock. Above me, the sky stretches out in pastel hues, the colors of early morning blending on the horizon.

I hardly register the beauty of the view. Inside, there's only darkness. I spent the entire night wandering through Halifax, restless, searching for a way out. But there isn't one.

It's over.

Ashton hates me. My dream job is gone. Once again, my parents will be so disappointed in me they won't even be able to hide it. But most of all, I'm disappointed in myself.

I head toward the ferry, hearing the gentle lapping of the waves against the sides of the boat, and the creaking of ropes and wheels as the passengers at the front of the line begin to board.

Ashton spent his whole life dreaming of sailing away, and today I'm the one who just wants to run. Because here in Halifax, trapped in the prison of my own thoughts, I can't stand another second.

I step out onto the deck. Around me, there's a bustle of activity. Soft murmurs, laughter, the cries of seagulls overhead. Everything sounds so cheerful that I feel like an outsider.

The ship's engines hum as we pull away from the dock. I lean against the railing, watching the Halifax skyline and the clinic gradually shrink into the distance.

Fragments of memories from the past weeks drift through my mind.

Ashton's smile.

His pain.

The desire to be there for him.

The warmth of his skin.

The taste of his lips.

The hope we shared.

Bittersweet, I relive our time together once more.

I see his pain, and he sees mine.

I open my heart to him, and he opens his to me.

I see who he is, and I show him my true self.

Does he really believe I've been pretending this whole time?

The wind brushes through my hair, a salty taste lingers on my tongue. And as we approach the other side, the outlines of Dartmouth become more distinct. The buildings, the trees, the people on the shore come into clearer view.

Just like my view of what happened yesterday. Ashton was hurt. Deeply. Finding out that I was the one who changed his life forever must have been a shock.

I bite my lower lip until I taste blood. Because I know that the way things turned out is partly my fault too. Once I realized what I had done, I should have told him right away. I shouldn't have been such a coward.

Did I cling to my pain and fear the same way I used to, without realizing that someone else might be drowning too?

Maybe. Because one thing is certain:

If I had trusted my first instinct about Ashton's true character back at Halifax High and looked more closely, I wouldn't have added fuel to his fire. Maybe he would have left me alone eventually. I wouldn't have set that damn shed on fire, and his father wouldn't have beaten him.

All of this became clear to me after Ashton was admitted to Halifax Harbor Hospital. And now I sense that it's happened again. In my panic, I stopped trusting the feelings between Ashton and me. Out of fear that Ashton wouldn't forgive me, I stayed silent.

I was too busy running from my guilt, even though I should have apologized right away.

All of this weighs on me, but what happened yesterday can't be undone—no matter how much I wish it could.

That doesn't mean there's nothing I can do. I lift my chin, take a deep breath. And make a decision.

No one can change the past. But as long as I'm breathing, I can make things right. As long as my heart is beating, I can make better choices. And as long as the hope of what I felt between Ashton and me still flickers inside me, I can find a way to save at least one of us.

And that's him.

The ferry docks, but I won't disembark. While the other passengers leave the ship, I gather my strength. Because what lies ahead of me now is the most important thing I've ever done in my life.

An hour later, I burst into the apartment.

"Hello? Anyone home?" I call into the hallway.

Sonora pokes her curly head out from the living room doorway. Her smile fades when she sees me. "What happened to you?"

I slip off my shoes. "Didn't sleep."

"I can see that." She strolls over to me. "But why?"

A sigh escapes my lips.

"Ashton." Sonora's grin reveals her dimples. She nods toward the kitchen. "Coffee?"

"Definitely." Because even though I can barely keep my eyes open, I still have a lot to do.

"So, what's going on with your patient?" Sonora asks, switching on the coffee machine.

My fingers drum on the gray marbled countertop. "He's worse than ever." Oh God, just saying it makes me feel sick.

With a quick flick of her hand, Sonora brushes her curls out of her face and opens the drawer with the coffee capsules. "What happened?"

I tell her what happened yesterday. Admit that I was fired and include all the medical details she needs to understand the issue. "It's pancreatitis, and it could become acute," I conclude a few minutes later. "I saw Cullen's sign, so maybe. I wasn't sure. But if it was there, then he might need emergency surgery."

"Wait a second." Holding a coffee capsule in one hand, she taps her chin with the other. "Yesterday my colleague was called in for a consult about a case of pancreatitis." She bites her lower lip. "How did it go again?"

I look at her expectantly, my pulse quickening. "What did she find?"

Absentmindedly, she places the capsule into the coffee

machine. "She confirmed the pancreatitis, but said surgery wasn't necessary."

What? I'm instantly wide awake. "That's a mistake!" I reply sharply. "There were Cullen's signs. They were still faint, but they were there."

Sonora grabs my arm. "Not every case of pancreatitis—even when Cullen's sign is present—requires surgery. Many cases can be treated conservatively."

That's true, but the risk is too high in this case. "Ashton's underlying condition still hasn't been diagnosed. It could be affecting the course of the pancreatitis. We can't treat him like just any other pancreatitis patient," I say urgently. "If your colleague didn't take that into account in her assessment and he isn't closely monitored, there's a risk of internal bleeding and necrosis." I swallow against the nausea rising in my throat. "Organ failure is possible, too!"

Ashton could die. Because I didn't save him in time with the right diagnosis of his underlying illness. My God, I should have asked for help days ago. Instead, I tried to solve his illness on my own, just to prove to Dr. Young that I'm a valuable person who can make an important contribution.

What a selfish bitch I was—again!

Panic crawls coldly up my back, grips my neck with a firm hand, and presses heavily on my shoulders.

"Hey." Sonora picks at her fingernails. "Have a little faith. My colleague knows what she's doing."

And if she doesn't? Even if the risk were minimal, I'd still have to act. And this time, not alone. "I need your help," I say. I've spent so long thinking I had to do everything on my own that the words now feel foreign on my tongue.

"What can I do?" she asks, eager.

Tears spring to my eyes immediately, because I didn't expect the feeling that comes with those words.

Relief.

I'm not on my own anymore—I have people around me who will support me.

"Your new boss is supposed to be a real authority in the field." I look at her intently. "Come with me to the hospital and help me convince him to personally give Ashton a full evaluation. And if surgery's needed, then I want your boss to do it—no one else." I hope I'm not asking too much of Sonora. After all, she hasn't been working in the department for very long. Who knows how much she can even…

"Got it," my friend cuts off the spiral of thoughts spinning faster and faster in my head. "Let's go."

"Really?" I can't help but look at her in disbelief.

As if it were nothing special, she shrugs. "Of course, what did you think?"

I pull her into my arms right away. "Thank you, that means so…" I can't go on—my voice fails me. But I'm sure she knows what I meant to say.

Sonora pats my back. "We've got this, it's no big deal."

That's exactly right. *We* have got this. Because while Sonora does what she does best, I'll do what I do best. "You'll operate—if necessary—together with your boss, and I'll work on solving the mystery of his underlying condition." That damned underlying condition that keeps triggering new secondary symptoms, each one more dangerous than the last.

This has to stop before it's too late.

She nods firmly. "Sounds like a plan."

Then we shouldn't waste any more time. Together, we rush out of the apartment, jog all the way to the clinic, and hurry up to the second floor, where the surgical department is located.

Out of breath, Sonora stops in front of a white door.

Dr. Ethan Stone, Head of Surgery, I read on the nameplate.

"Ready?" my friend asks, placing her hand on the handle.

I nod, gasping. "Ready."

She knocks briefly and pushes the door open. Behind the desk, which is cluttered with medical records and other documents, a doctor rises—one who far exceeds the reputation that precedes him.

He radiates even more competence and confidence than anyone claims.

"Dr. Wells?" His brow furrows as he fixes his gaze on Sonora. "What can I do for you?"

I step forward. "We need your help," I say, and it's already the second time in just a few minutes that I've spoken those words.

Hurriedly, I explain who I am and outline the history of Ashton's illness. "I believe his pancreatitis needs to be assessed differently in light of this," I say in conclusion.

He walks over to the window, a thoughtful expression on his face. "What's his ID?"

I exchange a hopeful glance with Sonora. "P010424-060. A colleague from surgery saw him yesterday and…"

"Hold on." He stops me with a gesture. "A surgeon has already assessed the case?"

"She has." I search for the right words, but none come. "But—with all due respect, sir—she may have made a mistake. Possibly." Oh God, I shouldn't be speaking to him like this.

He fixes me with a stern expression, and rightfully so. "What gives you the right to malign my colleague like that?"

Sonora steps beside me and raises her hands in a calming gesture. "Please, Dr. Stone." The way she says his name is strange, almost as if she's exchanging a secret code with him. "Give Dr. Taylor a chance."

He glares at Sonora angrily, then his gaze shifts to me. "If a doctor from my team evaluates a case, that assessment is sound."

No. Everyone makes mistakes. If anyone knows that, it's me. "I saw Cullen's sign, which indicates severe pancreatitis. Combined with his unclear overall health status, I believe this is a highly delicate situation that requires special attention," I reply as respectfully as possible, because one thing is certain: giving up is not an option.

"My colleague apparently assessed the situation as under control, otherwise she would have responded differently." He's clearly trying to stay calm, but his jaw tightens.

"Please take a look at the patient," I ask him again. "This isn't about who's right. It's about a human life." I raise my eyebrows. *Are you really willing to risk that?*, I ask him silently, because saying those words aloud to a senior physician would be an insult. I'm already sticking my neck out far enough as it is.

He looks back and forth between Sonora and me. Out of the corner of my eye, I see my friend nodding vigorously.

"All right. I'll ask the colleague to re-evaluate the situation." With that, he turns away and marches over to the desk.

"No," I say quickly, hurrying after him. "This calls for your expertise. You need to do it yourself."

Damn. Did I just give him an order, as if I were his superior?

I am just about to apologize when he spins around in anger. "I'll still be the one to decide who has to do what."

His nostrils flare, and he gives Sonora a strangely intense look. "This conversation is over."

"I can't allow that, sir. I'm sorry," I reply desperately, my expression pleading. "Not before you've agreed to see the patient."

A moment ago, I already went far out on a limb. Now I've lifted my legs as well and am dangling over the windowsill.

Sonora knows it too—I can feel her hand on my forearm. "Come on, June. Let's go. We'll find another solution," she whispers to me.

I maintain eye contact with Dr. Stone. There has to be something that could convince him. "He could die," I beg. What kind of doctor would he be if that didn't move him to act?

"I have work to do." There is something final in his words. "And now you'd better go. Immediately."

Behind me, Sonora draws in a sharp breath. "We will, thank you, Dr. Stone."

She grips my arm more firmly and pulls me toward the door.

If we leave this room now, everything might turn out fine. Ashton might not need surgery, and he could recover.

But what if the exact opposite is true?

The risk is too high.

There has to be something—damn it—that convinces Dr. Stone. Something more important to him than protecting his employee. Something that makes it impossible for him to refuse me his help.

I rack my brain feverishly as Sonora reaches for the doorknob.

Ohhh.

I've got it!

It's perfect—and it's my only chance.

"No." I clench my fists and turn to Dr. Stone one last time. "I'm sorry, but I have to insist that you come with us." His face flushes red. "Or do you want Paul West to find out that you refused to treat his son?" I ask, fully aware that this is the moment I throw myself headfirst out the window.

And suddenly—out of nowhere—fear flickers in his eyes.

Chapter Forty-Seven

ASHTON

June hasn't shown up again. One encounter with my father was enough to make her run for it. Why would she stay? The job's a lost cause—and that's the only thing she's ever really cared about anyway.

My chest rises and falls heavily beneath the blanket. Everything in me feels dark and hollow. Like the deepest interior deck of a ship no one would willingly enter.

At least Father is keeping his distance.

"It's going to be fine," I suddenly hear a woman's voice say out in the hallway.

"But…" a man begins to reply, but quickly falls silent again.

I push myself upright in bed as best I can. Over the past —I don't even know how many hours—I drifted in and out of consciousness. They must've increased the pain meds—at least I think so. My bed feels wonderfully soft, like it's made of cotton wool. And the colors in this room! Especially now, with the sun streaming in, even the white walls are glowing with vibrant light.

"You know it won't work without you," the woman whispers outside my door now, her tone conspiratorial.

No idea who the two of them are. I don't recognize the voices. Or am I just hearing them distorted? Maybe it's June, talking to someone out there?

June.

Her face appears before my eyes. So beautiful. She's smiling warmly—so warmly that I want to hug her. Kiss her and never let her go.

No. Screw her. All she ever wanted was the job, nothing more. Her reaction to that stupid daisy earring says it all. She started the fire, and then she didn't even have the guts to sincerely apologize to me.

"Let's see what's going on here," says the man standing at the door.

A second later, the door begins to open. A female doctor with hip-length corkscrew curls, who looks vaguely familiar, and a tall male doctor who could pass for a supermodel step inside.

"Mr. West?" He flashes a toothpaste-commercial smile.

I nod, confused, not entirely sure if they're really here.

"This is Dr. Sonora Wells, surgeon." The man gestures toward the doctor, who brushes back her mane of curls and winks at me conspiratorially. Sonora. I know a Sonora, don't I? "I'm Dr. Ethan Stone, Head of Surgery," he adds before I can place her.

"Yesterday they said I wasn't supposed to have surgery," I say, confused, because I'm pretty sure that's what they told me. Besides, I don't want new doctors. I want June—but the version of her I want doesn't exist.

This shouldn't be hitting me so hard. I should be mad at myself for letting her get that close in the first place.

"We'd like to examine this again." The doctor hands her colleague a medical file.

With a smooth motion, he opens it and skims through the contents. "Please lift your shirt," he says, turning to me.

Reluctantly. It wasn't fun yesterday either, when the other surgeon was here. Still, I push my T-shirt up. If there's one thing I've learned during these past weeks, it's that you're better off doing what the doctors ask.

The two of them position themselves on either side of my bed, pull on gloves, and lean over me. I feel a bit like I'm already lying on their operating table as they talk shop and point to the area around my belly button.

"Cullen's sign—not entirely clear, but still suspicious," says the doctor.

Her superior palpates my abdomen from the outside. A split second later, he narrows his eyes. "Please turn onto your left side," he instructs me in a strangely controlled tone.

With effort, I manage to roll onto my side. Now I can only see the doctor, who's peering curiously at my flank.

Suddenly, her eyes widen. "Grey Turner's sign!"

"We're operating," the doctor decides. "Immediately."

That sounds serious.

"Prep the patient, I'm booking the OR." His voice remains professionally steady, but I see the doctor hold her breath.

So it's not just serious—it's deadly serious.

Fuck.

"I'll assist," she adds in a tone that leaves no room for argument. "And I'll personally take him to the surgical ward."

He pulls off his gloves and tosses them into the trash can

next to the bed. "As you wish," is all he says before leaving the room.

"Hi again." The doctor smiles at me, her breathing quick. "I'm Sonora. June sent me."

June? I must be looking at her like a total idiot, because she gives me a mischievous grin.

"She asked me to look after you," she explains, quickly removing the IV bag from the stand beside me. Slowly, it dawns on me where I know her from—she's June's roommate. "She was sure you'd need the surgery, and, well, she was right." Sonora hooks the IV bag onto the arm above my bed. "She's a great doctor, you know?"

What is this supposed to be? An intervention to make me stop being mad at her? What does she think—that she can just send someone ahead to act out her little play again? She can't seriously believe this will impress me.

"I like your other face better. Looks less like you just bit into a lemon." She smirks and quickly ducks beneath my bed, as if she needs to check something down there.

"What's that supposed to mean?" I snap at her, even though it's not her fault. "If June has something to say to me, she should do it herself." Not that it would change anything.

In a rush, she unlocks the wheels of my bed. "Listen. I don't know what went on between you two…"

"And that's none of your business," I cut her off, because if June spilled any details of my past to her, I'm going to lose it—painkillers or not, even if they're coursing through my veins like glittery rainbow juice.

"Oh my God, calm down." Shaking her head, she reattaches the loose IV tube. "Can you just listen for a second?"

Do I have a choice? It's not like I can get up and leave.

She takes a deep breath. "The bruising around your

navel and sides indicates extensive retroperitoneal bleeding. Blood and other fluids from the inflamed pancreas are seeping into the surrounding tissue. That's a sign of a *very* severe pancreatitis." Her serious look sends a chill through me. "If this isn't operated on, you'll be six feet under before you know it, got it?"

I try to push back the panic that's taking hold of me, despite the painkillers.

"Good. I see we understand each other now." She quickly grabs the head of my bed and pulls, setting it in motion. "You can thank June alone that my colleague and I even came to take a look," she tells me as we head out.

That's… surprising.

Why would June send them? What would she get out of it?

She stops the wheelchair to open the door. "So in that sense, you probably owe her your life."

Maybe.

"Assuming you survive the surgery, of course."

That kind of dark humor doesn't amuse me. Maybe doctors need it to cope with what they experience in their jobs. But right now, I don't want to hear it. There's already too much fear inside me. Fear that I might never leave this hospital again.

"Like I said, I really don't know what happened between you two…" she continues, hurrying back to me.

This time I don't say anything. I've learned my lesson. And I'm slowly realizing that this won't be the only one Sonora has in store for me.

With a flustered expression, she steps behind me again. "But I do know that right now, June is doing everything she can to figure out the illness that's causing your problems," she says, pushing my bed into the hallway.

No, she's not. June left when there was nothing left for her to gain. Didn't she? "What makes you so sure?"

My bed rattles so loudly down the hallway that Sonora leans down so I can hear her. "A little trust wouldn't hurt you, you know."

Trust? In June? I don't know.

We reach the elevator, and Sonora, panting, presses the call button. "Doesn't matter. You can think whatever you want but let me tell you one thing." She points her index finger at me. "If you keep acting this stupid after the surgery and still don't get that your life is all that matters to June, you're going to lose her."

But I already have. Because the June who made my heart beat harder with each passing day over the past few weeks doesn't even exist.

But what if she does?

What if she really is trying to find a solution to my problem right now? Even though her dream job is already gone? When she set my boat on fire back then, she didn't know what she was doing. What if everything else I accused June of was nothing more than unfounded assumptions?

Even that accusation from back then. The one that started it all. Yes, yesterday during our argument, she tried to explain to me that she had always loved her mom. That I was the one who misunderstood the situation and jumped to the wrong conclusions.

My God. If that's true…

"Oh yeah," Sonora says with a nod as the elevator doors open. She busily pushes my bed inside and presses one of the buttons. "Looks like something's finally sinking in."

That's possible. I just don't know how to deal with it. Except that it's doing something to my pulse. And to my stomach. Something that's anything but painful.

But there's something else overshadowing it: fear.

Fear that I might not wake up after the surgery. Fear that I won't get the chance to reach out to June. June and I—we've already had two chances. What if there won't be a third for us?

The elevator doors open.

"Welcome to the place where miracles sometimes happen," says Sonora, pushing me briskly down the corridor of the surgical ward.

My heart grows heavy. If there's one thing I've learned in life, it's not to believe in miracles. But now, in this moment, as the double doors to the OR swing open, I want to believe.

Chapter Forty-Eight

JUNE

Tense, I shift back and forth on the wooden chair. Sonora snuck me in so I could be there for Ashton's procedure. Behind the glass wall that looks into the operating room, he lies. I can't see him—only Sonora, standing at the table in her blue surgical gown and colorful cap. She's surrounded by nurses, the anesthesiologist, and surgical residents. Next to her, Dr. Stone is just being helped into her gloves.

I should feel relieved that the two of them are finally operating on Ashton, yet I can barely breathe. So much could go wrong.

Too much.

And if something terrible happens in there, I'll have to watch helplessly from out here.

Nausea rises in my throat.

I can't let myself think about that, no matter how hard it is. Sonora and her boss are making sure Ashton is stabilized. In the meantime, I'll tackle another challenge—one that's just as important.

Ashton's inflamed pancreas must be a new symptom of

his underlying condition. Treating it is one thing, but it won't save him. Only a proper diagnosis of his actual illness can do that.

And finding that diagnosis is my responsibility.

I open the laptop I brought with me. As I press the power button, I think about how to continue my search for Ashton's disease.

Over the past few weeks, I've ordered countless tests and examinations, yet none of them have brought me any closer to the answer. What if there's something I've overlooked? I run through every detail in my mind, so intensely that I barely notice what's happening in the OR.

"Fever, abdominal pain—both occurring in episodes and each time accompanied by different secondary symptoms," I murmur, moving my index finger across the touchpad to navigate to the browser. "No long-term medication, no environmental toxins, no tropical disease, no occupational exposure."

For a moment, I glance up; everything in the OR seems calm. The team is focused, and the heart monitor shows a perfect sinus rhythm.

Everything's fine, June. Everything's fine.

"No lupus, no neurological disorder, no arthritis." I look away and open the medical database on my computer. "No hereditary diseases."

Stop.

Instinctively, I freeze mid-motion.

I don't know what it is that makes me pause, but something's off. To focus better, I close my eyes.

"Hereditary diseases," I say over and over again, until Ashton's father appears in my mind.

His hair is as dark as his son's, but there's something else about his appearance—something that doesn't show in Ashton's face.

The nearly black eyes, the equally dark brows. The tanned skin.

He looks... Mediterranean...

Hmm.

Ashton's family might have Mediterranean roots on his father's side. Maybe from Italy.

Fever. Stomach pain. Mediterranean.

I massage my temples. Repeat the words once more, and this time I say them out loud. "Fever. Stomach pain. Medite..." Suddenly, I clap my hands over my mouth. "Familial Mediterranean fever!" I shout, even though I'm completely alone here and no one can hear me.

That fits! Doesn't it?

A genetic disease that primarily occurs in people of Mediterranean descent.

Ashton did say there were no hereditary diseases in his family, but what if no one knows about it? Not every carrier of a mutated gene shows symptoms, and maybe that's the case with this disease too.

I quickly type *familial Mediterranean fever* into the search bar of the online portal and dive into the first article I find about the illness.

Yes. Here it is. The disease doesn't have to manifest; it often goes undiagnosed because the symptoms can so easily be mistaken for a common flu.

Aha!

A new puzzle piece clicks into place in my mind. Ashton said he was sick a lot as a child.

My stomach has probably always been my weak spot. That's exactly what he said. And I asked how often he got sick.

What did he say again?

If only I had the medical file, everything would be easier. But it's in the diagnostics department — the one place I'd better avoid after getting kicked out yesterday.

I rub my temples. Maybe once every few months? Three times a year? I hear Ashton say thoughtfully, and a heartbeat later I see him in my mind's eye. There's that pained smile of his as he tells me how his mom used to make him peppermint tea and put a hot water bottle on his stomach.

Yes, yes, and yes again. That fits too!

With my heart pounding, I open the article titled "Accompanying Symptoms of Familial Mediterranean Fever." I've barely read the first few paragraphs when my breath catches in my throat again.

The joint and muscle pain, the pleuritis, the amyloidosis, the kidney problems. Everything Ashton has had since he was admitted to Halifax Harbor Hospital fits my diagnosis.

Even the pancreatitis he's currently battling.

Involuntarily, I glance back into the OR, straight at the monitor displaying his vital signs. Heart rate, blood pressure, and oxygen saturation are all stable.

Everything is fine.

With sweaty hands, I move the mouse pointer to the next article, which covers diagnostics. As expected, a specific genetic test is required to confirm the diagnosis.

So I need a blood sample. But how am I supposed to get one?

Dr. Young.

I have to convince her to order the test. Because if Ashton's illness remains unidentified and therefore untreated any longer, he may never recover from the damage it's already caused. And his amyloidosis will return —possibly as early as tomorrow—and last time he was just damn lucky that the resulting kidney failure wasn't life-threatening.

I snap my laptop shut and jump up from the chair.

"Sorry, Ashton, I have to go," I whisper breathlessly, my eyes fixed on the OR. My fingers reach for the glass panel, brushing over the cold surface. "You've got this. I'll see you soon."

Hopefully.

Definitely.

With a heavy heart, I tear myself away and race out into the hallway. This time, I'm certain I'll do what I haven't been able to before: I'm going to save Ashton.

Chapter Forty-Nine

JUNE

I can't wait for the elevator, so I take the stairs. Clutching the laptop tightly under my arm, I race past the door to the third floor seconds later, skid around the corner, and tackle the final flight of stairs to the fourth floor, where the diagnostics department is located.

Made it.

I reach for the doorknob. At the same moment, the door bursts open from the other side—with such force that it hits me in the head with a dull thud.

I groan and reach for the throbbing spot on my forehead.

Damn, that hurts!

"June?" I hear a man's voice ask.

Of all people, it's Jaxon.

"Thought they kicked you out?" He takes a step back, his gaze drifting to my forehead, where a bump is probably already forming. "Heard it was a pretty brutal exit, too."

I respond with a grunt.

"What are you doing here?" He crosses his arms over his chest.

"I have something urgent to take care of." I barely manage to suppress a hiss as I touch an especially painful spot. Better not to mess with it any further. There's no blood, and that's the most important thing.

Jaxon lets out a laugh. "You do realize no one wants you here anymore, right?"

"I have to go in anyway," I reply, because there's no way I'm letting that stop me.

"You really don't get it." Jaxon pops a piece of gum into his mouth. "You lost, Barbie. And it's way too late to change that now."

"I don't give a damn about this stupid game." My tone takes on a shrill edge. "This is about a human life." About Ashton. About him getting better. About him being able to live his dream of sailing out into the world, instead of being stuck on dialysis, enduring endless hospital stays, or maybe even one day needing a kidney transplant.

He deserves to live.

To be free.

He snorts. "You really think no one's as smart as you, don't you?"

I don't have time for this. I reach for the door. "Let me through, Jaxon."

He steps in front of me. "In there," he says, pointing toward the entrance to the fourth floor, "are a bunch of doctors with way more experience than you."

That's true. "Nevertheless, I hold the key to Ashton's illness in my hands," I reply firmly.

His eyebrows draw together, panic flooding his expression. "Seriously?"

God, this is taking way too much time. "Seriously. So let me in already."

He squares up in front of me, defiant. "I'm supposed to help you? So I can lose my job too?"

This can't be happening. I clench my fists. I finally have a diagnosis that might actually be right, and now I'm not being given the chance to confirm it.

I glare at Jaxon, who looks more than tense. "Go home. You're done here," he says, leaning his back against the door.

"I need to speak with Dr. Young, and you're not going to stop me." Determined, I push him aside and reach for the handle.

"Well, tough luck. She's not here today." A smug expression creeps across his face.

Nonsense, I don't believe a word he says. "I want to see for myself," I hiss, step into the hallway, and hurry off.

"Security!" I suddenly hear Jaxon shouting behind me.

Has he lost his mind? I'm not a security risk!

"Security!" he yells again. "The blonde woman up front. Unauthorized access."

Why is he doing this?

Footsteps echo behind me. Fast and heavy.

I break into a run, heading straight for Dr. Young's office.

The footsteps grow louder.

"Stop," a deep male voice calls. "Stay where you are."

Not a chance. Instead, I pick up the pace and reach the boss's office before he can catch me.

Gasping for air, I turn toward the door. That's when I spot the sign dangling from the glass panel.

"Today, I'm saving my own life for a change," I read, followed by a winking smiley face.

Fuck.

"Your ID, please." Panting, the security guard steps up beside me, bracing himself on his thighs.

"I forgot it at home." I try to muster an innocent smile.

His brow furrows. "Then I suggest you go get it—quickly."

"Thanks, I will," I reply, already lost in thought, wondering how I could order Ashton's blood test without Dr. Young's help. I probably shouldn't bother asking Jaxon.

"She doesn't work here." That was Jaxon, who had apparently followed us.

The security guard tilts his head. Beads of sweat creep into the creases on his forehead. "Is that true, miss?"

"I'd better go now," I say instead of answering.

"She's dangerous!" That was Jaxon again, and he said it so loudly that every staff member who had just been walking down the hallway stopped and turned to look at me.

Is he out of his mind? Does he want the job so badly that he's willing to have Security escort me out?

"Why are you doing this? You already got the job," I say to Jaxon, but he just glares at me with fury in his eyes.

I lower my eyelids to avoid the accusing stares of my former colleagues and turn to leave. First, I'll get to safety—then I'll find another way to get to Ashton's blood.

"Escort the lady outside," I hear Jaxon growl.

A hand grabs my forearm and holds me back. "Come with me, ma'am."

"That's not necessary." I try to pull my arm away from the security guy, but that only makes him grip tighter.

His smile reveals crooked teeth. "I've got my orders, sorry."

With those words, he steers me further down the

hallway toward the elevators. He's just doing his job, I know that. The real problem here is Jaxon.

"She should be banned from the premises," he calls after us. "This woman is a threat to our patients."

Heaven help me, why can't he just let it go?

The elevator doors open, and we step inside. "You're making a huge mistake," I warn the security officer as we descend.

He stares straight ahead, his jaw tightening stubbornly.

"You're endangering someone's life." He has to understand that, and he needs to hear in my voice how serious this is.

The elevator stops, the doors slide open. "After you," he says dryly, signaling for me to exit the cabin.

"Is that what you want?" I ask, growing more anxious. "Do you really want someone to die because of your bad decision?"

Without answering, he grabs my arm again and pulls me with him through the lobby.

"Hey, you can't do this," I scream in panic. "Please, just listen to me…"

We reach the door, and he steps outside with me.

"I need to order a blood test. It's a matter of life and death for the patient…"

"Please, don't make this any worse than it already is." He pushes me down the stairs. "Leave. If I see you lurking around here again, I'll have to be far less gentle with you than I was just now. Is that clear?"

I hold his gaze, unyielding, and he does the same.

"Clear," I snap back a few seconds later and turn to leave. Not a chance, I think, hiding behind the next corner where he can't see me.

I tilt my head back and look up at the façade of the Halifax Harbor Hospital.

How on earth am I supposed to get back in there?

Chapter Fifty

ASHTON

I lift my eyelids. They're heavy. The world looks blurry.

There is bright light.

Black streaks.

Darkness.

I try again. For a split second, I see the ceiling tiles. I know where I am.

My hospital room.

Did I pass out?

Blinking, I try to sit up. A sharp pain forces me back down. I reach for my stomach.

A bandage.

Why?

"Ashton?"

Is someone there?

"He's waking up."

My mouth is dry. I want to say something, but my throat feels rusted shut.

Waking up?

Waking up from what?

"Everything looks good, Mr. West. The operation was a success."

"Operation?" I hear myself croak, my voice strangely distorted and unreal.

That's right. I had surgery. I force my eyelids open again.

The supermodel-looking surgeon from earlier smiles at me. "Good morning."

Slowly, more of my memory returns.

I'm alive.

Still.

"You have a visitor," he says, then his face disappears from view.

"June?" I ask, because that's all I can think about right now. More than anything, I want to see her familiar face and hear her say that everything will get better from here on out.

"No, my boy," I hear Father say.

Of course she's not here.

Because I hurt her. With the accusatory way I confronted her. With my refusal to listen.

That was wrong.

She has to know how much she means to me, and that everything that happened back then doesn't matter to me anymore. Not even the fire. But this damn illness ruins everything. It chains me to this bed, keeps me from fighting for her.

Groaning, I close my eyes. "I just need June. Where is she?" I ask weakly, drifting into a half-sleep, even though what I should be doing is jumping out of bed and going after her.

Chapter Fifty-One

JUNE

Fidgeting, I shift from one foot to the other, and although I do everything I can to steady my breathing, I just can't manage it.

It's taking too long. Hours have passed without me making it back to the ward. One of the security guards caught me every single time. No matter which route I tried to take to reach the diagnostics department, I didn't stand a chance.

I have to try Dr. Young again. She's my only hope. With trembling fingers, I dial her private number, which I tracked down after a long search online.

The dial tone rings in my ear.

Once. Twice. Three times.

"Come on."

It keeps ringing steadily.

"Pick up!" I pace back and forth in front of the hospital wall.

A click. Followed by a voicemail message I could recite by heart at this point.

"Damn it." I shove the phone back into my pocket.

I've already left her three messages, begging her to get to Halifax Harbor Hospital as soon as possible. Another one won't make a difference.

This isn't working. I can't wait any longer.

I have to find a way to get in there.

What else could I do?

A call snaps me out of my brooding.

It's Sonora. "Sorry I didn't get back to you sooner, I had to take care of some urgent... things," she says after a brief greeting.

"Did everything go well?" I ask breathlessly, pacing along the dirt path I've already worn into the grass in front of the hospital.

"Yes, the surgery was successful." She sounds relieved. "It was touch and go—he had heavy bleeding—but… well, everything turned out fine."

Something in her tone makes me suspicious, though maybe I'm imagining it. My nerves are shot—things like this can happen. "No lasting damage?"

"No," she says. "Everything's fine, June."

Thank God. I lift my gaze to the sky—it's overcast, but it's never looked more beautiful.

At last, I manage to release the breath I've been holding. "I don't know how to thank you."

"Don't mention it," she replies in a casual tone. "We're friends—we help each other. It's nothing special."

My eyes start to burn. I quickly wipe at my eyelids. "It absolutely is," I manage to say before my voice gives out.

"It'll take a little while for him to be fully conscious. But he should recover quickly," says Sonora. "You can talk to him later this afternoon."

I'd love nothing more. But how am I supposed to do

that if I can't get into this damn clinic? I glance up at the façade towering over me like a fortress.

"Oh, and one more thing." Sonora laughs on the other end of the line.

"Hm?" I ask, staring absentmindedly at the countless windows, none of which are open.

"Your Ashton is quite the hottie."

My Ashton.

Despite my tension, I have to smile. "Oh yeah, he definitely is," I agree, but quickly shift back to what matters most right now.

If I can't get into that clinic, I'll have to find another way. And that way might be Sonora.

"Would you do me a favor?" I nervously tug at the hem of my shirt. "I need a blood sample from Ashton. For an MEFV gene test."

"I'm already on my way to the next surgery," she replies apologetically. "If I'm late for that…"

Goddammit.

"I need that sample!" There is panic in my voice. "Without it…"

I stop mid-sentence.

Yes, I need that sample.

But it doesn't have to be fresh.

Right! My God, why didn't I think of that sooner?

"Yeah?" Sonora asks curiously.

"I have to get to the lab," I say hastily, as excitement surges through me again.

There's no danger inside the lab itself. I just need to get into the building, that's all.

"What do you want to do there?"

"Over the past few weeks, I've taken countless blood samples from Ashton. Each sample is stored for a while after analysis—in case a test needs to be repeated, for example," I say, more to myself than to Sonora. Hopefully, one of the vials will be suitable for the genetic test.

"Clever," she comments appreciatively.

"I have to go. Thanks for everything," I whisper breathlessly into the phone and end the call.

I hurry off, keeping close to the wall, trying to find an entrance the security isn't watching. I scan for open windows but don't spot any. Eventually, I reach the loading dock where laundry and meals are delivered.

A truck is parked at the gate, and a young woman is unloading fresh gowns, pants, and surgical shirts.

I rush toward her. "Emergency," I shout, because I can't think of anything better. "Let me through."

She immediately steps aside, and I slip past her into the clinic. I've never been in this part of the hospital before, so I charge blindly down the hallway. No one is around, not even at the spot where I find the elevator. I press the call button.

The lab is on the first floor, directly above me. The route couldn't be shorter, and the chances of getting there unnoticed are high.

Hopefully.

The elevator stops, and the doors slide open. I exhale sharply and step inside. On the way up, I undo my ponytail and shake out my hair. It's not like no one will recognize me now, but at least I look a little different, and I can hide my face.

A bright *pling* announces my arrival on the first floor. I press myself against the elevator wall as the doors open, revealing the hospital corridor.

No one is here.

I venture outside, walk to the lab with my head down, and push open the glass door.

A cacophony of voices reaches my ears. I glance up briefly. There are at least ten doctors, all crowded in front of the counter with their patient files, loudly demanding their test results.

How am I supposed to get through that?

"Slow down," I hear a woman call. "Please calm down."

I recognize the voice. It's the woman who helped me with the test results last time.

Tension grips me. If I can convince anyone to help me, it's her. But how do I reach her?

"June?"

I don't dare lift my eyelids. A pair of high heels appears in my field of vision. Is that…?

"Hey, what are you doing here? They said you…"

Yes. It's Olive. Thank God!

"I know," I reply quickly, pulling her aside with me and looking at her pleadingly.

"Say, is that a bump on your forehead?" she asks, studying me closely.

I wave it off. "Listen, I really need some test results. It's urgent."

She scratches the back of her neck, her silky hair swinging to the side. "Wait—what? You ordered tests? How's that even possible?"

I shake my head. "No, the test still needs to be ordered. Would you do it for me? Patient P010424-060, an MEFV gene test. Blood samples should already be available." It's the third time today I've asked someone for a favor. And once again, I feel that it's the right thing to do. No one fights alone. Together, we're so much stronger.

It's easy to see that she's overwhelmed by my request. "Am I committing a crime by doing this?"

"You're most likely saving a life," I reply, nodding emphatically. Then I quickly let my hair fall back over my face. There are just too many people around who might recognize me. "Especially if you can find someone to run the test right away."

Even in the best-case scenario, it takes several hours to get an initial indication. A detailed analysis will take weeks —I can't afford to wait that long anyway.

I look at her questioningly. "Don't you always bribe the lady with chocolate from the vending machine?" Yes, she does! It was less than two weeks ago that she told me that right here in the lab.

She grins mischievously. "Oh, so now you're fine with it? Just the other day, you acted like it was totally unethical."

That's true. But… in this case, it's right. Right now, Ashton is weakened from his surgery. If he has another flare-up— even if it's milder than the last— he might not survive it.

"I was being stupid the other day." I never thought I'd say those words out loud. I always wanted to be the perfect June. The one who gets everything right. The one who knows everything. The one who fights first and foremost for herself and the recognition that comes with it.

But that's over now.

Today, I'm just June. The one who makes mistakes sometimes. The one who doesn't know everything— and that's okay. The one who fights for others.

A warm smile spreads across Olive's face. "Alright, but you'll tell me what this is all about later, okay?"

"Deal." I repeat Ashton's identification code so my friend can write it down, then pull her into a hug. "Thank you! Thank you, thank you, thank you." My heart is racing, and it feels like it's pumping pure hope through my veins. Soon, I'll have Ashton's results as a first indication. "I'll be waiting at the other end of the hallway. Behind the green plants."

"So it is a criminal offense after all," Olive replies with a mischievous grin. "June, June, June. Where is this going to end?"

She winks at me and hurries off to order my test. In a rush, I sneak out of the lab before anyone can spot me. On the way to my hiding place, Olive's question echoes in my mind.

Where is this going to end?

The answer is crystal clear to me: where all dreams end.

Outside on the steep cliffs. On the rock where Ashton and I will stand, holding hands as we gaze into the first of countless sunrises—all of them belonging to us.

With a wistful smile, I push aside the broad leaf of the houseplant and squeeze into the corner behind the pot.

This is where I'll wait for the next few hours, my thoughts with Ashton and the moment he described to me.

As soon as I have the test results in my hands, I'll run to him. And no one will stop me—not even hospital security.

Chapter Fifty-Two

ASHTON

The next time I wake up, my eyelids feel lighter. I know where I am, and I know I actually have another chance to finally make things right with June.

I push myself up to look around. A groan escapes my mouth, and dizziness hits me right away—but unfortunately not enough. I still recognize that Father is sitting in the visitor's chair.

"Don't you have anyone to throw in jail?" I'd love to scream at him, but I don't have the strength. The words leave my mouth sluggishly.

He moves his chair closer to my bed. "I haven't worked as a judge in twelve years."

I don't care. My mistake. I asked him a personal question. Won't happen again. "Where's June?"

"Who?" He crosses his legs with an innocent expression.

I could puke, just because he's here acting like this. "Dr. June Taylor, my doctor."

He wrinkles his nose. "That incompetent blonde?"

"Don't call her that," I snap at him, and suddenly there's energy in me where there was none before. "You don't even know her."

He immediately raises his hands. "I'm not here to talk about her."

But she's all that matters. "Besides that, we have nothing to talk about."

He exhales heavily and folds his hands, as if he needs to collect himself. "How much longer do you plan on going on like this?"

He really doesn't get it. "Until you disappear and never come back."

"I won't do that," he replies, his tone inappropriately gentle.

Stubbornly, I stare at the ceiling. What am I supposed to say to that? There are no words left in me for him.

"Because I have something to tell you." His voice suddenly turns brittle.

I glare at him angrily. "Whatever it is, I don't want to hear it."

He swallows, his fingers gripping the arms of the visitor's chair for support. "I'm aware of that."

Well then, that settles everything. "So why are you still sitting there like an idiot?" I ask him in exactly the same scornful tone he used to ask me questions.

He flinches, pretending my words hurt him. "Please, let me finish."

"Where's June?" I repeat, because the idea that I'd want to have a conversation with him is just too ridiculous. Besides, I need to talk to her. I need to tell her that I finally understand what happened between us back then. That neither of us was truly guilty or innocent. And that I love her.

He shrugs. "I fired her."

"You can't do that." Who does he think he is? Mister All-Powerful?

"As chairman of the Halifax Harbor Hospital, I have the final say in all personnel matters," he replies, visibly confused. Then he suddenly pauses. "You didn't know that?"

Of course not. How on earth was I supposed to know that?

If you really believe I'm such a terrible doctor, then do it. One phone call to your father is all it takes, I suddenly hear June say in my memory, full of despair.

Did she know? And if so, since when?

Tell him what I did. Clear your name. Destroy everything I've fought for my whole life.

She wanted to come clean, but she was also afraid. Terrified. Afraid that I would tell Father who burned down that damned place. Out of revenge. And to finally throw the truth in his face, to make him see that he was wrong not to believe me.

And as angry as I was with her in that moment, it's actually understandable. I have to clear this up. She needs to know I would never do that to her.

"I have to see June. Right now." I push the sheet aside with effort.

"You're staying here," Father snaps. His voice is stern, but there's a strange flicker of fear in his eyes. "That woman is completely incompetent. Be glad you're rid of her."

"Have you lost your mind?" I yell at him. "Firing her was a mistake!"

Now he furrows his brow, and if I didn't know better, I'd even think he was sick with worry. "She examined you for weeks and didn't have the faintest idea what was wrong with you. Dr. Taylor played with your life!"

And how exactly is that any different from what he did? Didn't he play with my life too—and in a much worse way than June ever could have?

"She's a brilliant doctor. And if you were willing, just once, to look people in the eye instead of right through them, you'd know that." He'd see who's being honest and who's lying. But he's never been capable of that. "You're a selfish bastard who only sees the world from his own perspective. Someone who twists everything to fit his own narrative."

Saying that to him feels incredible. Only now do I realize how long that truth has been lying dormant inside me. And no one but June is the reason I finally understand it.

After all, she was the one who made me see that nothing in this world is purely black or white, or simply good or evil. It was through her that I came to understand something we all too often forget: that each of us sees the same thing in a different way.

Once again, I pause. I'm so surprised by the thought that suddenly takes hold of me.

"You almost managed to turn me into the same asshole you are." But I'm not. I'm not like him.

He looks at me, defeated. His lower lip trembles.

And in that moment, I know—it's time to prove that I've truly understood what June taught me.

"Why did you go after June like that earlier?" I ask seriously.

He lifts his shoulders with a sorrowful expression. "I was so worried about you, I lost control."

Yeah, right. "You don't even believe that yourself."

"A lot has changed over the past few years," he says now, so quietly I can barely hear him.

So he wants to talk about the past. Fine, let him. Because I know, no matter how painful it gets, I have to ask him this one question—the one I hadn't even cared about until three weeks ago.

"I don't care about the past few years. I just want to know one thing: Why did you tear me apart like that after Mom died?"

Father lowers his eyelids and shifts in his chair, as if he can't find a comfortable position.

"You hated me so much," I continue, since he clearly doesn't want to answer. "Why?"

Now his fists clench. "You were a terrible child, Ashton. You made my life even harder than it already was."

Excuse me? Is he seriously playing the poor dad card?

"That's bullshit and you know it." He has to tell me the truth. Only when I know his side of the story will I be able to move on. And I want that more than anything. "Why?"

"You were always getting into trouble, always causing problems." His expression tells me how baffled he is that I even asked the question. "The incidents at school, the smoking, the fights. And then you went and set the shed on fire!" With every word, he sounds a little more defeated.

"That wasn't me. When are you finally going to get that?" I don't even know why I'm reacting to his damn lies. Talking to him is pointless.

He jumps up from his chair. "Be a man for once and own up to what you did!" he yells at me, his eyes glassy with tears, confirming what I already knew.

I shake my head as I look at him. "You'll never change."

And that's his damn problem, not mine. "But you know what? I don't give a shit. I don't need you."

I never have. But there's someone else who does need him, and that's the only reason I still put up with his presence.

Chapter Fifty-Three

JUNE

Three agonizing hours after Olive ordered the genetic test, she hands me the results. Shaken, I take them and scan the data.

"Positive," I whisper soundlessly.

Ashton most likely suffers from familial Mediterranean fever. A more precise test will confirm it, but this result is enough of an indication to begin treatment.

"Oh no," I hear Olive say sympathetically.

I look up. "No, this is great!" With the right treatment, Ashton's prognosis is very good. We'll get the fever attacks under control, and he'll be able to lead a mostly normal life.

Olive smiles. "Well, if that's the case… what are you still doing here?"

That's exactly the right question. "I've got to go." Grinning, I squeeze past my friend. "Thanks again—couldn't have done it without you," I call out as I'm already heading for the fire escape.

Taking the elevator to the fourth floor would be too

risky, so I open the heavy metal door and listen into the stairwell.

No one there.

Clutching the test result to my chest, I tiptoe up the stairs. My pulse quickens with every floor I manage to pass unnoticed.

Just two more floors.

My breathing is shallow, and the paper in my hands begins to ripple from the moisture of my skin.

Just one more floor.

What was that noise? Is someone there?

I lean over the stair railing and look down. My heart nearly stops when I spot an orderly two floors below me.

As quietly as possible, I dash upward.

Just half a floor to go.

There's the door up ahead. And from that door, it's about a hundred meters to Ashton's room. How am I supposed to cover that distance without being seen?

Just one more step.

With trembling fingers, I reach for the door handle. The orderly's footsteps in the stairwell are getting louder.

I press down the handle, pull the metal door open, and peer out into the hallway.

There are five orderlies standing together in a group. Three doctors, a handful of patients stretching their legs. A pharmaceutical sales rep is just opening her case to hand out sample packs to the head nurse. And my friend from security, wearing safety shoes and a radio clipped to his belt.

He's standing next to a colleague by the elevator to my left. Ashton's room is on the right.

I hastily brush my hair into my face. My heart is pounding in my throat; I can even hear my own blood rushing in my ears. Air is trapped in my lungs.

One more deep breath in.

Exhale.

Go.

I slip quickly through the door, turn immediately to the right, and weave my way past the orderlies.

"Was that just…?" a man's voice says.

Even though it hardly seems possible, my pulse quickens even more. I pick up the pace.

"Yes, that's her! What's she doing here?" a woman's voice chimed in. She must have been there earlier when Jaxon loudly called me dangerous.

Not good. Not good at all.

"Security!"

That was it.

I have to run.

Clutching the test results tightly, I took off. Adrenaline surged through my body. It was like I was in a tunnel—I couldn't feel anything. No burning in my lungs, no exhaustion.

"Stop," someone shouted.

Ashton's room was the fifth door on the left. I could almost see it.

"Dr. Taylor, stop right now!"

I clenched my teeth and kept running.

Only three doors left.

I can do this.

All of a sudden, it feels like I'm running into an invisible wall that stops me dead in my tracks.

"Didn't I tell you not to show your face around here again?" a man's voice growls in my ear. Only now do I realize he's grabbed me from behind and stopped me mid-run.

His arms wrap around me so tightly I can't move at all. The sharp scent of his aftershave fills my nose.

"Let me go!" I scream at the top of my lungs, struggling in every direction.

His grip is too strong. "You're coming with me, nice and easy," he pants.

I hear a metallic clinking sound. My eyes fixed on Ashton's door, I frantically search for a way to break free.

Only fifteen meters separate me from my goal.

The security guard forces my arms behind my back. I feel cold metal against my right wrist.

Handcuffs? Is he serious?

Once again, I try to break free, once again I fight against a force I can't overcome.

And then it happens. He yanks the test result from my left hand and, just a split second later, the second handcuff snaps shut.

How am I supposed to get out of this?

Do I have to give up?

My muscles give out, and the security guard hooks his arm through mine.

Out of the corner of my eye, I see him pull his radio from his belt. "Tim to the fourth floor, please. Unauthorized entry, one person in custody," he says, breathing heavily.

No, no, no! I have to do something!

More and more employees gather around us, whispering to each other, pointing at me, laughing.

I shake the security guard's arm. "Let me go, you're hurting me."

His radio crackles. "Copy."

Still breathing heavily, the guy turns away to clip his radio back onto his belt.

He misses the holder. "Come on," he mutters, and I suddenly realize he is distracted for a moment.

In a flash, I raise my foot and kicke his shin with all my strength. He collapses with a sharp cry, and I take the chance to shake off his arm. Then I run like I'd never run before in my life.

Straight toward Ashton's room.

Suddenly, it sounds like a whole herd of elephants is chasing after me. All the staff on the ward—and maybe even more—are hot on my heels.

I'm almost there.

If my hands weren't tied behind my back, I could have reached out and grabbed the doorknob. But as it is, I have no choice but to lunge straight at the door.

I slam into the door with a loud thud, pain flaring in my upper arm.

Chaos erupts behind me. A hand touches my shoulder.

Another one to my hip.

"No!" I scream in terror, then throw my entire weight against the door handle.

Chapter Fifty-Four

ASHTON

Out in the hallway, commotion begins. My attention, however, stays fixed on Father, whose dark hair is trembling. Maybe from rage. Maybe from fear. I don't know, and I honestly don't care.

"I don't need you," I repeat the words I said earlier. "But June needs you. So for once, let me give you some advice: Be a man and admit that you made a mistake when you fired June." That's all I want from him. Just this one thing, then he can disappear forever.

With a loud bang, the door swings open. June stumbles in, faltering and falling to the floor.

Are those handcuffs on her wrists?

An entire armada of hospital staff storms into the room behind her. Nurses, orderlies, a security guard. That other doctor who first told me about the game—what was his name again? Jaxon, I think.

The man in black immediately lunges at June. "End of the line," he growls gruffly, grabs her, and hauls her to her feet.

"Let go. Now," I demand, but no one responds. I catch Father's eye. "Do something!"

"Ashton!" June shouts over the commotion. "I know what's wrong with you now."

We lock eyes. Her hair is a wild mess, her face flushed bright red. A large bump stands out prominently on her forehead.

Father raises his hand. "Silence," he bellows, and everyone immediately falls quiet.

A few people even lower their gaze. Now June's boss, Dr. Young, enters the hospital room. Today she's not wearing a lab coat, but her expression is filled with concern. She stops beside June, who is still struggling to break free from the security guard's grip and gives her a questioning look.

"What's going on here?" I hear Father ask, alarmed. Then he turns to June. "You have no business being here."

Has he lost his mind? June just said she's figured out what's wrong with me, and that's all he has to say? Before I can yell at him for it, June opens her mouth.

"I'm aware of that." She lifts her chin, and I spot a scrape beneath it. "But I won't let something this minor stop me from doing what's right."

I can't help but grin. The way she stands up to Father—so bold and confident—I like it.

With a gruff grunt, Father instructs the security guard to remove the handcuffs.

June groans as she rubs her wrists. "Thanks."

"You've got your chance—use it," Father says to June. "So out with it. What's wrong with my boy?"

My boy. Give me a break…

With a professional smile, she fixes her gaze on him. "Your son has familial Mediterranean fever, a hereditary autoimmune disease that's easily treatable…"

"Impossible," he cuts her off with a snort. "If there were hereditary diseases in our family, I'd know about it."

Anxious murmuring fills the room. Dr. Young gently reaches for June's arm. "Come, Dr. Taylor, let's take a calm look at this together."

June shakes her off, her eyes flicking to me. "Not every hereditary disease manifests in everyone, and this one often goes undetected for generations," she explains to me. "The stomach pains you had as a kid, the frequent fevers—that was all because of this illness."

"He really was sick a lot as a child," Father mutters.

Dr. Young furrows her brow.

"Yes," I confirm as well. Though I am surprised my father even remembered. After Mom died, he ignored all of my symptoms. Because I was a burden to him. Although... if I remember correctly... When Mom was still alive, he used to take care of me lovingly whenever I was sick. At least as often as his work allowed. I had forgotten, but now I remember. He wasn't perfect, but he was a good dad.

Back then.

June gives me a grateful nod, then looks expectantly at my father, whose expression clearly shows his confusion.

"Can you prove your theory?" Dr. Young asks, earning a stunned look from that Jaxon guy.

A radiant smile spreads across June's face. "I can. The test results show clear evidence."

A shocked murmur ripples through the room. "Can that be true?" someone whispers.

"And where are these test results?" my father asks her. He almost sounds hopeful.

"Um..." She glances around, searching, and she isn't the only one. Except for her sleazy colleague, everyone is scanning the floor feverishly; some even leave the room to check the hallway.

My father wrinkles his nose and turns to me. "And I'm supposed to rehire her?" he asks incredulously.

"Yes," I reply dryly.

Over Father's shoulder, I see June's bewildered expression. "You just…," she whispers urgently, and a split second later, a wave of tender longing washes over her face.

My heart instantly starts beating faster. "This job has to be yours," I say loudly enough for everyone gathered to hear. "And Father agreed earlier to give it to you." I fix my gaze on him. "Isn't that right?"

He fidgets with his suit pants, glancing back and forth between me, June, and Dr. Young, as if searching our faces for an answer.

My God, why is he making such a fuss?

"Isn't that right, Dad?" I press again, this time even more forcefully. There's only one way out of this for him: to give in. And I'll make sure he does.

June starts trembling all over. "Mr. West…," she begins, but Father silences her with a wave of his hand.

"That's right," he mumbles quietly.

A mountain lifts off my chest in an instant. "Thank you," I whisper to him in relief, even though he's the last person I owe anything to.

June's dream is coming true, and that's worth a thank you.

"No! This is *my* job." Jaxon glances around frantically, as if searching for someone to confirm that this isn't really happening. But no one pays him any attention.

Just a breath later, a nurse enters the room. In her hand, she holds a sheet of paper, which she hands to Dr. Young. "The test results," she says softly.

June's boss lowers her gaze to the results. Seconds drip by as slowly as honey, while everyone in the room seems to hold their breath.

Now the corners of Dr. Young's mouth twitch. "Familial Mediterranean fever. Congratulations, Dr. Taylor, you've solved your case."

June's eyes shine with joy—but only for a moment. Then her expression turns strangely serious.

Why? She got the job, and she diagnosed my illness. Earlier, she even said it was treatable. And she has my whole heart, too.

Still, she now steps toward Father with a tense expression. "There's one more thing left unresolved."

Excuse me? What does she want now?

Chapter Fifty-Five

JUNE

I could say thank you, smile at Ashton's father, let the joy rise within me, and savor the feeling that this ending is a good one for me.

I could call my parents, be the daughter who never disappoints them, and celebrate with them the most spectacular party of all time.

I could walk up to Ashton, hug him, and press my lips to his. Tell him how much he means to me and that I can't wait to stand with him on the cliff's edge and watch the sunrise together.

I could do all of that now—and just three weeks ago, I would have believed it was exactly the right thing to do.

But the time I spent with Ashton changed me, so now there's only one thing I know for sure: whether something is right or wrong often depends on the light in which we see it.

What I'm about to do is wrong for me.

No, it's more than that.

It will cost me my dream. But for Ashton, it's as right as anything could be. It will give him the peace he deserves.

"What's she doing?" someone murmurs.

"Shhh," another person hushes.

"She's crazy," Jaxon sneers.

Maybe I am.

Crazy.

But in this case, and for this man, there's nothing I'd rather be.

I catch Ashton's questioning glance, let him see in mine that everything's okay, then turn to face his father.

"Before you hire me, there's something you need to know," I say, addressing all my colleagues and the boss.

Suddenly, it's so quiet I can hear the seagulls screeching through the closed window. Tension fills the room—I think some of my colleagues are even holding their breath. Countless eyes rest on me, full of expectation.

Ashton's eyes are among them. And in them, there's a kind of love that gives me more strength than anything ever has before.

"About Ashton. And about what really happened during his time at Halifax High." My voice trembles slightly, but I don't let that stop me. I look this terrifying man—who made Ashton's life hell for years—straight in the eyes.

His brow furrows, though only slightly.

"None of the things the principal punished him for were actually his doing." I exhale shakily, and I hear Ashton draw in a sharp breath.

"June, don't—" he begins.

No. I won't. "It was entirely my fault. I was the one who kept falsely accusing Ashton," I continue, keeping my gaze fixed on his father.

Clearly confused, he rubs the back of his neck.

"I made up cruel stories about him and made sure he

got into trouble." With those words, at least some of the guilt leaves my mouth. For so long, I thought standing up for myself was the right thing to do. And I didn't realize that my hatred only created more hatred.

Fabric rustles behind me. "What's wrong with Barbie this time?" I hear Jaxon whisper, hungry for drama.

There's nothing wrong with Barbie.

Absolutely nothing.

For a moment, I look at Ashton. His face reflects a whole range of emotions, disbelief chief among them. He gently shakes his head, as if trying to stop me from going on. Maybe because he knows what's coming next.

I shake my head in return, letting him know he can't stop me. Then I turn back to face his father.

"How could you do that to my son?" Rage dominates his face. The veins at his temples bulge. "Get out of this room. Right now," he hisses through clenched teeth.

"I will, don't worry. But only when I'm done," I reply firmly. Because I'm not finished. Not even close. "I did all of that. I lied, I deceived, and I spread hatred." I press my index finger to my chest. "And on top of that, I was the one who set fire to your shed thirteen years ago, in early summer," I say loud and clear.

Mr. West gasps for air.

I step closer to him. "Ashton had nothing to do with it. He was innocent—all along." Tears sting my eyes. Tears of guilt. Tears of release. Tears of disappointment in myself for not owning up to it sooner.

And tears of fear.

Fear that my next words won't have the effect I hope for. Fear that instead of healing what I want to mend, I might end up breaking it even more.

"You punished him for my sins," I finish, my heart pounding.

Ashton's father stares at me. First with doubt. Then with sorrow. "You're fired." His icy voice fills the room.

I nod awkwardly. I knew it would come to this, but it still hurts. "I'm aware of that," I reply tonelessly.

"But that's only half the story, isn't it, Dad?" I suddenly hear Ashton say, his voice rough.

I see a flicker of guilt cross Mr. West's face. A murmur ripples through the people in the hospital room. "My God," someone whispers in disbelief. "What else is coming?"

Ashton clears his throat. "It's the half you've only seen a fraction of so far: the tip of an iceberg beneath which a monster sleeps."

I know what monster he's talking about. And from the look on Mr. West's face, I can tell he does too.

"This monster be—"

"Everyone out of here!" Ashton's father roars, his face flushed crimson, making everyone in the room flinch. "Now!"

My colleagues hurry out of the hospital room, and even the security guards disappear. As the room empties, I glance uncertainly at Ashton.

Should I go too?, I ask him silently.

He gives me a gentle smile. "Stay," he asks, and that's all he needs to say for me to understand what he's feeling.

I smile back. Nod at him. And I feel the thousand pieces my heart shattered into after our fight slowly coming back together. I feel myself healing. And I hope with everything I have that Ashton feels the same.

Maybe his father is protesting beside me, but I barely register it. In this moment, all I see is Ashton, and it feels like we're infinitely close, even though there are still several feet between us.

"Is that true, Ashton?" I hear Mr. West ask in a remorseful tone. "What she just claimed… about your mistakes… is all of that true?"

Chapter Fifty-Six

ASHTON

I turn my head toward my father. "Every single word," I answer his question, and then something happens that I never would have expected.

My father, the strong man who fears nothing and no one, suddenly looks small and weak.

Seeing him like that makes the wall I built inside myself years ago begin to crumble. Just a little. But even that is more than I ever thought possible.

"June only did those things because I was a complete asshole to her," I add, because I no longer believe in half-truths. And he'll have to face the whole truth today as well. "An asshole you made me into."

He exhales shakily, deep lines forming on his forehead.

"Why?" I ask again, just like before, hoping he'll give me a different answer this time. An honest one. "Why did you do it?"

For a while, he struggles to find words. June is chewing on her lower lip, and in her expression I can see how deeply she feels for me. And how much she hopes Father will finally answer my question.

He clears his throat now. The corners of his mouth droop, and he lowers his eyelids. "Because after your mom died, I was so full of grief and anger that I lost myself," he finally admits.

And it dawns on me why he hasn't told me this until now.

Because it hurts him.

And it hurts me too, because I can't help but think of her. Of the warmth that left my life with her. Of the unconditional love she gave me.

"Every time I looked at you, I was reminded of why she was in the car."

Because I needed a gift for Jeremy. She only went out because of me. "You blamed me for the accident."

"She was the light of my life." His expression is tortured now, full of longing. "Without her, there was only cold. I was lost, couldn't see reality. Today I know her death was fate. Chance. Bad luck. Whatever it was, the point is, you had absolutely nothing to do with it."

Sometimes a single moment can change everything. That's how it was when Mom died. That's how it was when I saw June coldly reject her own mom at school. And that's exactly how it is now, in this very moment.

I look at my father. I see the last rays of sunlight falling on his dark hair. I see the deep lines etched into his forehead, the sorrow written all over his face.

I see him. Without the shield that used to surround him. Standing before me is a man who lost everything years ago.

"I didn't want to hate you, and I hated myself for doing it anyway. Work was all I had left. My lifeline, the thing that kept me alive." He lifts his gaze, looks at me intently. "In my office, I was safe."

"From me," I add, because I know that's what he means. "From what you saw in me."

With his lips pressed tightly together, he nods. "I wanted to forget. Just forget. Leave the grief and the anger behind me."

I understand that—better than he might think. But our story isn't that simple.

"I was angry too." The memory settles heavily on my chest. Mom's death was senseless. So unfair. So wrong. "And I needed someone to be there for me." Someone to show me how to grieve. Someone to help me escape my own darkness.

Shaking my head, I fix my eyes on Father, who buries his face in his hands.

In that moment, I feel June sit down beside me on the bed. Right in the spot on my mattress where she used to sit so often. The one from which she held my hand, stroked my arm, and listened to my heartbeat.

She is by my side.

Right where she belongs.

Her fingers intertwine with mine, her thumb gently stroking my palm.

It means, I'm here. Whatever happens, I'm here.

Dad's gaze drifts into nothingness, and he blinks rapidly. "Back then, I should've taken care of you. If I could turn back time…"

Would he do everything differently? I don't know if I can believe that. Too much has happened.

I shake my head wearily. "But you can't." No one can. Everything we do, and everything we say, stays in this world forever. "You broke me," I say flatly.

I was his victim. And June was mine.

"I know." Dad slumps even further. "And not just since today."

What does he mean by that? I tilt my head questioningly.

"After you left, I was tormented by guilt. How could I stand in court day after day and judge people for their actions, after I had hurt my own son?"

He takes a deep breath. "That's why I resigned from the bench, found a therapist, and worked my way up at Halifax Harbor Hospital. Here, I can do what I couldn't before: help. Fix things that are broken. Make a difference."

Make a difference? My father?

I glance at June, who looks just as puzzled as I am.

"During therapy, I realized what had happened. To me. And to us," he continues.

I see wistfulness on his face and sorrow in his eyes. I see how hard he's struggling with himself.

But that's not all.

Beyond that, I see that June and I weren't the only victims. He was one too.

Fate put him through a harsh trial, and he failed it. Just as June and I failed ours.

"If you knew the whole time, why didn't you ever reach out?" If someone had told me three weeks ago that I'd be asking that question to my father of all people, I would've said they were insane.

He buries his face in his hands. "I was ashamed."

And I wouldn't have listened to him. That much is certain.

"When I found out you were here, I thought it was my chance. But you were so…"

Cold. I know. And I also know it wasn't right.

He looks at me apologetically. "I didn't know how… it was so hard to find the right words…"

Swallowing hard, I nod. "I understand," I say, and I truly mean it.

Until Mom died, he was a good dad—not perfect, since he was often away—but when we spent time together, I always felt his love. After the accident, all he had for me were harsh words. He didn't seem to know any others anymore. And neither did I, not until I saw June again here at Halifax Harbor Hospital. And for that reason alone—because of her—I can help him today with the right words.

"You're sorry," I say.

He nods, pain etched into his face.

"And you know that June is innocent." We all are—somehow. And at the same time, we're not.

He nods again.

"And you also know she's a great doctor," I continue.

This time, he raises his hand to stop me. His gaze shifts to June. "That's true."

Her fingers tighten around mine. I hear her breathing, uneven and shallow.

"I hope it's not too late." Father gives June a warm look. "Welcome to Halifax Harbor Hospital."

Chapter Fifty-Seven

JUNE

With tears in my eyes, I nod to Ashton's father, who smiles at me from a few meters away. "Thank you."

This job was everything I ever wanted. What I had dreamed of for years. What I thought I absolutely needed in order to be happy.

But the only thing filling my heart in this moment is the feeling of intertwining my fingers even tighter with Ashton's. The knowledge that I'm allowed to be proud of myself for what I've done between Ashton and his father by bringing the truth to light. And the sense that this is the beginning of something that will never end.

My gaze drifts to Ashton—my Ashton—who smiles at me, relaxed. Not like the Ashton from back then, when we first met. But like the Ashton of today.

The storm in his eyes has finally calmed, and a new feeling spreads inside me—one I've never known before.

A flicker of hope.

Deep in my heart, hope flickers—that no one has to be forever broken by their fate. That we can heal, someday, and that it can be love that drives back the shadows life has cast upon us.

"Without you..." Ashton says softly.

I place my index finger on his lips. "Shhh," I whisper, because I know there are no words that could express what we both feel.

Without me, he wouldn't be who he is today. But without him, I wouldn't be who I am either.

He kisses the tip of my finger tenderly, his gaze locked with mine. I can sense how fiercely his heart is pounding in his chest—because mine is doing the same.

Filled with love, I lean over him. A smile plays on his lips, his breathing is uneven. I let my fingers glide across his cheek, gently burying my hand in his hair.

Our noses touch, I breathe in the scent of his skin, his warmth envelops me. A quiet sigh escapes both our lips at the same time, just fractions of a second before they meet.

I sink. Into this moment, where everything is right. Into our kiss and the promise it holds.

Chapter Fifty-Eight

ASHTON

Two weeks later

I pull up my jeans and button them. Slip on the T-shirt and the leather jacket, then step into my sneakers. Finally, I zip up my bag.

It's almost time.

With a relieved breath, I step up to the window and open it. Mild sea air flows in, accompanied by the sound of waves, the screeching of seagulls, and the hum of boat engines chugging through the harbor.

Behind me, the door swings open with a scraping sound. "Hey," I hear June say softly, and she's already nestling against my side. "You ready?"

I wrap my arm around her shoulders and brush a kiss on her cheek. "Mhm," I murmur, overwhelmed by the wave of happiness rushing through me.

In just a few minutes, I'll be leaving Halifax Harbor Hospital. With my travel bag in one hand and June in the other. With a surgical scar that will soon heal, an illness already responding to treatment, and a new outlook on life filled with gratitude and love.

I'm more than ready.

"Well then..." June grins at me but makes no move to step away.

I tilt my head to kiss her. "Well then," I murmur against her lips. "Let's get out of here."

We turn to leave, and June grabs my bag, pointing out my fresh scar, then walks ahead. At the door, I turn around one last time. My eyes drift over the bed, the round visitor's table, the window. Yes, even the crack in the ceiling.

My stay in this hospital changed my life. Still, I never want to come back here again.

Smiling, I close the door behind me and reach out my hand to June. "So, tell me—how was your case review?"

Her cheeks glow pink as she talks in a waterfall of words about things I don't understand in the slightest. But I don't have to, because I can see how happy it makes her—and that's enough.

"... and besides, I'm now sure that Dr. Young has a big heart. So big, in fact, that she has to hide it behind her sarcastic façade to keep a cool head in the daily grind of the clinic," she finishes.

"And your colleague? That Jaxon?" I ask as we reach the hospital lobby, because until yesterday, it wasn't clear whether he'd be allowed to stay at Halifax Harbor Hospital.

So far, June has only mentioned that his case had apparently taken an unexpected turn. And that this was the reason Jaxon did everything he could to hinder her in solving my case after she was dismissed. In the end, I suppose everyone is fighting their own demons—even him.

"He won't be allowed to stay." She lifts her shoulder with a sorrowful expression. "The MRI Dr. Young ordered showed that..." A wistful look takes over June's face. "His patient has bone cancer. If he had ordered an X-ray at the very beginning, he might have caught it sooner." Her voice suddenly turns quiet and infinitely sad. Gently, I stroke her hand. "Sometimes a single moment can change everything," she says thoughtfully.

I stop in the middle of the lobby, pull her close, and kiss her gently. "Sometimes for the better," I remind her, because the fact that we found each other again was exactly that—a moment that changed everything for the better.

"Sometimes for the better," she repeats with a smile, resting her head against my chest. I know she can hear my heart beating—strong and steady—and we both know it's thanks to her.

I sway her gently back and forth as my gaze drifts through the lobby and then upward. On the first floor, I spot my father, leaning on the railing with both hands, looking down at us.

Now he raises his hand, a cautious smile flickering across his face.

I still don't know what the future holds for the two of us. Over the past two weeks, he's visited me often. We talked about Mom, about how much we both still miss her. We remembered her together, and that felt comforting.

I return his greeting with a nod.

Maybe one day I'll invite him over.

Maybe.

Time will tell.

I kiss June's forehead, gently push her away from me, and gesture toward the exit. "Come on, a new life is waiting for us."

Together, we take the last few steps toward the sliding door, which opens for us. Hand in hand, we step outside and turn the corner toward the parking lot. There, Jeremy is leaning against his Porsche, waiting to pick us up.

When he sees us, he comes toward us. June nudges me gently away from her and steps aside.

"Hey," I say to my brother, spreading my arms. "Good to see you."

For the blink of an eye, he looks at me, bewildered. Then overwhelmed. And then, for the first time in thirteen years, I pull him into my arms.

Epilogue

JUNE

One month later

Did Ashton really just say that?

When he woke me up ten minutes ago in the middle of the night, I feared something terrible had happened. But there was that determined look on his face, and I quickly realized that an idea was burning in his eyes.

A completely absurd idea that he just presented to me.

"You can't be serious," I say, taking a step toward the half-finished boat in his shed.

In disbelief, I run my fingers along the bow. I can feel the love he poured into this boat. The longing that drove him all these years. And the passion with which he crafted every single piece with his own hands.

He steps behind me, his chest brushing against my back. "I've never been more serious." His words make his torso vibrate against me.

I turn to face him. "You don't have to do this." Not for me, if that's what he's thinking. "This is your dream, your scars have healed, your illness is under control. You can set sail, every day if you want to." Feel the freedom, breathe in the sea breeze, enjoy life. He shouldn't give up any of that because of me. "As long as you promise to always come back here," I add, even though I know he wouldn't dream of doing otherwise.

His gentle smile sends warmth through my chest. Tenderly, he brushes a strand of hair from my face. "I don't need to come back to you," he says softly. "Because I don't want to leave anymore."

So that's how it is. "I think I understand."

It's similar to how things were with me and my parents. For so long, I wanted them to be proud of me, and I didn't realize that I was the one who needed to be proud of myself. The party my mom had planned never happened, even though I got the job. Instead, I just visited them and told them everything I hadn't been able to say before.

And it turned out to be much more than I had realized up until then. Most of all, what seventeen-year-old June had kept hidden from them.

I lean against Ashton's chest.

He clears his throat. "All my life, I wanted to run away. From Halifax. From my father. From the past." Gently, he rocks me back and forth. "Today, I have no reason to run anymore."

That's true, he doesn't. On the contrary, he has so many reasons to stay.

In Halifax.

With me.

Despite the past.

Smiling, I rise up on my tiptoes. "Let's do it," I whisper against his lips. "Whenever you're ready."

He takes my face in his hands and kisses me. "Now. I'm ready now," he says as we pull apart, looking at me intently.

I nod, still unable to believe he actually wants to go through with it. Even so, he walks to the gate and opens it. The cool morning air drifts in; it's still dark outside.

"Will you help me?" He comes back and positions himself behind the boat.

I step beside him, we place our hands on the bow and set the wheeled platform beneath the boat in motion.

Together, we push the boat onto the wide meadow in front of the shed. Ashton brushes his hands off on his pants and looks at his handiwork, barely visible in the dawn light.

Is he thinking about not going through with it?

Before I can ask him, he pulls a lighter from his pocket and flicks it on.

I look into the flame. "Are you sure?"

He nods. "Thirteen years ago, fate made me want to run away. And when I was admitted to Halifax Harbor Hospital, it forced me to stay," he says, lost in thought. "But you made me forget all of that."

My knees go weak.

"You are my past, and you are my future." In the firelight, he looks at me with meaning.

I meet his gaze and exhale shakily.

"What's about to go up in flames is my pain. It's my hatred and it's my rage." He smiles gently, then picks up a thin branch from the ground and holds it to the lighter.

The fire crackles to life, smoke rising into the sky. I watch it climb, watch him disappear into the twilight of the breaking dawn.

"I don't need any of it anymore," I hear Ashton say. "All I need…" He lowers the burning branch to the cloth covering part of the bow. "…is this one life with you." With those words, he sets the cloth on fire.

The flame licks high, its heat reaching me, yet I step closer to stand by Ashton's side. Together, we watch as the fire devours more and more of his boat.

My hand finds his.

We stand side by side, saying nothing. For minutes. With the smell of charred wood in our noses, the crackling of splintering boards in our ears, and the taste of smoke on our tongues.

In silence, we say goodbye. To everything Ashton is leaving behind forever in that moment.

As the first rays of sunlight creep over the horizon, Ashton gently pulls me close. Arm in arm, we stroll forward toward the sea. To the place where the waves crash against the rocks. To the place where the salty spray reaches our faces.

Side by side, we look out at the new day. It isn't the first time we stand here, but today, it feels like it is.

"One day we'll stand out on the cliffs," I whisper, just as Ashton has done back in the hospital. In a moment when neither of us knew whether we'd ever live that dream together.

"We'll hold hands and watch the first of countless sunrises, all of them ours," he adds, his gaze fixed on the horizon, where the sun slowly rises from the sea and paints the sky in soft shades of pink.

In the warm light of the new day, Ashton turns to me. Ash flakes cling to his dark hair, and damp streaks shimmer on his cheeks.

This is a moment in which everything changes again. Because the feeling I have carried with me for weeks now becomes certainty.

In the depths of my heart, I *know* that no one has to be broken by their fate forever. I *know* that we can heal, someday, and I *know* that for Ashton, that day is today.

Right now, in this very moment, we both feel it. Because in his eyes, I see the reflection of that one feeling that is now taking hold of me more powerfully than ever before:

A glimmer of hope.

Next in the Halifax Harbor Hospital Series

vinci-books.com/ATwistOfFate

He was forbidden. Loving him could cost her everything.

Falling for my boss was a mistake—especially when my surgical career is built on a lie. Dr. Ethan Stone is brilliant, untouchable, and drowning in guilt. Hospital rules and dangerous secrets collide, and no matter what I choose… I lose him.

Turn the page for a free preview…

A Twist of Fate: Prologue

SONORA

I always knew that the rug I'd swept my past under might one day lift in the winds of fate. But that it would happen here, of all places—in Halifax Harbor Hospital—I never would have believed.

My chest tightens. I don't want to do it. I don't want to see the shards I've so carefully buried.

But there they are.

Right before my mind's eye.

In them, I see myself—and I know that telling the truth is my only chance to shake Ethan awake. It will save him. But at the same time, it will take away everything he's ever held dear.

He'll never forgive me for it.

You're going to lose him, Mom whispers inside me, heavy with meaning.

"Yes," I say tonelessly, my eyes fixed on the door he just walked through, because I know it's true. "No matter what I do, I'm going to lose Ethan."

Thick tears well up in my eyes, tracing cold, wet paths

down my cheeks before falling from my jaw like they're dropping off a cliff into nothingness.

I'd rather jump into the darkness with you than stand in the sunlight without you. Those were Ethan's words, back when neither of us knew that we would never have either one.

And suddenly, it's no longer about whether we can keep our jobs or save our love from falling apart. Because both are utterly impossible.

There's only one thing left I can do right: I can save Ethan's life—and that's exactly what I should do. Even if it means each of us will leap into our own darkness. Because that thing we were searching for together, that one destiny shining for both of us—it doesn't exist.

A Twist of Fate: Chapter One

SONORA

Three and a half weeks earlier

When life deals you a bad hand, you have two options: you either surrender to your fate and fold before the game even begins, or you bluff until you win.

I've been bluffing for years—because stopping would mean ending up right back where it all started.

That can never happen.

Not even now, as the carefree laughter of my roommates June and Nyla drifts from the living room behind me while I step into the hallway, my heart pounding. The smell of the spinach pizza, which I had deliberately smeared into the ends of my hair just to have an excuse to leave the room, clings to my nose. Five minutes ago, it was delicious—now it makes me nauseous.

Lips pressed tightly together, I glance around at the chaos of moving boxes, a jumble of mismatched shoes, and half-assembled furniture.

Where did Nyla just say she left the mail?

There. On the box labelled *Kitchen*.

My nausea worsens as I reach for the mail.

Before I can go through the stack, the front door of our newly established shared apartment swings open. Olive—whom the four of us cheekily call our Glamour Lady—sweeps in on high heels. A delicate fragrance, as subtly elegant as she is herself, surrounds her.

"Oh dear," she says, eyeing my pizza hair and setting her shopping bags down on one of the boxes.

Dior. Gucci. Valentino. At the sight of the logos on Olive's shopping bags, a flurry of numbers instantly adds up in my head to a dizzying total. Still, I flash her a cheeky grin.

"Don't you think the green of the spinach goes perfectly with the dark brown of my hair?" I strike a model pose, then gesture toward the bathroom door behind her. "I'll clean it up real quick. The others are in the living room." Or rather, in our future living room, because at the moment, "construction site" is probably the more fitting term.

"Alright, see you in a bit." She smooths out her already wrinkle-free Marlene Dietrich trousers and turns to leave, then pauses. "Did we already get mail?"

My heart skips a beat. "Just ads."

"Let me see, maybe there's something interesting in there."

"Don't tell me you secretly shop at discount stores," I reply, hoping to distract her, and raise an eyebrow suggestively.

"Hey, Olive, we're in the living room!" I suddenly hear Nyla call out.

Olive furrows her brow in confusion. I point to her high heels. "You're kind of hard to miss," I say with a mischievous smile and disappear into the bathroom with the mail before she can ask me again.

Relieved, I close the door behind me and listen outside. A few clicks of high heels. Cheerful greetings. Laughter.

Thank God.

I exhale all the air that had built up inside me over the past few seconds. Then I turn to the mail.

Needlessly, my fingers tremble as I reach for the flyer on top. Even if the letter is in there today, it's not a big deal at all.

Beneath the flyer, I find a fashion magazine that Olive definitely subscribed to. Followed by…

There it is.

Fuck.

I just needed two more weeks—nothing more—they could've given me that.

But the fact that they sent the letter isn't even the biggest problem, because the envelope doesn't just bear my bank's logo—across the address field, the words Final Notice are emblazoned in oversized capital letters.

For a moment, I close my eyes. "Dear God, please let Nyla not have seen this letter when she picked up the mail," I whisper pleadingly, because that would make something I totally have under control and that's absolutely unimportant look like the exact opposite.

If my roommates find out I'm broke, they'll start asking questions. And even if I stay quiet, they'll look at me in that certain way. The one I swore I'd never have to see on anyone's face again.

I tuck the chemistry textbook under my arm and grab my bag. There's no need to check the time—I already know I have to hurry.

"Hey, Sonora, wait up," Chris calls after me.

"Gotta run," I reply, striding toward the classroom door, one hand protectively holding the dangerously torn strap of my bag.

He catches up to me. "There's a party at the pier later. It'd be cool if you…" He lowers his gaze awkwardly, his fingers fidgeting nervously. "It's a Valentine's Day party for… um…"

"Couples," I finish his sentence and immediately bite my tongue.

He's been trying to ask me out all school year, and every time it breaks my heart to turn him down—even though I think he's sweet.

He nods hopefully. "I thought maybe we could… only if you want to, of course…"

Hurting him is the last thing I want. Still, I shake my head. "I can't today," I say, trying to keep my voice light.

His disappointment is written all over his face. He tugs at his Burlington sweater. "Okay, maybe another time then."

I wish it were possible, but that day will never come.

"Mhm," I say, pointing to the oversized clock on the wall. "I have to go, sorry."

I wave to him and make my way as quickly as possible to my rusty VW van, which I parked today a few blocks from the high school in front of a hardware store.

It doesn't have central locking, so I fish the key out of my jeans pocket and insert it into the lock of the sliding door behind the driver's seat. Just to be safe, I glance around before opening it.

No one's watching me. That's good.

In a flash, I slip into the van, close the door, and switch on the small lamp, since barely any light makes it through the cardboard I've taped over the windows.

My waitress uniform lies on the mattress, next to a stack of medical textbooks from the library and the bag where I collect my dirty laundry. I change at record speed, tie my hair into a ponytail, and grab the bright pink cap.

As I slide the van door open with a flourish, I suddenly spot Chris.

He's standing less than two meters in front of me. With my scarf in hand, he peers over my shoulder into the van.

Great. "What are you doing here?"

"You forgot this," he says, handing me the scarf without looking at me. Instead, his eyes are fixed on my van.

I wish I were tall enough to stand in front of the bus and hide all its flaws. The rusty spots, the chipped paint, the dents.

Seconds of silence pass.

"So, uh…" he says, nervously running a hand through his hair.

"Yeah, I live in that bus," I say with a casual shrug, trying to make the situation easier for him. "It's a pretty awesome life, so full of freedom." The nights aren't cold at all and it's really no problem to find a new parking spot every few days, preferably close to the last one so I don't waste too much gas getting there. "A boring apartment wouldn't be for me." With electricity, running water, a fridge, and parents. Who needs all that anyway?

I watch as his body slowly tenses up. "Do you have a bathroom in there?"

"Of course," I lie, even though I know it wouldn't make a difference if he found out I shower at the gym. It's going to happen anyway.

Yeah, it's starting.

He looks down at the ground.

And now his gaze starts at my shoes and slowly travels upward.

He sees the holes in my sneakers—maybe he's really noticing them for the first time. Just like the frayed hem of my uniform. The faded T-shirt. Now he realizes I'm not wearing any jewelry. Not on my fingers, not on my wrists, not around my neck.

He wonders why he never noticed before. How he couldn't see that I'm not the princess he thought I was, but a damn Cinderella.

And now he's relieved I kept turning him down, so he doesn't have to be ashamed of his penniless girlfriend.

I take a deep breath to brace myself for what's about to happen next.

Here we go.

He looks at me. With that pitying expression people give a stray cat limping down the street, looking for something to eat.

That's exactly how he's looking at me. Even though the beat-up VW van behind me is just the tip of the iceberg.

Time to shut this down before he gets any ideas about asking uncomfortable questions.

"I'd really love to treat you to an espresso from my Black Luk," I say as smoothly as if I actually had the most expensive coffee machine in the world in my van. "But I've got to run. Rain check, okay?"

He looks away, embarrassed. "Okay."

I hadn't thought about that in ages—and even now, I shouldn't be, as I continue to stare at the bank letter in the bathroom of our shared apartment.

Chris never asked me out again, nor did he mention the espresso I'd promised him. Instead, from that day on, he and his friends looked at me with that one particular expression. Just like everyone else in my life who knew more about me than they should have.

As if poverty were all I was. As if I had no goals, no hopes, no dreams.

"Bullshit," I mutter bitterly. I *am* more than that, and I *have* more than that. So much more.

Determined, I fold the letter and slip it into the back pocket of my overalls. Then I tug down the neckline of my T-shirt and look in the mirror.

The tips of the butterfly's wings on my sternum peek out. I trace the lines of the tattoo with my index finger.

"We'll get through this together, Sonnygirl," I hear Mom whisper. *No, I'll get through this. On my own*, I answer silently, because that's the way it is.

"Pull yourself together," I tell the woman with the dark eyes, whose thick lashes finally stop fluttering. "You're a surgeon, you're starting your new job at Halifax Harbor Hospital tomorrow night, and in two weeks you'll be able to make your loan payments again."

She nods with resolve and lifts the corners of her mouth.

This is so much better than before. This woman is me.

I rinse the pizza crumbs out of the ends of my hair and step into the living room a little later. Autumn is home by now. She's just stuffing something that looks like an employment contract into her overflowing book bag. Her long red hair falls into her face.

"I think I've had enough pizza for today," I say, pressing both hands to my stomach as if pizza were the only thing weighing on it.

Nyla's gaze flicks to me, and I immediately try to read her brown doe eyes to see if she noticed the warning about my student loan from the bank when she dropped the mail off in the hallway earlier. Is that pity in her expression? Does she look at me a second too long?

Even if I don't know for sure, I want to believe that my secret is still safe as I settle onto one of the moving boxes I'd already used as a stool earlier. Autumn makes herself comfortable on the not-so-clean floor, sitting cross-legged. Nyla studies the food options, absentmindedly playing with her oversized earrings. Olive pushes aside the clear plastic cover on the couch and pats the seat cushion before sitting down. June, the fifth member of the group, smirks as she lets down her ponytail, making her look even more like Barbie than she already does.

None of my four roommates really know me. None of them will ever find out who I truly am or what I've done. For a split second, I wonder if the others are hiding something too. If they also have a rug under which a past lies buried—one they'd never uncover at any cost.

I quickly shake off these unnecessarily complicated thoughts. Everything is perfectly fine.

The five of us are not only going to crush this shared apartment life, but also our new jobs, which we're starting tomorrow at Halifax Harbor Hospital. Each of us will be working in a different department, but we all have one thing in common: we'll be doing it with the same wide grin on our faces.

"You know what?" June, who managed to snag a trial contract for the highly coveted specialist position in the diagnostics department, lets her gaze wander around the room.

"Wha?" Autumn asks with her mouth full.

A warm smile spreads across June's face. "I think this is going to be amazing," she says, voicing exactly what I'm thinking too.

About the Author

Belinda Benna is an award-winning author whose moving romance novels are filled with emotion, allowing you to lose yourself between the lines and find yourself at the same time.

Experience stories that will make you cry, laugh, and fall in love—each with a message that will stay with you for a long time.

www.ingramcontent.com/pod-product-compliance
Lightning Source LLC
LaVergne TN
LVHW030916080826
845145LV00013B/2913

* 9 7 8 1 0 3 6 7 2 6 6 1 4 *